When sin stains your soul, he tattoos your skin...

Tattoo artist Nathan Ink is more than he seems. An angel living in secret on earth, he forces his clients to face their flaws by tattooing images of their sins on their bodies, but this glimpse into the soul often results in his clients' deaths. Although Nathan avoids the other angels, when they ask him to keep an eye on Faye, a nephilim being stalked by another of her kind, he reluctantly agrees.

The angels have kept Faye in the dark about her stalker, but to keep her close to Nathan, they've tasked her with investigating the high mortality rate of Nathan's clients. Despite her distaste for his methods, she finds herself fighting a growing attraction to Nathan, and discovering he's not a rogue after all forces her to question her own mission. When Faye learns her stalker is another nephilim who intends to use her to breed a new race of hellish beings, teaming up with Nathan may be the only way to prevent a genocide.

Nephilim

By Mary Ann Loesch

KENSINGTON BOOKS

Kensington Publishing Corp.

www.kensingtonbooks.com

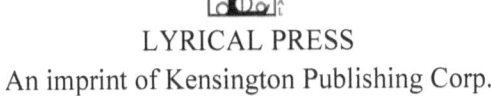

LYRICAL PRESS

An imprint of Kensington Publishing Corp.

First Electronic Edition: July 2011
eISBN-13: 978-1-61650-293-5
eISBN-10: 1-61650-293-2

First Print Edition: July 2011
ISBN-13: 978-1-61650-726-8
ISBN-10: 1-61650-725-X

Printed in the United States of America

Chapter 1

The angel stood outside the tattoo shop and listened to the hum. The red neon sign attached to the building blinked the words "Hell's Leak" and cast dark circles under his eyes. But the humming...oh, how it tempted the angel to go inside the sterile little shop and let it trickle through the senses until his body pulsed with it. That was one of the vices of his kind. The flick of a silver lighter, traffic lights swaying in the wind, a soft swirl of motion from a child's pinwheel...these things transfixed the angels and allowed life's little accidents to catch them off guard.

Inside the shop, the hum of the tattoo gun stopped, and a man with inky black eyes placed the instrument on a table next to him. The loud, heavy sound of metal music replaced the noise of the gun, and as if sensing the anomaly outside, the man turned around. A hint of cruelty grew in the stubborn lines of his features as he stared through the glass at the angel. He shoved a lock of his long, black hair away from his face and frowned.

Azal.

A small ray of hope flickered in the angel's chest at hearing the other man acknowledge him in his thoughts. But the man turned his attention back to the intricate design he branded onto his client, uninterested in communicating further. Disappointed, the angel turned up the collar of his long overcoat and walked away.

Though a cold January night, a crowd surged down the street. Frosty puffs of breath swirled around the people hurrying to nightclubs and bars ready to get drunk or laid. Their eagerness and desperation perfumed the chilly air.

Sloth, the angel thought. Absolute sloth. Why isn't anything done about it?

But he wasn't here to worry over these sweating, sinning mortals. There had been a breach of gigantic proportions. If it didn't get fixed, they would all pay.

Azal stopped in the middle of the sidewalk, disrupting the flow of foot traffic. Ignoring the colorful comments painting the air around him, he closed his eyes and concentrated. The woman was on the street somewhere. He could smell her voice--light, but whiskey husky with a touch of smoke to it. He blocked out the stench of pizza and stale beer, letting his senses search.

There. He had it. The sound of her pulled the angel past the scents coloring the sin-infested street, beyond the raucous metal music from one of the clubs, through the steam and smoke of a blues lounge, and to the tiny little piano bar called Black Cat.

The angel flinched at the tinkling sound the gold bell above the door made as he pushed it open. Not wanting attention, he quickly moved to a back table in the room, noting the place was almost empty for a Friday night. Good. Less people made it less likely his attention would be drawn elsewhere. And he needed to be focused. The woman was important.

"Can I get you something?" A waitress smiled down at him. Her black hair shimmered in the glow of a dim candle placed on the table. Above snug black pants and a white T-shirt, the bar's logo stretched across her breasts. According to the small glossy nametag pinned on the tight shirt, her name was Barb. She tapped a foot before crossing her arms, and Azal realized he'd inadvertently been eyeballing her cleavage. "What would you like to drink?"

"Vodka tonic." Azal opened his mind to listen to her thoughts. They trailed behind Barb as she walked away, a leaking balloon of disgust.

Asshole. It's always about the tits. Who does he think he is? Too bad he's so cute. I really dig the scar.

He smiled and touched the long scar that ran from his hairline down the side of his face. These humans. So beautiful in every way, and yet so fickle. Such an appealing reason to make his many frequent trips between the veil.

He forgot about Barb as the reason he'd been drawn to Black Cat walked onto the stage. Her sequined green dress swished as she sat on the bench of the black Steinway piano parked center stage. A cheer went up from the small crowd, and she gave her blond hair a modest pat. She smiled, bright and vivacious, but the angel noticed it didn't match the coolness in her green eyes.

"Thank you," she said with a slight Texan drawl. Azal remembered how she liked to portray herself as an innocent country girl when she performed, born to the simple life. This persona always brought a smile to his face. She was far from innocent. "My name is Faye and I'm here to sing the Vodka Set tonight."

Another cheer went up from the audience. Faye smiled and began playing an old standard, My Funny Valentine.

"Here's your vodka tonic." Barb placed the drink on the table and liquid sloshed over the side of the glass. Flustered, she grabbed a napkin to clean it up. The angel wrapped his hand around her wrist and gently pulled her toward him.

"I'm sorry for my earlier offense," he whispered. "But don't worry. Good fortune will come to you tonight."

Confusion flowered on Barb's face and her black hair fell forward, a curtain shutting off the world for a moment. He kissed her. A little spark of light sizzled between them before Azal pulled away and severed the connection.

Barb stumbled backward and ran a finger across her mouth. He could tell she was not quite sure what had happened, the memory of it already fading. Azal watched her walk unsteadily away. As she passed the stage, his gaze met Faye's. The angel shrank back into the shadows, but knew it was no use. She'd caught his scent. Faye finished the song and nodded good-naturedly at the audience as they applauded.

"Ya'll ever see that old movie The Outsiders? The one with the kid called Ponyboy?" Faye smiled at the eager nods in the audience. "My favorite part is when they read the Robert Frost poem Nothing Gold Can Stay. You know, 'Nature's first hue is gold, her hardest color to hold.'"

The angel felt the beginning of nervous butterflies in his stomach.

"It's about how we all start off life being gold and pure. As we get older we lose some of the gold of youth. I guess we can't be innocent forever." She chuckled, but it was a harsh, bitter sound to Azal's ears. "Stevie Wonder sang a song in the movie called Stay Gold, and I have an old friend here tonight that I'd like to sing it to. Now I know it's not really a Vodka Set song, but this friend is special, so I figure we can make an exception."

Faye sang the first notes into the microphone. As her sweet tone enchanted the drunks, the angel fought the urge to laugh. Stay Gold. He knew how Faye felt about his tarnished soul--not one drop of gold left in it by her estimation. Hadn't she told him so the last time they'd met? Back then it seemed ludicrous that an angel of his caliber would be less than 14kt. But now...well, the world and heaven had gone and changed on him.

"Oh my god!"

Faye stopped playing. The bar's attention focused on the waitress, Barb, who jumped up and down, holding a scratch off lottery ticket in her hand. "Oh my god!"

Faye smiled. "Now look, honey, you better have a good reason for interrupting my song."

Barb rushed around the bar, her body quivering with excitement. "I won! I won the lottery! Look!"

Faye eyed the ticket the woman held, her gaze narrowing. She glanced in the direction of the angel. "Well, good for you, Barb. No one deserves it more than you, honey. Hold on tight to that ticket now. I wouldn't want your good fortune to evaporate. Fate has a way of turning on you, doesn't it?"

Barb hurried off, still squealing with excitement.

"Well, this is turning out to be quite an evening. An old friend comes to call and a new friend wins the lottery. Vodka Sets are meant to be dreary 'round here, but I'm just not feelin' it tonight. Tonight feels more like a tequila night," Faye said.

Laughter and scattered applause ran through the crowd.

"Okay, folks, give me five minutes to adjust the set list and I'll be back."

Faye made her way toward his table, nodding and smiling at the regulars who called out to her. The angel took a deep breath, surprised at how nervous he felt. Angels weren't meant to feel emotions, but that had never been true of him. As she moved closer, she seemed to throw off the country girl persona that disguised the tough woman underneath. Maybe it was the green dress, the swish of the hips, or the way she held her chin--he could tell she would be difficult to win over tonight, and he needed to win her over. Everything depended on Faye.

"What the hell are you doing here, Azal?" she asked, losing the Texan drawl.

"Hell?" Azal said, sipping from his drink. "Must we bring hell into the conversation so soon?"

"I'll bring whatever I want into the conversation. Answer the question."

"Sit down." He grinned good-naturedly when she remained standing. "All right, Faye. Stand. If you need to prove you don't take orders from me, fine, but you'd probably be more comfortable sitting."

"Why are you here, Azal? I know it's not just to chat. You angels are too busy screwing things up to stop by and actually visit."

Azal ran a finger over the rim of the glass and smiled at her. "Can I buy you a drink for old times' sake?"

"Well, you could, but I think Barb just quit due to winning the lottery," Faye said. "Since you are the angel of good fortune, I'm going to assume you had something to do with that."

"I merely rectified a small error I made earlier."

"Can't say it's not a good thing. Poor kid is broke." She peered down at him. "I know you have a freakish obsession with Earth women and their boobs. Were you looking at her tits?"

"Maybe a little."

Faye laughed and pulled out the chair. As she slid into it, her nails drummed on the table. He hated the way she always appraised him. No doubt her sharp mind had already catalogued the changes she read in his face.

"I liked the song," he said when she didn't speak. "Stay Gold. You haven't lost your sense of humor."

"Figured you'd appreciate it. You still towin' the party line on that?"

Azal stared at the candle. Here was the moment, and yet he hesitated to bring it up.

"Don't get lost in that amber glow," Faye snapped. "I hate that transfixion shit."

He kept his gaze on the candle, but smiled at her words. "Faye, you know me too well. It would be easy to slip into the rhythm of the flame and watch it bounce back and forth, a tiny unappreciated miracle. But that's not the way of it tonight. Tonight I need to talk."

Faye eyed him warily, then reached out to grasp his drink. She sipped carefully, her eyes never leaving his face. "So talk. This is your chance. You're lucky I'm in a relatively good mood."

"For now."

"Cut the cryptic bullshit, Azal, and get to it. Why are you here?"

"I need your help. Or more to the point, God needs your help."

"It's always something with Him, isn't it?"

"I'm serious."

"I'm sure you are."

"God has a job for you. An important job."

"Then He can take care of it Himself. I quit the business a while back, as you may recall. I haven't seen hide nor hair of

God or His angels in seven years."

"Only because you refuse to let us in. God is in everything. The wind. The rain. It's all got His fingerprint on it--"

"You can stop right there!" She drummed her fingers on the table again, struggling to keep her anger in check. "Don't give me that sanctimonious crap. I've heard the speech. It's all a load of horseshit hidden by flowery words. Those flowery words let me down."

"Faye, what happened to you was…unfortunate."

"If you say it was all part of God's plan, this conversation will end now."

Azal sighed. How was he going to reach her? He tried again.

"We have a problem, Faye. We've got a rogue."

"A rogue?"

"Yes. We have someone whose intentions might no longer be of a divine nature. We would like you to find out what he is up to and how far off the path he's strayed."

"No."

"Faye--"

"I'm not helping you."

He'd been afraid of this. Total resistance was not unexpected, and it wasn't as if he could blame her. Seven years had not eased her bitterness. She'd lost everything, and no one, least of all him, had stopped it. Her eyes glittered in the candlelight and Azal opened his mind, trying to probe her thoughts.

She shook her head as if swatting away a fly.

"Stay out of my head. That path is closed to you." She sat back and studied him a moment. "A rogue, huh?"

"He's a symbolist. Works as a tattoo artist down the street at a place called Hell's Leak."

"Charming. What's his story?"

"He brands people with his designs and then…well, odd things happen to them."

"What kind of designs?"

"Symbols for the seven deadly sins."

Faye grinned. "No, shit? I didn't know you guys ever did anything creative. What's his name?"

"Nathan Ink."

"Catchy. So he tattoos people with symbols for the seven deadly sins and then odd things happen. Big deal. Isn't that your thing? Don't angels get paid to teach people lessons in mysterious ways?"

"Faye, you know better than that. As an angel, it's my duty to guide those who have lost the path to righteousness."

"The bullshit's getting pretty deep in here, Azal."

"He's killing people, Faye. His designs bring about the death of those who sit in his chair. Killing is not what angels are meant to do."

"Hah!" Faye took a small drink of the vodka tonic. "Maybe you should review your Old Testament history. Or mine."

"Faye," Azal grabbed her cold hand and squeezed. "He's killing innocents and taking their free will. There was a time when you wouldn't have stood for that."

Faye jerked away from his grasp and rubbed her forehead. Azal knew he'd gotten to her. A healer by nature, death was not welcome around Faye. She'd always strived to alleviate ailments or cure sickness. Even her small business, a plant nursery called The Flower Pot, thrived under her nurturing touch.

"Faye?" Azal allowed the desperation he'd been holding back to color his voice.

She looked at him intently. "There's more to this than you're telling me. You could send any number of people after this rogue to take care of him. Why me? I'm not even an angel, just one of God's happy little accidents. A freaky anomaly."

"Nathan Ink won't talk to the other angels. Shuns them completely. With your...unique background, I thought you might have better luck with him." He looked away. "So will you help me?"

Faye picked up his glass and downed the rest of the vodka tonic. As she got up she pinched his cheek, pausing to trail one finger down the scar on his face. "Tell you what, I'll think about it."

Azal watched her saunter away and felt his chest fill with hope. It wasn't a definite yes, but better than a solid no. He touched his hand to his cheek where the coolness of her hand still lingered. After a moment, he got up and made his way out of the bar.

It was a start.

Chapter 2

Sixth Street still bustled at one in the morning. The clubs overflowed with people whose smiles were tinged with alcohol and merriment. Though the bars would shut down in an hour, music pounded the air as each establishment competed with the other to bring in the clientele. Sidewalk carts worked overtime to keep up with the demand for bratwurst on a stick and the sweet joy of fried dough covered in powered sugar. Flat-chested girls in hemp tank tops, the scent of patchouli clinging to their bodies, cranked out homemade jewelry and reveled in the un-hippy smell of profit. Less innocent pleasures were available nearby, all one needed was to know where to look.

Some thought Las Vegas had cornered the market on the seven deadly sins, but as Faye walked along Sixth Street, she knew it wasn't so. Austin, Texas could give Vegas a run for its money any day. Oh sure, things were definitely bad in Sin City, but it wasn't caused by demons or the devil. That was always such a hard concept for believers to grasp. There were no demons or devils. Just angels who manipulated the odds and influenced free will. And that was really the key. In Vegas, free will was easily swayed. The sins of envy, gluttony, lust, sloth, greed, wrath and pride were always on display. Texans were still a little more modest, but that didn't make them any less vulnerable.

Several tattoo shops catered to the drunken masses in downtown Austin, and Faye wondered which belonged to Nathan Ink. What had Azal called it again? Hell's Leak.

The old familiar resentment reared up within her at the thought of him. She hadn't seen Azal in seven years, though he'd tried to make contact with her on more than one occasion. He'd never gone so far as to drop in on her before, preferring to throw simple signs in her path designed to express his presence. Faye ignored them. For a while he had cajoled and pleaded with her in her dreams until she'd performed a ritual to block him. Once, in an almost charmingly human approach, he'd sent candy and flowers. She'd tossed them in the trash. As if such trifles could soothe or win her over. Please. The angels and their Almighty leader had blown any chance of her help long ago.

So why am I looking for this Nathan Ink?

The rush of IH 35 traffic a few blocks away made her think longingly of her own car parked beneath the overpass. She wished she was safely in it, driving home to her apartment. Just the thought of the little room located above her plant nursery caused Faye's frustration at Azal to grow. If it weren't for him, she'd be there right now, not trudging around Sixth Street looking for some damn rogue angel.

Faye stopped. Though she knew to be wary of this part of the street, which had less foot traffic and more potential for danger, she closed her eyes, pressing a hand to her forehead where a tiny pain formed. She rubbed at the spot, but the pain grew, and with it came a sound, small at first, then gradually growing into a buzz.

Here we go, she thought. Time to pierce the veil.

Faye opened her eyes. She stood next to a dark and empty shop, just one of many on the east end of Sixth Street that took up the lower half of a two-story building. But something changed in the air. A shape shimmered next to her, caught between the veil of this dimension and the next. She blinked her eyes, letting her hand drop away from her forehead, and willed herself to relax.

"C'mon then. Show yourself."

Faye opened her senses, the pain in her head overwhelming her as it always did when she first looked beyond.

Stay calm, breathe, she reminded herself. This is all part of the process of seeing what others can't.

After a moment, the shimmering shape next to her solidified, and the pain lessened as a shop came into view. Light poured from the windows, illuminating the sidewalk that only moments ago had been dark. A red neon sign hung outside the door blinking the words Hell's Leak.

So it was not for everyone to see.

The only customer Faye could see inside the shop was a young man with brown hair. He sat motionless in a red chair, a light smile on his lips and a dreamy detached glow in his eyes.

His black and green boxer shorts were shoved up his thigh as a woman with milky brown skin rested a hand on his shoulder. Her eyes were shut and a serene smile played on her lips. In her other hand the woman held a brown leather book, which she pressed to her chest. Faye could clearly make out the word emblazoned in dark red on the cover.

Sinz.

Another man leaned over the customer's naked thigh. His long black hair fell forward as the tattoo gun in his hand emitted the loud buzz she'd heard earlier.

"Nathan Ink," she said out loud. "In the flesh."

Faye glanced at the shop's walls, which were covered with the same familiar symbols and designs she had seen on the walls of numerous other tattoo shops. Flaming skeleton heads adorned one area, along with variations of sexy succubae and devils. Anchors, flowers, tiny Mickey Mouses, Celtic symbols--it was all there. Her gaze swept across the work area where two stations were set up with the young man occupying one. Black and white tiled floors shone under the fluorescent lights, and Faye figured the inside smelled like a mix of rubbing alcohol and Pine Sol.

Nathan Ink put the tattoo gun down. She couldn't hear their conversation, but she could tell he had finished the design when he rubbed salve across the tender skin. Faye stood on her tiptoes and tried to get a peek at the tattoo. No luck. Nathan covered it with a loose bandage, and the young man pulled up his jeans, looking dazed. The woman smiled, took his offered card and ran it through the credit card machine. A few moments later, he left the shop, bumping into Faye as he passed.

Curt. His name spilled from his mind with ease when he brushed her shoulder. Self-conscious, he straightened his blue flannel shirt and moved away, leaving a sweet scent behind that reminded her of being in a bakery.

"Nice cologne. Not very masculine, though," she muttered and debated whether or not to follow him.

Faye looked back at the shop. The woman was busy cleaning up, but Nathan stood at the window staring at her. He tilted his head to the side, and a little prickle of heat ran up the back of her neck. He tried to get inside her head.

She smiled, shook her finger at Nathan and then followed the young man, wondering which of the deadly sins he would fall prey to.

Curt meandered up Sixth Street, his gait unsteady. She couldn't decide if he was drunk, or if it was the pain from the tattoo. Deciding to pull Azal's trick, Faye opened her mind.

Damn thing stings. What was I thinking? The thread of his thoughts were sluggish, slurred.

She almost lost him in a throng of laughing young women celebrating a bachelorette party, but his thoughts floated easily in the air above the garish, heavily made up faces of the women, and she was able to hang on.

Bitches. Fucking bride. Probably looking to get laid one last time. Maybe I should help her out. Bet that faggot from earlier wouldn't make fun of me now. Got a real cupcake tattoo tonight. Faye pushed through the girls, smiling and congratulating the bride who swayed on her feet. With a push of the mind, Faye suggested to a bridesmaid it was time to take the future bride home. As the bridesmaid sang her new idea to the bridal party, Faye picked up the thread of Curt's thoughts once more.

Hope this tattoo helps me get laid. She's a fucking beauty. Proves I'm not a damn queer.

She quickened her step and found her target in line outside of Hoek's Pizza. The black lights attached to the front of the walkup window gave the young man's face a wan look, and illuminated the dark circles under his eyes. Restless, he shifted back and forth on his feet and then too quick for anyone else to see, a glow of light pulsed through his body. He stilled. Faye watched him reach down and gently touch the covered tattoo. Then he leaned forward, and she could have sworn he smelled the hair of the woman standing in line before him.

Would love to run my hands over her body…she's got a fox tail too. Bitch must work at that strip club…maybe she'd like a little extra cash.

Curt reached forward as if he meant to carry his thought out, but then stepped back.

What the fuck! Can't go around touching women. She wouldn't be interested, anyway.

A second pulse of light flickered through Curt. The woman in front of him turned around, her eyes glittering in the black lights. She wore a skin tight blue dress, leaving nothing to the imagination. A miniature fox tail, about the size of a lucky rabbit's foot, hung from a bracelet on her wrist. Faye recognized it as the emblem for the strip club, Foxy's. The dancers employed at the seedy club roamed Sixth Street on the weekends, often passing out the little fox tail ornaments to help drum up business. Rumor had it they occasionally worked out side deals with the customers for other favors.

"You smell so good," the woman whispered. Confusion grew on her face and she reached out to touch the man's chest, causing the strange light to flicker through him again. "So...yummy, like vanilla icing. My name is Heidi. What's yours?"

"Curt."

"Curt. I like it." Heidi smiled, though her eyes were murky and baffled. She tilted her head, causing her glossy black hair to drift to the side. "Want to go back to my place for a private dance?"

"But I don't know you." Curt took a step back. Faye grinned. Though his thoughts traveled a sexual path, Curt reacted as if he were unused to the attentions of a woman as worldly as Heidi.

"So get to know me." Heidi closed the small gap he'd put between them, touching his chest again.

Curt stepped back, repulsed.

What the hell's wrong with this guy, Faye wondered. I bet that's not the usual reaction Miss Hotsie Totsie there gets.

"C'mon." Heidi grasped his arm, and Curt shuddered at her touch, but followed her out of the line.

Intrigued, Faye shadowed them to an alley, listening to Curt's thoughts.

She's actually into me! So why am I so turned off?

Faye peeked around the corner of the alley.

"I can't wait. Screw the dance. I need this right now." Heidi pushed Curt against the wall with a possessive kiss, rubbing her lithe frame against his. She touched his lower body, and another burst of light shot through him. He moaned, and encouraged by the sound, Heidi grabbed his arms, pinning Curt against the building. "That smell is driving me crazy!"

Faye stepped back and heard Heidi giggle as she pounced on Curt again. A little late night porn was fine in the confines of your home, but a peep show in the alley...not her thing. She shouldn't have followed Curt in the first place. The pulse of light charging through him had probably only been his hormones reacting to lust. It was the sort of thing her special skills allowed her to pick up on from time to time, and not always something she cherished. It didn't mean anything odd was going on. Faye had seen stranger things happen on Sixth Street. After all "Keep Austin Weird" was the city's motto.

"Dammit, Azal." She leaned against the wall outside the alley, frustrated.

He'd done it to her again. Piqued her interest enough to investigate something that was none of her business. She'd sworn off this stuff a long time ago. Time to call it a night.

"Goddammit!" Heidi's curse rang out from the alley. "What

the hell is your problem?"

Faye peeked again. Curt looked down at his crotch, a bewildered, embarrassed expression on his face. Heidi stepped back, stamping her foot.

"I don't believe this," she said, and gestured to Curt's pants. "You wanted me. I know you did. I felt it. You don't dance for men every night and not know when they want to fuck you!"

"Yes...yes, I did...I do," Curt said, fumbling for the words. "This has never happened to me before."

Heidi lunged toward him, trapping his mouth in a lurid lip lock. Curt's hands reached up and shoved her away.

"Stop," he said, panting.

Heidi, her face red, stalked out of the alley. Curt's thoughts floated in the chilly night air.

What the hell happened? I couldn't...damn...and she was hot! A stripper too! Fucking tattoo. She shouldn't have brushed against my leg. Hurt like hell. Almost seemed as if the tattoo twitched. No wonder I couldn't keep it up.

Curt walked out of the alley and Faye could have sworn she heard soft feminine laughter. No one else was around. Odd.

And interesting too, she had to admit. Just the sort of thing Azal must have known would intrigue her.

"This is not my problem," Faye said, watching the young man limp off. She glanced heavenward and spoke louder. "Azal, do your own dirty work."

She strode down the street toward the parking lot under the overpass. Since the bars were closing everyone was headed in the same direction. She allowed herself to be pushed along, caught up in their drunken merriment. Images of various people's nights passed through her head.

Stay out of people's heads. You've pried enough for one night, Faye.

Before she could follow through on the thought, a tingle of anxiety crawled up her spine. Something was about to happen. Trouble was coming. She braced for it.

Up ahead a homeless person stepped forward from the shadows. In his hand, the silver blade of a knife flashed under the streetlight. With a quick thrust, he stabbed a female passerby. The woman dropped to the ground, her hands instinctively coming up to shield herself. The homeless man continued to slice into her as she lay on the cold sidewalk. The crowd of people with the woman stepped back, unsure in their drunken haze of what to do.

Someone screamed, breaking the paralysis of the crowd. People shoved one another in their haste to get away, careening into those who pushed forward to help. The chaos attracted the attention of a group of frat boys across the street who charged over, their bellows of surprise adding to the mayhem. Everything happened at once and yet to Faye, it felt as if the whole scene moved in slow motion.

"Call 911," Faye shouted to a bystander. She grabbed the arm of the homeless man and shoved him against the wall. His hazel eyes moved back and forth frantically and then for a brief second focused on hers. Recognition flashed in his eyes and an image of an ornate cross popped into her head. Before she could process it another bystander stepped forward to help subdue him. With a guttural cry, the homeless man kicked himself free and took off into the dark night.

Faye dropped to her knees and placed a hand on the woman's forehead. Blood pooled around the body, but Faye saw she still breathed, though her eyes were wild with pain. She pressed her hand harder and the woman's name popped into her head. Julie.

"Julie? Can you hear me? Blink if you hear me," Faye instructed.

Julie blinked.

"Good. Hang on, honey. Help is on the way."

Faye probed with her power, getting in Julie's head. Flashes of her as a child. Julie at five with a gap-toothed smile. Julie in high school as the prom queen, brown feathered hair fluttering. Kissing her first serious boyfriend in college. Pissing off the homeless man who'd stabbed her. He'd asked for money and she'd blown him off.

"Further. Go further," Faye murmured, feeling the beginning of the pain.

There. Faye's mind probed past the images and into the warmth of the human body.

"Too late." A deep sadness washed through her as she observed the fatal wounds that even now caused the lifeblood to drip away. Nothing could be done. "Julie, look at me. I know you're scared, but I can help. I can make the cross easier."

Panic fluttered in Julie's dark eyes. She struggled to speak. "H...help...me..."

With as much power as she could muster, Faye focused on the wounds in the torso. All sounds muted and fell away until there was just the erratic beat of Julie's heart. Faye's first instinct was always to heal, but in this case, that wasn't an option. Instead, she delved into the ocean of pain Julie felt and removed it. Her power surged forward and flowed back with waves of Julie's pain. She gasped at the cold shock of taking it in, and watched the young woman give a small peaceful sigh as life slipped further away. Closing her eyes, Faye whispered a quick crossover prayer, feeling the soul lift from the body. When she felt Julie pass through the veil without incident, she released the young woman's hand.

Sirens screamed and pandemonium ruled the street. The shocked crowd surged around Julie and Faye. Faye crawled back, trying to escape the faces and hands that seemed to be everywhere. Someone grabbed her shoulder, pulling her away from the cluster. Nausea built within Faye, and though her vision clouded, she managed to stand. The hand on her shoulder moved down to her elbow, and she blindly followed the person guiding her away from the chaos.

"Stop please," she whispered. "I'm going to throw up."

She bent over and vomited on the sidewalk. Clouds of black dust came from within her, dissipating as they hit the ground, leaving only a foul smell behind.

"Jesus, lady, what the hell did you eat?" A Goth kid leered down at her, his lip ring shimmering in the night. Faye fought the urge to reach up and give it a hard yank.

"Move on," a voice instructed the kid. The deep, rumbling tone carried the hint of a threat, and the Goth kid scurried on his way.

"Thanks for your help." Faye wiped her mouth and looked up at her rescuer.

Two inky black eyes stuck in a harsh pale face that stared down at her. Long, shiny black hair framed the face, falling to just below the man's massive shoulders. He wore a T-shirt that read Fuck with me. I dare you. No one in his or her right mind would have done such a thing. Just above the collar of his T-shirt, a long black tattooed line appeared, running around to the back of his neck. She knew exactly who the man was.

Nathan Ink.

Chapter 3

Nathan stared at the woman. He'd sensed the commotion on the street before it occurred. Curiosity had driven him from his apartment above Hell's Leak to see what would happen, though he had no plans to intervene or stop the event. That wasn't his place.

As he stepped outside, Nathan could smell her. She'd stood outside the shop earlier, her blond hair shimmering like a halo in the red neon glare of the Hell's Leak sign.

Ahh...a new client. Let's hear the hum of her sin.

But she'd walked away after shaking a finger at him, almost as if she knew what he'd been thinking. And then there was the hum. Though he always had the metal music he favored cranked up in the shop to block the grating tone of the ever-present hum, it usually managed to rise above everything else, pleading to be noticed, but not with the woman. He'd heard nothing that singled her out as being special enough to sit in his chair.

Maybe she was strong enough to resist temptation.

Or maybe she was one of the Others. The thought made him frown. What could they want with him?

When he'd seen her take the dying woman's pain, Nathan's first instinct had been to withdraw. He hated dealing with the piousness of the Others! Yet the woman's scent was different, not quite angelic. It drew him down the street almost against his will.

"You smell earthy. Ancient. Not like an angel." He watched her steady herself. Whatever she'd done for the dying woman came with a physical price.

"So you're saying I smell like old dirt?" She brushed off her skirt.

"Maybe. Who are you?"

"Faye McCoy." She stuck out a shaky hand, which he looked at curiously.

"What do you want?"

"To get off the street for starters."

"Who sent you?"

She dropped her hand and glanced around. The cops were interviewing witnesses. Pretty soon someone would turn around and point her out. He could sense her anxiety and tried to look within her head at her thoughts.

"That doesn't work on me," she said, turning back to him and touching her head. "I learned a long time ago how to block my thoughts."

The admission surprised Nathan and he tilted his head to the side, studying her. "C'mon." He expected her to follow him back to his shop, but she hesitated, chewing on her bottom lip. "You wanted to get off the street."

"I'm not going into your shop," she said.

"Why?" The sudden stubborn plant of her feet intrigued Nathan, as did her refusal.

"I'm not…comfortable with that."

"If you want to get off the street, the other option is my apartment upstairs." He smiled and let his wolfish gaze wander down her body. "Comfortable with that?"

"Do you ever tattoo people from your apartment?"

"No."

"Okay," she said, but he heard the wariness in her tone. "I'll go up."

She kept pace with his long strides as they headed away from the noise of the crime scene. Nathan noticed she fidgeted with her dress, glancing nervously behind them as he unlocked the street door next to the shop. As they climbed the stairs, he found her smell a distraction. It surrounded him in the small stairwell, tickling his senses, though he still couldn't quite place it. Something not fully human. At the top of the stairs they stopped in front of a green door. Nathan muttered his password and it slid open.

"Well, that's a new one. I thought doors swung open," Faye said.

"I created a vision for anyone who might be too curious about me." Nathan peered into the room. "I don't like letting people in my true domain."

"We could just have easily gone to a coffee shop," Faye pointed out. "But you don't seem like a coffee shop kind of guy."

They stepped into the apartment. It wasn't much, just one big room that stretched across the second floor of the building. Dusty books were stacked floor to ceiling, and boxes teetered on top of one another. Toward the back lay an old white mattress with the sheets tangled in a heap. In the middle of the room sat a stained couch that might have once been a fashionable red. A few feet away, the matching recliner sagged at the bottom, and its lumpy stuffing poked out from various holes in the upholstery. A worn coffee table covered with newspapers, pizza boxes and a baited mousetrap sat between the couch and the recliner.

"Hmm.... I think I'd rather see what the tourists view when the door swings the other way. Your domain is a mess," Faye said, her gaze sweeping over everything as she brushed off a spot on the couch and sank down. She touched a hand to her forehead.

"Does it hurt to do what you do? To take someone else's pain?" Nathan asked. She shifted on the couch, the motion causing her short dress to ride up a little.

"Yes," she said.

"Then why do you do it?"

"I can't help it."

"The call is just too great for you then?"

"No." Defiance glimmered in her eyes as she turned her attention back to him. "I don't have a call. I ignore anything that resembles a call. I just feel compelled to help people when they need it."

"So you work for the angels?"

"Not anymore."

Nathan shut the door and strode over to the windows behind the couch, staring out into the night. The cops still worked on the homicide down the street. The red and blue glare of their presence flashed on the walls of the surrounding buildings.

"I saw you before," he said, sensing her tense again. "You were standing outside my shop. Most people only see an empty building, but not you. You could see it, but you didn't go in."

"I'm not really interested in getting a tattoo."

"Few people can resist the temptation to come inside Hell's Leak once it's revealed to them," Nathan said. When she didn't respond, he prodded. "You followed one of my customers."

"I did, but to tell you the truth, that was a letdown. Nothing much happened there."

"That you saw."

"Unless his tattoo has something to do with his inability to, shall we say, close the deal with a woman, then what I saw wasn't too exciting."

Nathan gave a low chuckle. "The tattoo has everything to do with it."

"Maybe you're overestimating your skills."

"Check the papers tomorrow. You might change your mind."

Faye looked at the newspapers spread out on the messy coffee table.

"Are you a big fan of the Austin American Statesman, Mr. Ink?"

"I keep track of current events. Especially if they pertain to me."

She picked up one of the papers, and scanned it. Her brows knitted . Nathan wondered if she would see them. Would she be able to tell which articles related to his clients?

"Azal sent you," he said. Her fingers stiffened on the paper before she tossed it back to the table.

"Not exactly."

"But you know him."

"Unfortunately."

"Do I detect a hint of dislike for Azal? The lucky one? The bringer of good fortune,"

"He's a showoff." Faye stood. "And, yes. He visited with me earlier tonight. Azal thinks you are a rogue angel, that you tattoo people with designs of the seven deadly sins."

"I do. That's not a secret among my kind."

"Azal is under the impression the mortality rate of your clients is high once you've tattooed them. He wants me to investigate you, see how far rogue you've gone."

"And will you?"

"I don't play for the Heavenly All Stars anymore."

"Then why are you here?"

"Pure chance," she said. "You caught my healing act on the street. I hadn't decided if we were going to meet at all."

"Some angels might call that fate," he said, marveling at her resistance to the confines of a higher power. He couldn't help but admire it.

"I'm no angel," she said.

Nathan nodded, pushing away the grin that sprung to his lips. He concentrated on her cool green eyes, trying once more to probe her thoughts. She shook her head at him.

"Uh-uh. That path is closed. Stay out of my head."

He ignored her, trying to get past the basics. She was about medium height with blond hair, which she wore pulled up into a loose bun. Bustier than the average girl, she was definitely not unpleasant to the eye. Athletic legs probably meant she jogged or walked a lot. He liked the way her feet looked in her green high heels--delicate, but ready for an ass kicking. She appeared to be in her late twenties or early thirties, but he knew that could just be a glamour spell. The interesting thing, the thing that made him curious, was the scent she carried. She had the soft smell of the ancients and yet, it was just as she said. Faye McCoy was not an angel. So what did that make her?

"I'm twenty-seven," she said, and grinned. "I know you were wondering."

"All right. So your name is Faye McCoy, and you have some sort of gift that allows you to take pain from others," Nathan said, and leaned against the windows. "You're in touch with angels, though you claim not to work for them, and best I can tell, you are not one of us. Does that about sum it up so far?"

"You forgot about the part where I'm supposed to investigate your rogue activities," she said.

"Right. Azal is making you his errand girl."

He had to give her credit. She managed to ignore the goad in his words. Faye closed her eyes, and Nathan felt a slight pressure in his head as she tried to probe his thoughts. Though impressed with her tenacity, he kept his mind locked. At his warning look, the pressure faded away.

"You must be very special if Azal came to me." Faye moved closer. Her scent wrapped around him, and to his surprise, he felt a stirring of desire. "We didn't part on good terms."

"I am special."

"Especially arrogant maybe. I believe your sin is pride." She laughed. "I haven't seen anything that leads me to believe you are above average. So far my best summation is you are a messy angel who asks a lot of questions, and is rude enough not to offer a glass of water to someone he knows is in pain."

"I don't have any clean glasses." Nathan picked up one of the newspapers from the coffee table. "Take this. It might assist you in your investigation. I think you've recovered enough to slip away unnoticed now."

"Trying to get rid of me by providing dirty secrets, are you?" She took the paper, folding it under her arm as she started for the door. Once there, Faye turned back to him. "You can't fool me, Mr. Ink. You gave me the tourist version, after all. This pigsty of an apartment is what you wanted me to see. It didn't work, you know. I can pierce the veil to the truth."

She closed her eyes. With a wave of her arm, the room transformed. The boxes, books and clutter vanished, revealing a tidy space. An ornate wooden bed replaced the old mattress on the floor. Art hung on sandstone colored walls capped at the ceiling by white crown molding. Several sconces placed about the room gave off various degrees of warm and soothing light. There were shelves and bookcases, holding all kinds of trinkets and oddities as well as books. Tucked into the wall between two CD racks filled with music sat a massive stereo system. The small spotless kitchen area revealed a stainless steel sink, refrigerator and stove. A glass cabinet held amber glasses and light brown plates.

"You must really like IKEA," Faye said.

Nathan heard her high heels click on the stairs as she left, and a few seconds later, she appeared on the sidewalk. She walked away without looking up.

He found he wanted her to look up.

Before he could examine the feeling, another figure standing on the opposite side of the street caught his attention. The glow of a street lamp illuminated the worry on his old colleague's, Azal, face. How the angel of good fortune had changed!

Well, that's not my problem, Nathan thought, and drew the shade down on the window. Settling on the red couch, he opened a carved brown box on his coffee table, pulling out a pack of American Spirits and a crystal ashtray. As he lit a cigarette, his mind lingered on Faye and the job she had been commissioned to do. He knew there were some angels who considered his methods unconventional, but still, he got the job done. If he couldn't take a little creative license with the work, then what was the fun in being an angel?

With a gentle wave of his arm, he cast out his power and the wall sconces dimmed. Better. Now he could think.

What did Azal really want? Why send Faye to check on him? The rogue label--just a convenience, a red herring. Perhaps the time had come to pull back the veil and take a peek at the other side. Get the latest gossip, as the mortals were found of saying. He preferred to have no contact with such things. The longer he stayed on the earthbound side, the better he understood the vices of humans. Nothing like wallowing in the muck and mire of sin to help you appreciate your job.

"Dammit." Nathan stubbed out the cigarette. "Let's see what we've got."

Hands pressed together in prayer pose, he took a long breath and focused on first blocking out the noise of the mortals. The city sounds faded away until only the hum of sin, the only sound Nathan could never completely shake, remained. With his eyes closed, he whispered an old Hebrew chant. A soft swirl of wind tickled his body, lifting his hair and engulfing him in a wave of peacefulness as he slid into the comfort of being behind the veil. A strong sense of homecoming coursed through him.

A new sound nudged at his keen sense of hearing, desperate for his attention, but Nathan kept his eyes closed. It grew louder until he recognized it as weeping. Higher and more melodic than the cry of humans, it was heartbreaking and beautiful all in the same moment.

"An angel is crying," Nathan whispered.

"There's more," Azal's strong voice rang in his head. "So much more, Nathan. Your brothers and sisters need you."

"What's going on, Azal?" Nathan felt his head would burst as the lament and mourning grew louder, heavier. There were feelings here he couldn't quite absorb. Under the anguish, another emotion brewed and threatened to bubble over. Fear.

"Angels are dying." Nathan could barely hear Azal above the roar of sorrow. "We need your help, Nathan."

Nathan covered his ears and tried to block the rush of noise. He pushed himself free of the veil, his body soaking up human essence like a balm as he returned to Earth. He opened his eyes, relieved when the sounds stopped. After a few deep breaths, he tried to stand. Dizziness forced him to steady himself before moving toward the kitchen. He rummaged in his cabinets looking for the small vial he kept hidden behind the spices.

Gulping down the amber elixir in the bottle, Nathan staggered toward the bed. He fell against his sheets, grateful for their softness, and managed to roll over so he stared up at the ceiling. His heart pounded, threatening to burst free of his mortal shell. He couldn't shake the deep sorrow he'd experienced.

What had been happening behind the veil? What had Azal said?

The soothing effect of the amber liquid forced its way into his aching head. Just as he succumbed to it, Azal's words floated back.

Angels are dying.

Chapter 4

Faye couldn't sleep. She tossed and turned, little snatches of a dream flittering in and out of her subconscious. The part of her aware that she dreamed tried to push away the dark vignettes, but only succeeded in pulling herself further in to the seedy depths of another person's mind.

Faye could never completely make out the face of the black-haired boy in the dreams, but she felt his emotions, heard his thoughts. There were times she caught a clear glimpse of his eyes, or the twist of his mouth, but other than that, his face remained a swirl of gray in her mind. She watched him prowl the city. The dark alleys and cross streets offered infinite places to become one with the shadows, and were as familiar to him now as his childhood home had once been. Of course there was nothing left of that old white house with its peeling paint and shoddy floorboards. He'd made sure of that. The fire that burnt the building to the ground had been magnificent to watch, and the sense of freedom that came with it--Faye knew he'd do it all again in a heartbeat.

The knife kept him going. Faye watched him crouch down, pull the weapon out, and caress the blade. A tiny drop of blood welled at the tip of his finger. The boy examined it, fascinated when the crimson liquid pooled and fell to the ground.

"Momma," he said. The knife had belonged to his mother, Faye was sure of it, and she knew the boy viewed the weapon as an extension of her. A little picture of the woman flashed in Faye's mind--tall with weathered skin and oily hair the color of dishwater. Her lifeless eyes reminded Faye of a shark.

The boy held the knife with reverence and examined the bone handle. There were carvings deep in the surface, along with letters written in an unfamiliar language. He ran a finger over them, tracing their bumpy outline, and smearing his blood on the handle. It seeped into the pores of the bone, leaving no trace behind to mar the knife's appearance.

The blade looked dull and dirty, but if flashed just the right way, it sparkled. One could almost hear it sing of the agony it rendered to those unlucky enough to be caught in its path.

He stood and swung the knife out at Faye, though she knew he couldn't see her. She watched him pretend to battle an imaginary opponent for a few minutes before delving deeper into his mind. Faye tried to get a sense of who the boy pretended to fight, but his only thoughts were of his mother. He wondered how Momma had gotten her hands on such a special knife. After all, she was just a common killer with no sense of the greater picture. He could only assume it had been given to Momma to pass along to him when the time was right. Perhaps it had been a gift from his father. Shame the man hadn't been around to teach him how to use it!

The boy had discovered on his own it could do more than just kill.

A man crept into the alley, staying just on the fringe of the shadows. Faye pulled a name from his head. Tom. Her heart quickened as she sensed his intentions--sex with the young teenager.

"Watch out!" Faye called, but her words were not heard in the dream. Helplessness planted itself in her stomach, a sick little flower that blossomed strong.

The boy turned and stared into the shadows before sniffing at the air. Urine, sweat and alcohol--Tom's body odor gave him away, and he lumbered out from his hiding spot.

"I'm not going to hurt you." Tom stepped toward him. Faye's heart beat faster, knowing the man lied.

"But I'm going to hurt you, mister, if you come any closer," the boy said, brandishing the knife.

Tom chuckled and took a tentative second step. "Don't make this hard. I hate it when they struggle."

The boy lowered his head, but not before Faye had seen anger flash in his eyes. She shivered and pressed a hand to her mouth, as Tom, with an overconfident swagger, edged closer to the boy.

"I promise to be quick, kid." Tom rested his dirty hand on the boy's shoulder and Faye felt the bile rise in her throat. She wanted desperately to intervene, to step forward and break the confines of the dream. Her heart pounded louder, almost blocking the sound of the boy's voice.

"Me too," the boy said as he plunged the knife into the soft belly of the man before him.

* * * *

Faye gasped for breath. Damn. She hated those dreams. They'd been occurring regularly the last few months, but whenever she woke up, she couldn't quite remember all the details. The boy always starred in them, though she struggled to remember what he'd been doing, or the contours of his features. Whatever happened in the dream, whatever sight she'd seen that caused her heart to race, would be erased from memory, though often the boy's residual emotions would remain behind. This time wasn't any different. Already the visions faded, but the sense of loss, of utter abandonment stayed. Or were those her own feelings? Sometimes it was hard to tell. Faye rolled over in bed and grabbed the little notebook on her nightstand.

Momma. She wrote the word down and circled it twice, knowing it meant something important. It was the key to…her mind struggled to make the connection.

"It's the key to…" she said, her voice shaky.

The significance of the word would not come. Frustrated, she placed the notebook back on the nightstand and sank down in her bed. The morning traffic rumbled outside of her apartment on busy Lamar Street. A soothing, normal Sunday morning sound, she relished in knowing her shop, the Flower Pot, would be closed. It was definitely a perk of being self-employed.

The Flower Pot had once been an old gas station leftover from the fifties. Faye had purchased it seven years ago, seeing the potential in the abandoned location and its unique two-story design. It had taken some time, but now the run-down gas station with its curved arches and old-fashioned feel was a small thriving florist and plant nursery. Flowers bloomed in bright pots outside. The exterior of the building, once a mixture of whites and greens, had been given a cheery yellow makeover. Painted daisies grew all over the sides of the shop, intertwining with the business' name printed on the front wall.

Faye escaped there, content to be one with nature, and satisfied her plant world would bring her peace. From time to time, loneliness crept in, but that's what her stint at the Black Cat was for. Most people would see it as artistic release, not a cry of despair. Admitting to such a feeling would have been tantamount to asking for help. That wouldn't do.

The small room above The Flower Pot served as Faye's

personal living space. Nothing more than a simple efficiency apartment, she'd done her best to create a soothing environment with soft brown and olive tones. The tiny kitchen and dining area appealed to Faye's need for open space--no places for unwanted visitors to hide.

This morning, as the last remnants of the unsettling dream slipped away, depression twisted in her stomach, battling with the anxious butterflies that had made it home when she'd seen Azal in the audience last night. Her gaze flitted for a moment on the only picture she allowed herself to have out and then just as quickly, she glanced away.

She hated being spied on, manipulated. For seven years, she'd managed to fill her time with things that kept her from wondering too much about the Others, and with the exception of Azal, the other angels left her alone. Fine. She wanted solitude. Yes, there were times when the loneliness almost consumed her, but she didn't need a bunch of pious hens cackling over her misfortunes, offering sage but useless advice. Speaking with Azal, agreeing to assist him in any way, was like opening the door for the rest of the angels. Would they start dropping in and asking for favors too? No way would she be going down that path again!

"Hell, no," she said to the empty apartment as she got out of bed.

She started the morning routine--stretch, start coffee, find food not expired in the fridge--and forced her thoughts to focus on Nathan Ink. Tall and good-looking in a hard sort of way, she couldn't help but admire the black, shiny rock star hair that swung loose and free at his shoulders. She pondered the tattooed line she'd seen running up from his chest and around his neck. What kind of tattoo would an angel have? And those big muscles--Faye wondered if angels worked out at the gym, or was that just the natural form of his mortal shell?

And what a sexy mortal shell it was, Faye thought, stirring her coffee.

His wary attitude gave her no clue about the real nature of his activities, which she was supposed to be checking on. Of course that was only if she chose to do so. Right now, that was feeling like a pretty big if.

A soft thud outside her door announced the arrival of the morning paper. She glanced at the clock and stretched again. Only six hours ago she'd helped someone cross to the other side of the veil. The after effects always took a toll on the body. She winced at the various aches in her muscles.

Faye opened the door and picked up the morning paper from the welcome mat, relieved the paperboy had managed to throw it up the stairs for once. Though winters in Texas were typically mild, barely getting below fifty, she didn't relish walking down the cool steps in her bare feet to fetch the Statesman. Faye slipped off the plastic cover and skimmed the morning headlines. The slight breeze rustled her hair, and a scent, delicate and soft, tickled her nose. Her senses went on alert.

"See anything interesting?" Azal asked.

Faye turned back to the interior of her apartment.

"I thought I smelled shit," she said, and pointed down the stairs. "Get out. I didn't say you could come in, Azal."

"I didn't ask."

Faye shut the door, frustrated. She moved about the room, snapping open the shades, which allowed light to flood the place. Azal stood in the center. Sunbeams gathered around his brown hair, giving him a glow that would have caused awe in most people. Faye had seen the show before, and while she might have still been impressed by it, she would never let Azal know that.

"Did you talk to Nathan?"

"Yes. I don't know why you bother to ask. I'm sure you already know the answer." Faye went into the small kitchen and opened the fridge. "Is this going to become a habit? Are you planning to drop in whenever you want?"

"I brought éclairs."

She peered at him from over the top of the refrigerator door. "What kind?"

"Chocolate covered."

"With custard or whip cream for the filling?"

"Whip cream, of course."

"Okay, you can stay for a few minutes, but only because I'm hungry."

"I figured as much." Azal watched her plop onto the sofa and grab the box he'd placed on the coffee table. "I like your apartment. And your shop. You've done well for yourself."

"Thanks."

"I see you kept the MG. Your father loved that sports car. I remember when he bought it, how proud he was to drive your mother around in it."

"Can we cut the small talk?" She didn't want to think about her father and the MG. It had taken her a long time to stomach driving it again, the memories almost too much to bear at first.

Faye picked up an éclair, and then offered the box to Azal. "You want one?"

"I need to know about Nathan. How did he seem to you?"

Faye bit into the sweet pastry, observing his body language. His shoulders were tense, and impatient energy crackled through him. "He seemed fine to me. I don't know the guy, so I don't know what his normal temperament is like."

"Did you notice anything odd?"

"He's an angel who tattoos people. Where should I begin?" At his small sigh of frustration, she continued. "He's in the habit of glamoring things so no one finds his lair or his shop unless he wants them to, but that's not out of the ordinary. Lots of earthbound angels do that in order to keep a low profile."

"True. What about his shop then? Did you see anything there?"

"I didn't go in, but I did watch him and an assistant finish a tattoo on a client."

"An assistant?" Azal asked, and Faye could almost see his ears perk up. He sat down next to her. "Man or woman?"

"Woman. Young and black with long dreadlocks."

"How did this customer seem when he left the shop?"

Faye bit into her éclair again, thinking back to Curt. He'd staggered on his way out of Hell's Leak, and there had been that strange glow flickering just under his skin. Not to mention Heidi and the way she'd been drawn to Curt by his smell.

"I'm not sure," she said. "I thought something was different with him. There was this light that pulsed through his body, but when I followed him...well, he turned out to be some average guy with a hard-on for every woman he sees. I think I was just picking up on his pheromones. It happens sometimes."

"The assistant's name is Judith. She's actually an apprentice, and we've been watching her closely for some time." Azal leaned back on the sofa. Faye stole a quick glance at him, surprised to see sadness crinkling the lines around his eyes. On impulse, she reached up and smoothed out one of his curls.

"You're tired. I've never seen you this bad off."

His eyes closed at her touch.

"Everything has changed," Azal said. "I loved you so much, Faye. I loved what was yours, and I'm ashamed that I lost them."

Her hand dropped like a stone. An image of Chris popped into Faye's mind, followed by thoughts of her parents. They were all gone. Dead. Doomed to be murdered when their protector was distracted. All a part of God's plan. Her gaze flicked to the picture frame on her bedside table.

"I try not to think about what happened," she said, getting up. "I try not to think about you or the other angels. I'm surviving."

"Yes, you are. But are you living?"

"Let's talk about something else."

"Fine." Azal snapped his fingers, and the television clicked on to Austin Daily, the local morning news program.

"Police are still trying to find the man responsible for a string of murders in the central Austin area. If you have any information, please contact A.P.D at the number on your screen," the newscaster said. "In other news, the body of a young man identified as Curt Brown, a student at the University of Texas, was found early this morning outside of a Fifth Street establishment. Authorities are still looking into the cause of his death, which has not been released at this time. Police say that foul play was not involved."

"Oh, shit." Faye felt the pain in her head grow worse. "Oh, shit. I should have kept following him. Maybe I could have saved him, or at least eased his pain when he passed."

"But then you would not have been there to help Julie cross over."

"You knew about that?"

"I sensed what was occurring."

"You could have stopped it. You could have helped."

"That was not what fate intended."

"Fate? Is that your excuse this time? Are you sure you weren't distracted again, caught up in the magic of the colors of a street lamp or something? No, that's not it. You were probably staring at a candle in some seedy bar, entranced by the miracle of its little dancing flame. You've been around for thousands of years, Azal, and yet some things never change!"

"Faye, you know how our rules work." Azal stood. "We can't save people if their time has come, even if it comes about by what could be construed as unnatural means. Fate has written the cards for every person's life the second they were born, and Julie's moment had arrived. It's unfortunate, and it was a terrible way to go, but at least she had you. You were fate's gift to Julie."

Fate's gift? Faye shook her head. An old argument, one they'd had many times before, and Faye knew there was no way to win it. Her mind rebelled, feeling free will determined fate, but there was no point in saying that to Azal.

She watched him move to the window. The sunbeams swirled

around him again, giving him the angelic glow artists so often tried to capture in paintings. "Curt is a different story. It wasn't his time, but due to Nathan Ink's interference, Curt's life ended. I believe Nathan severed the connection on purpose, without regard to fate and the natural order."

"Then why didn't you stop that?"

"Because we couldn't see it coming."

"Are you saying God can't tell what Nathan, one of his own special servants, is up to?"

Azal grew quiet, his face unreadable.

"Azal, you're not telling me everything."

"I've told you what you need to know for now." Azal turned from the window. "I need your help. You see, Nathan is still relatively young to this way of life. He still finds certain aspects of being an angel…distasteful. He doesn't play by the rules. The things his clients endure…"

"Like Curt? What really happened to him?"

"I want you to find out, but be careful."

"He can't read my mind. I've blocked him."

"Nathan is powerful. Don't forget that. I need to know more than ever where his loyalties are!"

The words echoed in the small room, and Azal crossed his arms, contrition on his face as if he'd given too much away.

"Why? Why is it so important? What are you not telling me?" Faye touched his arm causing a tiny spark. She knew Azal's feelings manifested themselves in various ways. When he was happy, everyone got lucky--in one way or another. His anger could cause a room to go up in flames. But sparks, sparks were a sign of defensiveness. Or secrets he didn't want to share. She stared down at the small scorch mark on her palm. "How worried should I be, Azal?"

"You can handle Nathan," Azal stepped back. "And don't worry. I'll be close."

"How do you know I can handle him? Have you seen my fate?"

"I don't need to. You'll be fine."

He faded away, leaving a soft glow in the air. She breathed in the scent he left behind, reminded of her father.

Don't go there, she cautioned herself. Focus on the here and now.

Faye wondered what would happen to Nathan if he turned out to be a rogue. What did God do to punish undesirable angels these days? Thoughts of her father pushed their way to the forefront of her mind again, and she remembered all too well how God had punished him. Would the same fate befall Nathan?

Would his soul be extinguished too?

Chapter 5

The midmorning sun burnt his pale skin. A nocturnal fellow by nature, the creature spent too much time honing his gothic palette to find the daytime agreeable. Oh well. This was worth a little jaunt out during the day. The brief moment he'd spent with Faye McCoy last night had stirred his curiosity, among other things. He'd almost forgotten what it felt like to have feelings other than disgust toward the humans.

Faye stood on the corner of Fifth Street, delicious and appealing in her ignorance of his presence. He'd gotten better and better at cloaking himself. Not even the angel on the opposite side of the street could sense him unless he willed it so! And that was saying something, considering the weight of his many sins. But he'd have a little fun with Nathan Ink later.

Right now was about Faye.

The creature smiled, and enjoyed the luxury of watching.

* * * *

Faye scratched her head, and pushed back a loose strand of her hair. She focused all of her inner sight on the spot before her, confident she had discovered the location of Curt's death. She felt the lingering energy left from his exit along with his last emotions. Panic. Terror. Confusion. Bliss. Lust.

Moving a few yards away, she placed a hand on the door of the Rainbow Cattle Company, a popular nightspot for Austin's gay community. The wood tingled beneath her palm, and Faye couldn't help but smile. Beyond the door lay an energy oasis where people came in search of confidence, freedom and love.

She moved back to the sidewalk and squatted down, noting the energy grew strongest in one spot. As she lowered a hand to touch the pavement, purple streaks of light leapt up to meet her palm. Residual life force.

Her mind became cluttered with images. Like a black and white movie playing only for her, she saw Curt as he must have appeared the night before, stumbling in front of the club. He'd lost the pants and shirt Faye had last seen him in and now wore only his boxers and a T-shirt.

A little giggle erupted from Curt. No...that wasn't quite right. It sounded more feminine. He looked down at his leg, a frightened expression skewing what would have normally been a handsome face. His hands shaking, Curt pulled up the edge of his boxers, revealing a tattoo of a 1940's pin-up girl with flowing black hair.

The pin-up girl's large breasts stretched her red and white checkered shirt, which was tied at the midriff. Her long legs were bare except for the tight blue shorts she wore. In each hand she held a milk pail. Both were about to overflow with creamy white liquid, and as Faye watched, a drop of milk ran down the sides of one of the pails. The tattoo giggled again, her mouth curving into a seductive grin, complimenting the amusement in her big green eyes.

Curt moaned and clutched his left arm.

The pin-up girl looked at Faye and winked.

Shocked, Faye jerked her hand away from the sidewalk and glanced around. A strange sexual current ran through her body, and she shivered. She wanted to probe further into Curt's energy, but couldn't chance calling attention to herself. The number one rule drilled into her head since she'd first discovered her powers as a child couldn't be violated. Be discreet.

The sidewalk to her left and right was clear of pedestrian traffic, but a quick look across the street showed differently. A man leaned against the wall of a building, his arms crossed, watching her. Still enough to be mistaken for a statue, his hair gave him away as the chilly wind caught strands of it, lifting them up in a breezy dance before they settled against his chiseled face.

Faye took a deep breath and met the blank gaze of Nathan Ink, glad of the passing cars separating them. Azal's early warnings made her cautious. Before she could decide what to do, Nathan appeared at her side, a slight grin on his face.

"Angels always make everything look so easy," Faye said. "Have you ever actually used a crosswalk before?"

"I find no reason to bother with such things." He nodded toward the sidewalk. "See anything interesting?"

"Yeah. Actually, I did." Faye tried to squelch the butterflies in her stomach. The last thing she needed was for him to sense her feelings. "How about you?"

"Just a woman on the sidewalk thinking deep thoughts."

"What are you doing here?"

"I occasionally take walks downtown on Sunday mornings. It's quiet. Care to join me?"

"I have work to do here."

"Walk with me. I find walking helps clear the mind," he said. "I'll even buy you a coffee at the coffee shop down the street to make up for my rudeness last night."

Faye shrugged, and pulled her jacket tighter. Screw Azal and his warnings. A golden opportunity to ask a few questions had presented itself and she couldn't let it slip away. "All right. But I want the good stuff. Not that Starbucks crap."

* * * *

Silent, they walked to the coffee shop. Nathan couldn't quite get a sense of what she thought or felt, and it bothered him. Mortals should be simple to read. He'd paid for their coffees, and allowed her to choose the direction their walk would take. He wasn't surprised when she slowly led them back the way they'd come.

"Mr. Ink, I'm going to cut to the chase," Faye said, sipping the coffee as they walked. "I want to ask you some questions so I can get on with my life without angels hounding me all the time."

He liked the way she talked. No bullshit. How rare to find someone not completely enamored by the divine!

"I want to start with the idea of you being a rogue angel. Are you one?"

Nathan smiled, not so much at the question, but at the nerve it took for her to ask it. He might not have been able to read her thoughts, but her body language made it clear she wasn't comfortable around him. Last night, he hadn't sensed that as much, but then again, that could have been due to the pain she'd been under from helping the dead cross over. Today was a different story, and he hadn't missed the way she'd kept a respectable amount of distance between the two of them as they stood in line at the coffee shop. Even now she made sure of her personal space.

"A rogue? Depends on what that word means," he said. "My job is to show people the path away from sin. I'm good at what I do, which is a problem for some of my…peers."

"Do you think you do your job right?"

Good question. Way back in the beginning, when his artistic gifts were first altered, Nathan had thought so. The path God laid down challenged him. Oh, the stories he could tell about the sinners he'd worked his magic on! But a great deal of time had passed. Much had happened in heaven and the world to change his thoughts and jade the joy of his art. Did he do the job right? He didn't know.

"I do the job my way."

"Tell me what happens when you tattoo a client."

"I brand their soul."

"What does that mean?"

"When I touch my clients, I get…impressions…little glimpses into their minds. These glimpses help me infuse the tattoo with whatever sin it represents."

"But you don't always work alone, right? Last night you had an assistant in the shop. She touched Curt's shoulder."

"Ah, yes," Nathan smiled at the memory. "Judith is very creative, and Curt's tattoo needed a special ingredient of desire. She helped provide it with her presence. The whole time I marked Curt's skin, all he could think about were the naughty things he wanted to do to Judith. I have to admit, she's pretty inspiring."

"I see." Faye looked away, but not before Nathan caught the slight trace of pink on her face. "Curt's sin was lust then? Lots of people suffer from an overabundance of that. How come everyone doesn't suffer the same fate?"

"Because they don't all sit in my chair," Nathan said. "Nor is everyone's lust as extreme as Curt's."

"What gives you the right to determine what's extreme and what's not when it comes to lust? It's not as if you're out there in the dating world."

"My credentials come straight from God. It's not your average Joe who finds his way to my shop. The sin, the need--it must be strong for the client even to view my establishment." Nathan tried to keep the irritation he felt at justifying himself out of his voice. "I also have to hear the hum."

"The hum?"

"Mortals always carry around a little hum. For most people it's a golden noise, the hum of life and opportunity. But there are some who waste opportunity, waste life, and their hum is different. It's a sound too harsh for your human ears to understand."

"So the hum is the calling card for your clients?" Faye stopped walking and turned to Nathan.

"Yes," he said. "It's how I recognize them."

She grew quiet. He watched her, reflecting that most of the mortals he met were clients, their sins so heavy he couldn't wait to get the job done and send them on their way. Conversation with his assistants could be stimulating at times, but they were always so full of questions about their own callings. Nathan found it easier to just be silent around them. It surprised him to find he'd enjoyed his talk with Faye.

"So what did you think of my tattoo?" He prodded while she remained silent. "I saw you stirring around the residual life force energy Curt left behind. I'm sure you got some inkling as to what his last moments were like. Tell me, what did you feel?"

"I don't understand everything I saw or felt," she admitted, and the pink rose in her face again, intriguing Nathan. He'd be willing to bet money she'd felt some of Curt's lust. "You called Curt's case of lust extreme. Tell me more about that. Make me understand you. Make me understand what I saw and felt."

His lips twitched, but he kept back the grin of pleasure.

"Last summer, Curt killed his best friend. This friend admitted he was a homosexual, and Curt didn't take the news well."

"I see,"

"No. I don't think you do." Nathan thrust his hands into his pockets. "See, Curt was a homophobe, but in reality, he had a strong attraction to other men. He couldn't accept that about himself, and as some do, he strove to be as masculine as he could. When the friend attempted to kiss him, Curt liked it."

"Let me guess," Faye said. "He might have liked it, but it went against everything he stood for. So he killed the other man."

"Basically."

"So then the tattoo, the pin-up girl, she did what? Taunted him with lust that couldn't be placed anywhere?"

"Oh, it could be placed somewhere. Curt just didn't like the option he was presented with." Nathan laughed, imagining the expression on Curt's face when he'd finally figured out what happened to him. That was the part Nathan always regretted. That he missed the big realization, the moment the client became fully aware of the cost of their sin. Residual life force memories weren't nearly as good for him as the real event. "See you didn't get to the end of the vision. You didn't see the part where all the gay men in Rainbow Cattle Company came rushing out, brushing against poor confused Curt, and causing him to blow his wad. The rush, the heat, the heart attack that followed--it must have been magnificent."

Faye stared down at the sidewalk. Oh, how he wanted to know her thoughts, to see what she thought of him. Was she repulsed? Angry? Appreciative? The exhilaration of sharing this made him almost giddy.

"Do they all die, Nathan?" she asked. "When they sit in your chair, is death what comes for them?"

"Free will is what comes for them, Faye. My tattoos help them realize they have choices. What they chose to do after leaving my chair is up to them. Curt had the opportunity to turn himself in for his crimes. The pin-up tattoo would have bargained with him over that, but some clients are too stubborn to do the right thing."

"If Curt had confessed, would he be alive?"

"More than likely."

"How do you know which design to choose for your clients?" she asked.

"I have a book called Sinz. It's old, been with me a long time. My designs are kept there. I've always had a knack for drawing, or scratching, as I used to call it. The tattoo calls out to the client when they walk into the door, matching their hum. I just find the right match."

"Are they all like Curt's? I mean, are they all tattoos of people?"

"No. Some are more traditional symbols. Like I said, the design I choose depends on the sin and the person." They walked in silence for a few minutes, and he allowed himself to breathe in her intoxicating scent. Damned if it didn't stoke a small fire of desire in him. To clear his mind of this feeling, he broached a new subject. "Azal must be happy you're doing as he asked."

"I suppose." They stood on the bridge of Waller Creek. "I'll just be happy when he's gone."

"I'd like to hear the story of why your faith in Azal was broken."

"Not today. Today is about you. I'm surprised you don't know my story, anyway. Angels are as bad as teenage girls when it comes to gossip." She flashed him a brief smile that dazzled him. "How come you don't hang out with the other angels?"

"I've found that after five hundred years, I work best alone. I'm pretty young compared to most of the Others, but I've already lost my love for the holy babble. I'd rather just do my job."

"Holy babble? Isn't that part of your job? Don't you spout holy babble when you tattoo the clients?"

"I tattoo sinners, but I don't offer them scripture. When they sit in my chair, they're past that point."

"And yet, somewhere in your core existence, you must buy into the crap that makes up the church," Faye said. "Your faith in God and what He has you doing must be strong."

"The church is just a building. I'm an angel," Nathan said. "I work for God, not the church, and yes, I believe in Him. I have faith in my Father."

"Good for you," she said bitterly, and stared down at the creek.

"If Azal offends you, why are you checking up on me? Why help him?"

"I don't know," she said, but he sensed the lie.

"Azal can be persuasive," Nathan said. "Perhaps this will heal the bad feeling between you."

"I don't like death." There was fire in her voice he hadn't heard before. "Or the angels that keep company with it."

Nathan's eyes narrowed, and his fingers tapped against the rail. At the ripe old age of five hundred, friends were not a necessity. Yet his heart tightened in his chest and coldness swept over him, washing away her scent.

"I'm sorry." The realization of what she'd said and how it applied to him grew on her face. "I didn't mean--"

"You know, when it rains enough," he said, ignoring her, "the creek below us fills up like a rushing river. Anything that falls into it is pushed along before getting dumped into Town Lake."

"I believe it's called Lady Bird Lake now."

"I'm a creature of habit." Nathan shrugged. "Did you read that newspaper I gave you?"

"Not yet."

"Look for a story about a young woman who drowned."

"Your handiwork?"

"I don't like to brag." He turned from the rail. "It's time for me to head back to my shop."

"Thanks for the coffee," she said.

"I'm sure I'll see you soon." With a nod, he turned and walked away, resisting the urge to look back when he hit the cross street. She was an interesting creature, though he didn't care for the prick of anger he'd felt at some of her words. And her comment about keeping company with angels that brought death--why had it got to him? It shouldn't have mattered in the least what a mortal--and a woman, for that matter--thought about his job.

But Nathan hoped she wrapped her investigation up soon. Something had happened to him while they stood together on the bridge that worried him. A strand of her hair caught in the morning breeze, lifting and falling like a feather, the perfect color of gold and brightening in the sun. He surprised himself by becoming momentarily transfixed by it. That shit was for novice angels, not veterans. He'd broken the habit long ago. How Azal would have laughed if he'd seen it occur!

And just what was between Faye and Azal? Whatever it was had shaken her faith in heaven. He heard it in her hum.

A familiar sound pricked at his ears, driving away thoughts of Faye. The hum. It filled his head, and he looked around, expecting to see a potential customer.

There was no one.

The hum intensified, shooting through him like daggers and leaving only dizziness behind. He reached out with all his senses, the invisible fingertips of his mind brushing against nothing. Whoever the hum came from stayed out of sight.

Sweat dripped down Nathan's forehead as he staggered to the door leading up to his apartment. Entering the room, he swept his hand toward the stereo. The harsh sound of Gwar filled the loft, but even they weren't enough to drown out the noise. His fingers shook and tingled with the hum, threatening to drop the tiny vials he removed from his kitchen cabinet. The sound gathered strength, and he gulped down the elixirs, blood trickling out of one of his ears. He fell to the floor, clutching the empty vials in his hands.

After a moment, the pain subsided. Healing blackness gathered around Nathan, and he closed his eyes, letting the elixirs do their job.

Something powerful lurked on the street below. He sensed it still. The size and scope of its sins had been almost too much for Nathan to listen to. But the angel knew it wouldn't be long before he or she found their way to Hell's Leak and his chair.

* * * *

Azal frowned. More and more he found that such a gesture was becoming common. Every time he caught himself making that face, it only added to his discontent. He considered it a sign he'd spent too much time earthbound. Humanity sunk its claws into his angel essence the longer he stayed, and quite frankly, that wouldn't do. He wasn't some mere fledgling. He was Azal, bringer of good fortune, a Power in the tier of the Hierarchy of Angels. Emotions, feelings, those were for lower angels and archangels. It was even understandable those beings would comprehend, even desire, human emotion. They, after all, had once been human.

Not like Azal and the Others. He supposed he couldn't be a hundred percent sure he'd never been human, but he had no recollection of an earthly life. He'd simply been made by God as a heavenly creature meant to be powerful and loyal to its master. His placement as a Power allowed him to drift in and out from behind the veil, and help humanity find its path. Azal found it to be a rather thankless job at times, which was yet another sign his angelic self blended too often with human essence. After thousands of years of being a Power, a warrior of the Lord, and a dutiful servant, it had only taken twenty years on Earth to break him. He blamed Raphael for that.

Azal frowned again and moved across the University of Texas campus, invisible to those around him. He ignored the students who hurried past, anxious to get their Sunday plans underway. Sex and alcohol consumption--the threads of their thoughts drifted to him making him wonder if anyone studied anymore.

He remembered watching Faye when she'd been a freshman at UT. She'd never known it, but he'd always kept a close eye on her. Raphael had insisted upon it, and because Azal often thought of Raphael as a tutor, a mentor of sorts, he'd agreed. Truth be told, it hadn't been such an imposition to pop in from time to time and check up on his young guardian. Occasionally, he would even make his presence known to her. They would spend hours chatting or arguing over philosophy, a pastime he enjoyed. Faye asked lots of questions, but remained respectful. Her father had done his job well. How he missed the old Faye, the one full of life, happiness and…love.

The mysterious creature he currently tracked hadn't been so lucky. Azal had gathered only little glimpses of the creature's upbringing, and understood it had been raised by a mortal woman with little explanation of its heritage or their ways. And yet somehow this unknown being, with no training, had learned to block even the most powerful of angels. Not only was such a thing frustrating, but dangerous as well.

That had always been the problem with nephilims. Rare and difficult to find, one never knew the true extent of their powers, either. Most were not as lucky as Faye. Both her parents had guided her, as well as a guardian angel.

What a joke that had turned out to be. Damn Raphael. If he'd only asked him to do some other task, some other favor that wouldn't have called him away for so long from the veil. It was one thing to pop in and out, creating good luck, but to linger on Earth…well, it weakened him with emotion. That mistake had cost Azal. And Faye.

Ahead, the UT football stadium rose. Azal slipped inside, moving through the interior to its core. The green turf stretched out, surrounded by empty stadium seats, which he ignored, preferring to sit in the middle of the fifty-yard line. The silence of the barren stadium comforted him, and the angel lay down to stare up at the azure sky dotted with puffy clouds. He stretched out his arms and legs, taking deep breaths.

"It's pretty, isn't it?"

Azal turned his head and spotted the old woman. She sat on the bench at the sidelines, her feet crossed comfortably in front of her. The cross around her neck glowed as she gazed at the sky.

"Yes," Azal said. "You did a good job with that."

"It's one of my better accomplishments. There's just so much beyond it. I thought the humans would have found more by now."

"They are advancing at a rapid pace."

"True. But sometimes I feel they're going in the wrong directions."

"Surely, it is how you deemed it. What could be wrong?"

"Shall we talk theology now, Azal? Is that really what you want?"

Azal sighed and sat up, twisting his body to face the old woman. "Tell me what knowledge you wish to impart."

"I'm here to check on your progress. I can't see clearly beyond the veil when it comes to my angels. Not one of my brighter moves I'm afraid. When I created my angel tiers, it never occurred to me I would need to check up on them. I trusted they would do my bidding, but angels, like humans, have evolved." The old lady stood and moved to Azal, placing her hands gently on each side of his face. "But I underestimated my children of humanity. I made them too beautiful, too smart and too tempting. They are strong indeed if they cause feelings in even the most powerful of my angels."

"Forgive me," Azal whispered. "I can't seem to stop the emotions that roll within me."

"Shhh….you've done nothing but what I asked," she said, but her voice grew stern. "I advise you to be careful, though, old friend. I couldn't bear it if you fell from grace too. It's been a long time since I had to destroy an angel, and you would be a great loss."

Azal nodded. He'd witnessed an angel's death one time. The power it left behind created a dying star in the sky.

"I've been unable to track the nephilim," Azal said, standing. "I can sense him from time to time, but he's slippery. I don't know who's taught him, but he's aware of us and seeks to stay hidden. The only signs of him are the bodies he leaves behind."

"And the symbols."

"Yes. If indeed those symbols come from him. This nephilim could be innocent of the crimes we attribute to him. Our source is still very confused."

"What are you saying?" The woman's eyes sharpened, glittering in the sunlight "Don't tell me you still suspect…are you referring to Nathan?"

"He is…a wild card," Azal said, but his voice softened. "I don't think he would do this to his own kind. I wouldn't have pushed Faye in his direction otherwise. He can protect her better than I can at this point too."

"She's still holding a grudge against you, isn't she?" When Azal nodded, the old woman said, "Sorrow is one of the more interesting character traits. It lingers in some people, clouding their judgment."

"That's why I haven't told her everything that is going on," Azal said. "I don't think she would be able to control herself if she knew the truth just yet. Gradually easing her into the knowledge is best, and I've put her on the right path several times today."

"What about Nathan? Have you talked with him?"

"He is resistant, as always, to speak with me."

"Find a way," the old woman said. "I'm fond of Nathan, always have been, but there are things about him that remind me now and again of Lucifer. Any sign of that scoundrel, by the way?"

"Nothing."

"I'm sure he's about," she said with a soft chuckle. "Nothing keeps Lucifer down, and I see his work everywhere."

"As you say," Azal said, and bowed his head.

"But see if you can't locate him too," she said. "It's been too long."

Azal nodded.

"And the Others? Have you discovered anything more?" The old woman twisted the cross at her neck. "Could they still be alive?"

"I feel it is as you feared. They are destroyed. I cannot sense them anywhere."

The old woman said nothing to this but took a step back. With a shimmer of golden light, she disappeared, but not before Azal had seen the slight slump in her shoulders.

Azal stared at the spot, sorting through a myriad of feelings. He longed to be traveling upward with her, free from this place, the feelings. But the work wasn't done.

Weary, he lay back down and stared at the sky, letting his thoughts wander free.

Chapter 6

Faye ignored the long line of people waiting to get a table at Katz's Deli and headed straight to the bar where her friend, Zenovia, worked.

"Vodka tonic," she said to the pretty bartender.

"Hey, girl." Zenovia's silver hoop earring swished against her dark hair as she greeted Faye. "Heard you had a great set at the Black Cat last night. Barb stopped in earlier today on her way out of town. Lucky bitch. That could have been my lottery ticket! She and I always go in together on those damn scratch off tickets. All the good stuff happens at Black Cat on my nights off! Not that I really had the night off, since I was busting my ass bartending here."

"So did Barb say where she was going?"

"The same place Barb always talks about going to." Zenovia splashed vodka into a crystal tumbler, following it up with tonic.

"Vegas?"

"Yep. I tried to talk her out of it, but you know how that goes. That girl's got no sense in her head." Zenovia placed a lime on the edge of the glass and slid it across the bar to Faye. "So where you been today? You look flushed."

"I walked over from my house. Before that I was at the hike and bike trail."

"And now you need a vodka tonic?" Zenovia grinned. "Most people drink water after they exercise."

"It was a hell of a walk."

Faye sipped the drink as Zenovia moved away to help another customer, but her thoughts dwelled on the spirit she'd encountered at Lady Bird Lake. She hadn't bothered to go home and check out the newspaper article as Nathan suggested. Why wait?

I don't need a newspaper article to locate a spirit.

Sitting in the warmth of the bar, Faye shivered. It hadn't been hard to find it. The residual energy of the obese young woman with desperate eyes trailed along the water's edge, a soft purple mist only Faye could see. A mermaid tattoo sagged against the folds of flab hanging from the spirit's naked back.

The dead woman stared at the water, but the mermaid--a slash of color against the gray skin of the ghost--swished her blue-green tail. Balancing a mirror in one hand, she used the other to smooth down her hair and pinch her cheeks until a soft blush arose in them. As the mermaid surveyed the results, she puckered her lips and blew a kiss to herself.

"Fat ass was a vain one. Once she had that gastric bypass surgery, she thought she was hot stuff," the mermaid said, glancing at Faye conspiratorially. "But in reality she was a bitch, a slut who stole husbands and boyfriends as if they were nothing. Isn't that right, fat ass?"

The woman shuddered, but did not turn around.

"If only she'd been this subdued in life." The mermaid swished her tail, causing the flab on the woman's back to wave like water. "We took a little swim together, and when it was time to get out, she didn't want to. She felt too beautiful as a mermaid, entranced by her face in the looking glass of moonlight. Big mistake."

A cruel smile broke out on the mermaid's porcelain face.

"The vainglorious bitch drowned. She puffed up like a fat, ugly sausage!"

The woman turned. Dark circles ringed eyes set in an oval face pale enough to see the blue veins running across it. Her wet hair held mud and leaves in its tangled strands, and the stench of the lake, mossy and damp, perfumed her. She covered her breasts, shivering, and said, "He did this to me."

"Who?" Faye asked.

"Nathan Ink."

Before Faye could question the spirit further, the woman vanished.

Back at her apartment, she'd scanned the newspaper. It hadn't taken long to locate the story of a girl found dead on the banks of Lady Bird Lake. Dated December, the brief article stated only the victim's name and the bare facts. Cassie Blanford. Age 21. Body discovered by morning joggers who strayed from the hike and bike trail around the lake. Cause of death was listed as drowning. There was no mention of tattoos or Nathan Ink, but the picture of Cassie showed a thin version of the ghost Faye had met.

She scanned the article next to it, which was about the Grim Sleeper, a serial killer the cops had been tracking for several years. Austin definitely had its share of murders, but deciphering which ones Nathan Ink caused would be a challenge. Faye sat back on her heels, thinking about the stack of newspapers she'd seen in Nathan's apartment. How many of the deaths in those could be attributed to him? And when you got down to it, what really made Nathan so different from the serial killer the cops were tracking? While she'd never looked up the actual profile of a serial killer, it wouldn't have surprised her if she found Nathan shared common traits with such an offender. Of course he got to hide behind the title of angel.

Zenovia's bright laugh broke Faye free of her reverie and squashed the twinge of anger she felt.

"Here's to you, Cassie Blanford," Faye said softly and lifted her glass. "Poor thing."

She sipped her vodka tonic and watched Zenovia, admiring the way the barmaid put everyone at ease. They'd been friends for several years, though Faye still tried to keep her at arm's length. True friendships had never come easy to Faye, because of the secrets about herself she'd been trained to keep. Of course the touching thing was often a problem too. Hard to keep friends when you automatically knew so much about them from a handshake.

Undeterred by Faye's standoffish behavior, and a hopeless romantic, Zenovia always looked for someone to match Faye up with who was, in her opinion, too often alone. Faye could never explain to the other woman she was alone by choice. In her mind, she'd had the best, and she wasn't the sort who could settle down with just any other guy. He would have to be tolerant, special, and most of all, open-minded.

Like Chris.

He'd been taken from her way too soon. They would have been married by now, maybe even have started a family. Chris always mentioned wanting kids, but Faye had been hesitant. She liked children. It was just…well, genetically she wasn't sure what would happen. Faye knew what it was like to be different, a child of genetic misfortune. Not just acne different or talk funny different, but way out there able to jump buildings in a single bound different. Would she be able to risk that for her kids? She just didn't know.

Her eyes filled with tears, which she wiped away. It didn't matter now. Chris was gone, killed seven years ago in the same accident that had taken her parents, leaving her alone in the world. They were far beyond the veil where she couldn't see them, and hopefully they couldn't see her. Some of her actions these past few years hadn't made her proud.

"You okay, Faye?" Zenovia scrubbed at a water stain on the counter. "You look a little down. Man trouble?"

"I'd have to have a man in order to have trouble," Faye said. "I'm fine. Just been a busy day."

"I know how to cheer you up," Zenovia said, and pulled out a copy of the Austin Chronicle already opened to the music section. "That band I wanted you to see is playing tonight at Antone's."

"I don't know," Faye said. "My ass is dragging. Dancing isn't really the cure for that."

"Oh, c'mon. A few drinks, a little fun--you'll forget all about being tired. Remember that night we tore it up with Carlos at The Continental Club?"

"Oh, I remember," Faye said. There were moments when she could still feel the hangover from their last adventure at the infamous Continental Club. And then there was Carlos...God, how could she ever forget that night? It had been one of the few times when she'd allowed her logic to take a vacation while she'd indulged her senses. But the shame, the guilt, the utter disloyalty to Chris--she'd felt in the following weeks had taken the pleasure away from the experience. "I'll think about it."

"Good enough for now." Zenovia glanced over Faye's shoulder and smiled. "Perfect timing. Here comes that guy I told you about last week. Mr. Blue Lagoon."

Faye grinned at Zenovia's enthusiasm as she waved the man over.

"Hi, John." Zenovia leaned over the bar to give him a hug. While she waited to be introduced, she took in his tall lanky frame, which ended in a shock of curly blond hair. "This is Faye."

"Hi, Faye." John turned and offered his hand. She shook it, bracing for the usual spark of information to jump into her mind. It was a skill she'd come to both dread and rely on. However, in John's case there was nothing. No childhood images or ex-girlfriends popped out. Just a sense of relaxation and calm. How rare! She could probably count on her fingers the number of times that had happened in her life. Some people were just better at naturally shielding themselves from her gifts than others.

"Nice to meet you," Faye said, intrigued.

He ordered a Lone Star and hung the gold-rimmed sunglasses he'd been wearing into the pocket of his shirt before saying, "You're the singer who works with Zenovia, right? At the Black Cat?"

"That's right." She watched him sip his beer, amused at the foam moustache it created on his face. "Do you live close by, John?"

"Yep. I'm an urbanite. I live in one of the high rises off Fourth Street," he said.

She gave an appreciative whistle.

"Those places are nice. You must do well for yourself."

"Well," he said and tilted his head to the side. "I'm actually not working right now."

"Oh, sorry. I didn't mean to be so personal."

"No, no, you're fine. It's no big deal." The easy smile returned, and Faye couldn't help but notice how cute he was. And tall. His looked down at her as if he knew a secret and said, "So, Faye, what do you think?"

"About?"

"The hair." He grinned and pointed at his head. "Zenovia told me you're a Blue Lagoon fan. Do you want to touch it?"

Faye laughed before she could help herself. She did have the urge to touch his hair. There was so much of it, and it reminded her of the actor in the movie The Blue Lagoon. She nodded and reached over, pulling on one of the soft curls.

"I never should have told Zenovia I liked Christopher Atkins. Has it always been like this?"

"Pretty much," he said. "My mom tried to cut it when I was kid, but it always grew back curly. Finally, I just gave up. It's cool, though, because chicks love it. Look at us. I just met you and already you're running your fingers through my hair."

"I knew she wouldn't be able to resist you," Zenovia said. "See if you can talk her into going to see The Crabs with us tonight."

"They're good," John said. "You should come check them out."

"What kind of music do they play?"

"Latin funk. Great for dancing if you're into that sort of thing."

Faye couldn't help but notice the way his gaze slid over her figure, and she wondered if he pictured the two of them dancing together, bodies pressed close, hips finding their own erotic movement. Hell, the thought of it gave her a tingle in places that hadn't seen action in a while.

"Could be interesting," she said, struggling to sound normal. Geez...what was with her today? Since touching Curt's life force energy, an odd feeling churned in her off and on all day. Lust. At one point during her conversation with Nathan, she'd been tempted to lean forward and kiss him, just to see if she could. Common sense had quickly reared its head, but still...And now here it was again. As she stared at John, sexual desire rose in her like a slow moving flood. She tried to focus on his words.

"The Crabs need lots of support right now. Their guitar player was killed a few weeks ago," John said.

"What's the story with that again?" Zenovia said. "The guitar player's girlfriend killed him in self-defense or something, right?"

"That's the rumor," John said.

"Uh-oh. I can tell by your tone you think the girlfriend is lying."

"Maybe," John said with a shrug. "Her story keeps changing. Originally she raved about some tattoo causing the musician to go crazy."

Faye's heartbeat picked up speed. Could it be the boyfriend was one of Nathan's clients? What were the odds of that? It was definitely worth checking out. And then she could have a justifiable reason for hanging out with John too.

"Sounds like some messed up shit." Zenovia slid a drink down the bar where a thirsty patron caught it.

"You girls are all a mystery to me." John grinned. "I certainly can't claim to understand any of you."

"Doesn't stop you from trying to get into our pants, though," Zenovia said, tossing her brown hair.

"No," John said good naturedly. "It doesn't."

Both of them laughed. Faye downed the rest of her drink and placed it back on the bar.

"You want another?" Zenovia asked.

"No. I've got to get home and clean up if I'm going out with you tonight," Faye said, and smiled at Zenovia's squeal of delight, but inside she fought a battle to stay calm. "Nice to meet you, John. See you later."

As Faye stepped outside of Katz's, the afternoon sun slipped away into the confines of dusk. An unearthly orange glow rested on everything, making the city sparkle. With her gaze, she followed the sparkle of light across the street where it settled on someone. Azal. She heard his voice in her head.

Stay close to Nathan, but be careful.

He nodded and walked down Sixth Street toward Congress Avenue, gently fading away.

"Asshole," she said, hoping her voice would follow him. "What are you really up to?"

Chapter 7

The house stereo at Antone's played a Michelle Branch song featuring Carlos Santana. People swayed along to the music, their voices rising above Santana's guitar as they drank their beer and cocktails. Nathan sat in the back, feeling out of place and wondering what the hell he was doing tapping his foot to a Michelle Branch song.

He supposed curiosity had gotten the better of him. His assistant, Judith, had left the Austin Chronicle open on the counter of Hell's Leak with The Crabs gig circled. Next to it, she'd printed: Wasn't this one of yours?

Nathan smiled at the advertisement, which labeled the evening concert as a tribute to the band's guitar player. Would Faye have picked up on this little gem? He thought it possible she might. He'd sensed the divine presence of Azal nearby all afternoon. Perhaps the angel of fortune manipulated the odds a little in order to get Faye to further her investigation of heaven's rogue? Nathan would put nothing past Azal.

Right now Faye stood in line at the club's entrance. Nathan watched her smile at the door guy, obediently letting him stamp her hand as she scanned the place. How long would it take for her to sense him? Probably less than five minutes.

The blue dress she wore gathered in a loose scoop at the front, tightened in the middle and then flared out in a sexy swirl around her legs. A black shawl hugged her shoulders to protect her from the chill outside. Her hair, pulled up and caught in a golden clip, hung down her back in a shimmering tangle. The style reminded him of a Greek goddess, though Nathan had actually met a few Greek goddesses in his time. They were just angels dressed to play a particular part.

None of them moved him as much as Faye did right then.

Damn! The thought caught him off guard again. Attractions did not come easily to Nathan Ink. Though he had met plenty of women throughout the centuries, the ones that caused a reaction in him on a physical level were few and far between. Not to mention forbidden. And yet, from time to time, he yearned. God's love was great and good, but still…he watched the humans and noted their affections for each other, the way they could attach to another being body, heart and soul. Even through his tough veneer, their actions confused and fascinated Nathan. It kept him from finding solace behind the veil.

The song changed, and the band Weezer started singing about an island in the sun. Faye still hadn't spotted him, and he continued to watch her move through the room, smiling and nodding at people she knew. He could almost see the sense of peace she brought with her greeting. A simple touch on the shoulder here, a squeeze of the arm there. She spread natural healing without even being aware of it, though he noticed she did the touching, not allowing anyone else to initiate contact.

The hum rang out, and he gritted his teeth against the pain it brought. He looked around, searching for the source. Hard to tell with all the people in the room. The sound soared above Weezer and the chattering of the crowd, smacking him hard with its power as it had that afternoon.

Nathan wavered in his seat, feeling as if little holes were being ripped in his fragile armor. The human tissue of his mortal shell could barely house the essence of an angel to begin with, and the human eye could not withstand his true form. Best to leave the club before he hurt someone.

Already the people around him sensed his strange energy. A couple near Nathan started to argue, their voices shrill with hysteria. Another woman fainted, her face pale and white as blood dripped from her nose. The man next to her swayed, and stared down at her with glassy eyes before vomiting on the floor.

"Nathan, can you hear me?"

A hand touched his shoulder. The pain subsided enough for him to focus on the worried face looking down at him.

Faye gripped Nathan's shoulder, sending another flow of her energy into him. "Is that better?"

"Yes," he said, and reached toward the glass votive on the table. He plucked a floating lily out and gulped down the water. Sweat broke out across his forehead, and as he ran a free hand over it, he noticed the sweat was tinged with blood.

"Take it easy. I don't know what's going on, but the strength of your anxiety is practically shaking the pillars of this place." Faye pulled a chair close to his and sat, never removing her hand from his shoulder. "What's happening?"

"I'm not sure. The hum...it's not like what I usually hear," Nathan winced as the tone sounded. "This is the second time I've heard it."

"When was the first?"

"Just after we parted this afternoon. It overwhelmed me then too."

"Here. Let me." The concern in her voice warmed him further. She reached over to touch her fingertips to his forehead, massaging gently, and he found the sensation soothing. "So who is it coming from?"

"I don't know." The pain subsided, lingering just below the Band-Aid of energy she provided. He reached for the soft hand massaging his forehead and held it. "Thank you. My human armor almost slipped. That would have been terrible for everyone here."

"But it didn't. No harm done, big guy." Her hand lingered a moment in his before she pulled it free. "You sure you're okay?"

"For now. I only came to Antone's to see who would turn up for the tribute concert."

"Really? Do you always take such an interest in your clients?"

"Don't you take an interest in your clients?"

"My clients buy flowers, and besides, we're not talking about me. Answer my question."

"I think there are other questions you should be asking, other beings you should be interrogating."

"What's that supposed to mean?"

The hum flared up again before he could answer, and he couldn't help the low moan that escaped him. Faye moved behind him. He felt her lush breasts pressed against his upper back as she massaged his shoulders and neck, and he wasn't sure what was better--the healing power she wielded or the softness of her body.

"Do you see anyone who looks like the cause of your pain?"

His gaze passed over the couples, the loners, the musicians gathered at the stage, the dark haired bartender hurriedly mixing drinks, an old woman sitting alone and watchful in the corner. Something familiar about her...

The music shifted, coinciding with a shift of energy provided by Faye. Now Lenny Kravitz sang an old song, Believe, from one of his earlier albums, and she hummed along.

"I always wanted to get this guy in my chair." Nathan tried to focus on something other than her intoxicating scent and the sudden jumble of crazy images involving Faye and his bed.

"Lenny Kravtiz?" Faye squeezed his shoulder and the warmth spread deeper into his body. "Please. He's too beautiful to be guilty of any major sin."

"We're all guilty of sin no matter how beautiful."

"Even you?"

"Are you saying you find me attractive, Faye?" Nathan smiled. Even through the veil of pain, the obvious discomfort the question aroused in Faye amused him.

"We are all beautiful in God's sight," she mocked and removed her hands. "How do you feel now?"

"Better." He stood, swaying just a little. She grabbed his arm, supporting him in a gesture he found both absurd and touching. Spotting the lily he'd taken from the votive, Nathan handed it to her.

"How gallant," she said. "Leaving?"

"Yes." He hesitated and then said, "Come by the shop later. I'd like to hear about how your…research…is going."

She studied him a moment. "I'm meeting some friends here, but I'll drop by later. Besides, I think I have some research to do here first."

"She's over on the other side of the stage, sipping an apple martini," Nathan said, enjoying the confusion on her face.

"She?"

"Yeah. What were you expecting?"

"Someone dead since that's what happened to both of your other clients I've checked on so far. I thought the musician was the one you tattooed."

"My client is alive," Nathan said. "Tara only wishes she was dead."

He left Antone's. The headache flared up slightly as he passed the entrance where eager Crabs fans were gathered to pay the cover charge. He almost knocked a tall man with curly blond hair over as he pushed past the crowd. Mumbling an apology, he trudged back to Hell's Leak, heading upstairs where he could take something for the damn pain in his head and prepare for Faye's visit.

* * * *

Faye watched him go. He had a nice ass. Of course he was an angel so what else could be expected? Angel's were supposed to be blessed with all the best attributes. Why not a nice ass? On the other hand, thinking about it like that made it somehow seem very wrong to Faye. After all, he was an angel.

I think there are other questions you should be asking, other beings you should be interrogating. What had he meant?

She would ask him that later. For now, she intended to focus on the only living client of Nathan's she'd come across so far. Faye slipped to the other side of the stage where a lone woman sat sipping her apple martini, stoically puffing on a cigarette.

Tara. That's what Nathan called her.

Tara listened to a small green iPod, and Faye reached out with her mind. A popular tune by Rage Against the Machine filled Faye's ears along with Tara's thoughts.

I fucking hate this place.

Tara ran a hand through her shock of red hair and puffed harder on her cigarette.

Fucking Tommy. It's his fault I'm stuck here dealing with the band's goddamned looks.

Tommy. Faye glanced at the large black and white photo placed on an easel at the front of the stage. Hispanic with cropped black hair, Tommy stared out at the crowd who stopped to touch the picture solemnly. Tara watched, her shoulders tight with tension.

Faye squared her shoulders and headed over.

"Hi," she said.

The woman looked up, distrust in her black rimmed eyes as she pulled one of the ear buds out.

"Yeah?"

"Is your name Tara?"

"Who the fuck are you?"

"I'm a fan of The Crabs. I think I've seen you here before."

"So? Look. I'm straight. I don't do the lesbian thing anymore." Tara rolled her eyes and started to jam the ear bud back in.

"I'm not hitting on you."

"Oh." Tara gave Faye a cursory once over. "Well, move on. I'm not in the mood to make new friends."

"I knew Tommy."

Tara's eyes narrowed.

"Who are you again?"

"My name is Faye McCoy."

"Have we met?"

"No."

"Were you fucking Tommy?"

"No."

"Well, how do you know him? Were you a fan?"

"Sort of. Shame what happened to him."

Tara looked away and her hand tightened on the stem of the martini glass. Faye reached out, hearing the young woman's thoughts.

Blood. So much blood. I didn't mean to hit him so hard.

"How did you say you knew Tommy?" Tara asked.

"I like guitars." Faye hoped Tara wouldn't ask any technical questions about the instrument. She'd never played a guitar in her life. "We ran into each other at Guitar Center a few times."

"He liked to hang out there on Saturdays." A shiny teardrop formed in Tara's eye. "He loved that place."

"You know, he always seemed like such an easygoing guy. I can't understand what would make him snap and go crazy," Faye said. "It's just so hard to believe a guy like that would want to hurt you."

"But he did snap." Tara stubbed the cigarette out. "He snapped and attacked me."

"Why?"

"I don't know."

Tommy loved that fucking guitar. He always paid more attention to it than me.

"Whatever happened to that guitar he liked so much?" Faye asked, fascinated by the woman's thoughts. She couldn't help but notice how heavily tattooed Tara's arms were too. How Nathan must have adored this particular client!

"You mean the red Washburn?" Tara ran a hand through her short hair again. "His precious Betsy?"

"That's right. That's what he called her."

"She was destroyed…in the fight. An accident."

I broke that thing in a million pieces. Made him see me finally. All those splintered pieces on the kitchen linoleum got his attention. Should've choked him with one of the guitar strings.

"Why did he attack you? Was there an argument?"

"I already answered these questions at the police station."

Tara pulled out another cigarette with a shaking hand. "Are you some sort of undercover cop they're using?"

"Was it a tattoo? Did you get a tattoo that started to make you feel...funny?"

"You're crazy," Tara said, but Faye hadn't missed the surprise that rippled across her face. "I don't know what you are talking about."

"Where is it?" Faye asked. None of the tattoos visible on Tara appeared to be Nathan's caliber of work. "I'd like to see it."

"No." Tara's trembling fingers flicked the lighter over and over, unable to get a flame. "I don't feel like talking anymore. Go away."

Faye reached across the table and lit it for her. Looking into Tara's eyes, she said, "I know you might not believe this, but I'm here to help you. Please...tell me what the design was."

Tara took a long drag of the cigarette.

"A guitar," she said, softly. "A red Washburn like the one Tommy called Betsy. It wasn't what I asked for. Why would I want some fucking guitar I hated tattooed on my body?"

She sighed and rolled up the sleeve of her black blouse. On her bicep lay a small red guitar. An exquisite piece of work, it looked as if it waited to be strummed.

"It's a little masterpiece," Faye said. She had a strong urge to run her finger over it, and an idea came to her. "Mind if I touch it?"

"Sure. What does it matter now?"

Faye reached out, feeling the guitar throb under her hand. It pulsed with harsh red energy. Wrath. Pressing harder, she heard the soft strum of a guitar chord.

Rage filled her. A vision of Tommy's death struck her hard.

Tara stood above the young man who lay on the linoleum floor in a pool of dark liquid, his head split open from a fall. His eyes were tinged with blood, and his tongue clicked against his teeth as he tried to speak.

A guitar strummed. Tommy's eyes darted around the room looking for the source before settling on the red tattoo emblazoned on Tara's arm.

Tara stood above him, the broken remains of his precious Betsy in her hand. With a vicious grin, she broke the cracked neck of the guitar off, tossing the rest aside. It landed with a discordant clatter in the corner of the small kitchen. Tara grasped the long piece of wood, its end sharp and jagged from the break.

"You never fucking loved me," Tara said, holding the stake

up high. "You only loved her."

With a mighty thrust, she brought the sharp end of the guitar neck down, piercing Tommy's skull. He convulsed on the floor.

"Who the hell are you lady?" Tara jerked her arm away, fear in her eyes. "Are you like him? Are you like Mr. Ink?"

"No," Faye rubbed at her head and tried to shut off the anger, Tara's anger, still coursing through her. "I'm nothing like him."

"You made the tattoo strum. I felt it. It hasn't done that since the night...since Tommy died."

Faye couldn't quite clear the infectious rage in her head. Thoughts of Nathan's clients swirled in her mind. How brutal his methods were. Despicable really. This particular tattoo might have influenced Tara's free will, but Tommy paid the price. How could Nathan justify that? She would make him pay, she would teach him a lesson, she would kill him if she had to, she would-- stop!

The little voice in her mind that repelled violence begged to be heard. Without caring what the other woman thought, Faye downed the rest of Tara's martini. The smooth liquid slid down her throat, cooling her emotions.

What the hell had just happened?

"Tara, listen to me. I don't know everything that has happened in your life, but this anger you have is driving you," Faye said when she'd regained some control. "That tattoo is very special. It feeds on the emotion you provide it. The only way to stop it is by dealing with your anger. Don't let it control you."

"What are you? A fucking shrink?"

Faye stood and placed a hand on Tara's shoulder. As she squeezed, a burst of energy shot through her hand and into the young woman. Tara quivered as if she'd been shocked with electricity. The power of the tattoo squirmed against Faye's own as she sought to pull some of its energy out of Tara.

She released Tara's shoulder. "Look at your arm."

"How did you do that?" Tara stared at Faye. "You made it fade a little. I thought you weren't like Nathan Ink."

"I'm not. I'm a healer. Now if you want to be healed all the way, you need real help. And yes, I'm talking about a fucking shrink. Maybe the more you let go of the anger, the more that," Faye pointed at the tattoo, "will fade."

A vicious headache grew in Faye's head, and she rubbed at her temples. The anger she'd absorbed churned through her system. She tried not to stumble as she moved away from the table, leaving a speechless Tara behind. Outside, the night air helped cool her frazzled nerves, but the feeling didn't dissipate.

She left a hurried message on Zenovia's cellphone, explaining her absence at the club and then, clutching the shawl about her, trudged down the street toward Hell's Leak. The more she thought about Nathan, the more Faye couldn't help but be disgusted by his job. Despicable! That was the right word for the man. Wait. She needed to stop thinking of him as a man. So what if he had a nice ass and sexy voice that rumbled when he said her name. He was still an angel with an overdeveloped sense of righteousness.

The evening breeze pushed through her hair, momentarily clearing her mind. He'd asked her to come by his place and so she would.

But she would bring a little of her own righteousness with her!

Chapter 8

Nathan watched the street from his apartment window.

He sensed Faye, and it amazed him that he never had before. How could a creature of her strength walk around town without his knowledge? True, Nathan had only been a resident of Austin for a few years, traveling from city to city, going to wherever the pull of sin was strongest. One of the first things he did in any new place was scan for other angels. Faye hadn't even been a blip on his radar.

That's because she is not an angel, he reminded himself and moved from the window.

Downstairs in Hell's Leak, he continued to probe the air.

Wrath. Though still a few blocks away, the feeling jumped from Faye's skin, skirting through the night air. Primed for a fight, the thought of an angry Faye, eyes flashing with green fire, tantalized Nathan.

Soon enough, he thought and unlocked the shop door, flicking on the red neon sign. Time she came in to Hell's Leak. He placed the Book of Sinz on the counter, crossed his arms and waited.

A few minutes later, the door swung open and she stepped into the shop. He thought the harsh, angry music playing on the radio suited her mood.

"You're angry." He observed the flush on her face and mottled red spots on her neck. The shawl slipped off one shoulder and dragged on the ground. She didn't need it, he felt the heat streaming from her skin.

"You're a monster, Nathan."

"I'm sorry you think so."

"Much as it pains me to agree with him, I believe Azal is right. Something should be done about you."

Nathan felt a soft prickling in his head. The nerve of the woman trying to get into his thoughts!

"You asked me to stay out of your thoughts. I think it only fair you give me the same courtesy." He walked over to his rolling chair and sat. "Tell me what's got you so steamed."

"What gives you the right to brand people in such a way?"

"We've been over this already, Faye. My gift affords me the right to do many things as decreed by God."

"God wants you to kill people?" She picked up the book on the counter, and it sparked at her touch. "Is that what this book gives you permission to do?"

"People have been dying in His name since time began."

"Don't give me that line. You're as bad as Azal when it comes to quoting company policy. I want answers."

"And I'm giving them to you. You just don't like them. I don't kill people."

"Tell that to Cassie or Curt, your former clients." Faye said. The anger gathered strength, and Nathan felt it tainting the room. "And what about Tommy? You know, the man killed by his girlfriend after she got a tattoo in your shop? How do you justify that?"

"I didn't kill him."

"Bullshit." She banged the book on the counter. "The tattoo might have caused Tara to do the dirty work, but it came from you. His death has your fingerprints all over it."

"It was her choice!" The walls shook with the force of his words. "I don't control what a client does after they leave my shop. My tattoos influence their free will, but it's still their free will. Every tattoo provides a moment, a hint of how the client could change their path. If they change, the tattoo loses power, though it stays on the body as a reminder."

"Like Tara's?"

"Exactly. Tara is an angry person. It got the best of her. She didn't have to do what she did, there was an opportunity to put things in perspective. She could have backed out, but she didn't, and the anger won."

"But Tommy...why did he have to die?" Faye pressed a hand to her forehead. "And why isn't Tara in jail? Shouldn't that be part of her punishment?"

"Faye, I don't have all the answers. It must have been Tommy's time," Nathan said. "And as for Tara, fate isn't finished with her yet. She could still be saved."

"I know. When I touched her tattoo--"

"You touched it?"

"Yeah. Unlike you, I tried to help Tara. I tried to heal her."

How would Faye's body and mind react to absorbing his work? Maybe that was the cause of her intense anger right now. The anger she felt practically punched a hole in the air before her. She'd also stirred Curt's residual life force energy, which would have been tainted with perverse lust. How had that been affecting her?

"Tattoos like mine aren't meant to be healed," he said, getting up. "It's up to the clients to heal themselves."

"The client? That's how you see them, isn't it?" She walked to the shop door and looked out. "Just a business deal."

"You're only seeing one side of the story here."

"I don't think so--" she began, but Nathan cut her words off by wrapping one of his arms around her waist, pinning her back to him. "What are you doing?"

He placed his other hand on her forehead. Sure enough, he felt the residual anger pulsing in her head just below his palm. Tara's rage waited to be reborn. He pushed against her skin, and his own power coursed through his arm, battling with hers.

"Leave it." She tried to pull his hand away from her forehead. "It will go away."

"So you know it's there?" He kept his hand in place, feeling the anger continue to pulse against his palm.

"It's not my first day using my powers, you know," she said. "I know what the side effects can be. I absorbed some of Tara's anger, so now I'm angry. But on behalf of all the people you've tattooed, I think I have a right to be."

"That's how Tara felt too. Entitled to her anger. Entitled to everything, because she'd had a rough time in the world. Instead of fixing her choices, she felt it should all just be given to her. Perhaps you have a little in common with her." Nathan closed his eyes and pushed with his powers, trying to pull out the bad energy. The room vibrated with a burst of white light, and he fell back, unable to hold onto her as she slipped to the floor.

Faye glared at him, the anger flickering in her eyes. He watched her struggle for control of her emotions, her chest heaving before she turned to the side and retched. A black cloud of dust came from her mouth, and he remembered seeing the same thing happen after she'd helped the woman who'd been stabbed on the sidewalk.

Nathan went to the water cooler and returned with a small paper cup.

"Better?" He watched her gulp down the water and wipe her mouth with the back of her hand.

She nodded and handed him the empty cup. As he walked behind the counter to throw it away, Faye got up off the shop floor and moved to the barber chair. He heard her shaky breathing, but no longer felt the powerful anger coming off her in streams. Some of her hair had slipped free from the clip and he reached over, running his finger over a strand. He tucked it behind her ear, noticing her breathing stilled.

"I'm sorry," she said.

"Nothing for you to be sorry about," Nathan said. "You absorbed a lot of energy today that wasn't your own. It's only natural there would be repercussions."

"No, Nathan. That isn't what I mean," she said, lowering her gaze. "I'm sorry, but I don't think what you do is right."

Her words shouldn't have surprised him. He didn't need approval from others, never had, not even when he'd been human. Yet the soft tone of her voice stung.

"May I look inside your book?"

With a nod, he reached over and handed it to her.

Faye's fingers traced the outline of the word Sinz on the cover, causing another spark to jump from the book.

"Careful," he said. "All my designs are stored in there."

"You draw them yourself?"

"Most of them. I've collected some designs from apprentices I've had over the years."

"Do the apprentices turn out like you?" She opened the book, gently turning the worn pages.

"Not exactly. They aren't angels. In the old days we called them prophets. They have a calling to serve, and manage to find their way to me. I train them on the art of being a scratcher and the importance of their talents."

"Scratcher?"

"It's what I used to call this sort of thing before I became an angel."

"How did you become one? I've never been clear on what the criteria is for angelicness."

"You have your secrets, Faye, and I have mine."

"Fair enough." She closed the book. "Do you have a favorite symbol you like to draw?"

"The cross." He laughed at the expression of surprise on her face.

She smiled too, the anger gone, and he marveled at her gift, again wondering at her quick recovery. He smelled the humanity in her, and yet it mixed with another scent, something old and rare.

"Nephilim," he said. "You're a nephilim."

"Yes." Faye looked away. "But I prefer not to focus on that too much."

"But I'm right? You're a half breed."

"How crude."

"How apt. Nephilims are creatures born of human females and angels."

"I don't exactly need a lesson on biology when it comes to this subject. Nor do I need you to tell me about how creating a nephilim is a huge no-no to God. My kind is the real reason the Great Flood happened."

"You're ancestors were a little out of control. And the angels who broke the law had to be punished."

"So he wiped the world clean of us." Faye rolled her eyes. "Yet here I am. Bet God wishes he hadn't made sex so appealing."

"I thought nephilims were giants," Nathan said.

"The males are very tall, but typically the female is the average height of a regular human being."

"Who were your parents?"

A shadow crossed Faye's face.

"I don't want to talk about them," she said and Nathan frowned. "But don't worry. I can tell you are a total rule follower. They were punished for breaking the laws of heaven if that's what you're concerned about."

"The punishment of other angels doesn't interest me," Nathan said. "I just have a case of old-fashioned curiosity, and I really want to know who they were. I've never met anyone like you."

Faye laughed.

"What a cheesy pick-up line! Did you hear what you said? I've never met anyone like you." She repeated the phrase and swung her legs off the barber chair to face him. "If we were in a bar, I'd throw a drink in your face just to be dramatic."

Nathan's dumbfounded expression made her laugh harder. The sound softened the mood, and he tried to picture her throwing a drink at him. Another image crept into his mind instead, one he acted on without thinking. Before Nathan knew it, he'd stood and his lips were on hers, a burst of sweetness lifting his spirits. She kissed him back, and he felt her longing, the sudden grip desire placed on her. He pushed against her, wanting more.

Her mouth devoured his with an aching intensity. Heat pulsed between them, and he picked her up. She gave a soft sigh and planted her lips on his throat, his neck. Later, he couldn't remember how they had gotten from the shop into his room upstairs.

Once in the room, he slid the door shut and pressed her against it. His hands roamed up and down her body, eventually lifting her dress. She moaned as he reached beneath the soft fabric to touch her, and he pulled her toward the bed.

"Wait." Her ragged breath matched his own. "Wait...I think I might still be feeling the effects of the day. I don't want you to get in trouble because of me."

Trouble? What was she talking about?

"You're an angel," she reminded him. "You are not supposed to be doing this."

Nathan blinked. The desire slipped a little but still pulsed underneath his skin. She looked so beautiful, flushed with her feelings, ready for the taking. What did she mean when she said she still felt the effects of the day? He sensed no leftover anger from Tara--only the strong pull of ardor and lust.

Lust. She is experiencing residual lust from Curt's life force energy.

"I'm sorry, Faye." Nathan released her. "You're right."

For once her sensory guard wall was down, and Nathan felt disappointment radiate from her.

"You asked about my parents," she said.

Good, Nathan told himself. Focus on something else. Don't think about how close you came to breaking the rules.

"Who were they?"

"Momma was a doctor. She met my father while working at Brackenridge Hospital. He'd come into the ER to check on a stabbing victim, and she caught him bending over the person, a white light coming from his hands. The man's wounds closed up as if nothing had happened. My father could have glamored my mother, making her forget what she'd seen, but he always said there was something about Momma, something in her eyes that made him not do it." Faye smiled. "They became friends and eventually lovers. How they kept it secret is beyond me."

"It was an angel sabbatical," Nathan said. "It's like a vacation from the job, a chance to mix with humans, and only given to those high up in God's angel tier. They're the only ones who can handle it for that long. Your powers become extremely limited, and the longer you stay on Earth during a sabbatical, the more you take on the human essence, slip into their ways. God doesn't watch his angels twenty-four-seven. He doesn't have to. We are supposed to be extensions of him."

"God punished them in the end," she said. "They were good people. The police said they were in the wrong place at the wrong time. A fire broke out in one of the derelict buildings where they'd gone to minister to the homeless. It spread fast. My family got caught in an explosion, but I never bought that story-- as if my father couldn't escape some fire!"

"What do you think really happened?"

"I think God checked up on my father and didn't like what He saw." The challenge in her eyes dared him to contradict her. "I think He punished my parents."

Nathan couldn't deny the possibility. Angel sabbaticals could last centuries and with no one monitoring them…well, one could get away with anything. A few angels did occasionally fall from grace during these times, hence the birth of the nephilim.

"Did any of the other angels know about your heritage?"

"A few. Some dropped by our home from time to time. I was never in on any of the conversations, but I know they always left my father weary and hurt. I hated seeing that most of all," Faye said. "He did nothing but love me and my mom."

Sadness surrounded Faye like an old worn coat. Nathan wanted to remove it and bring back the joy he'd seen in her earlier. But he knew better than to get close to her. He couldn't trust himself just yet.

"That's how you know Azal."

"Yes. My father always said Azal was our family's guardian angel."

"Must have been an honorary position. But honorary or not, guardian angels don't quit. He is still on your side."

"Fuck him. He dropped the ball seven years ago. He should have protected my parents. If he'd been a true friend to my father, a true friend to me, that's what he would have done," Faye said. "But Azal was…distracted. It cost my parents and my fiancé their lives."

"How long were you engaged?"

"Six months. Chris interned at the hospital where Momma worked. He assisted both my parents with their community projects, though he never knew the truth about my father." She shrugged and wiped at her eyes. "So there you have it. My sob story. You wanted sex and you got drama. Sorry."

"You absorbed a lot of energy today--Tara's anger, Curt's lust--it had to come out somewhere."

"Right. Good thing I didn't touch Cassie. The last thing I need is a case of vainglory." She turned to him. "Just so you know, I don't usually try to jump a guy's bones for at least a couple weeks after I've met him. Especially not some rogue I'm supposed to be checking up on."

"You made it clear you think I deserve the title."

"Make me think different." When he didn't answer her challenge, she asked, "What did you mean earlier when you said I needed to ask questions of the right people? Is there something going on I should know about?"

"Talk to Azal. This is his party, not mine." He intended to follow his own advice once she'd left. "By the way, you did the right thing in stopping us.

"Did I? It might have been right, but I'll tell you something, Nathan Ink, the sex would have been great."

She left, closing the door gently behind her.

* * * *

Azal waited for her on the street.

"Spying on me?" she asked as he fell in step next to her.

"Just making sure you're okay."

"Ah, doing the job, I see," she said. "Still acting as if you're my guardian angel."

"Yes." Azal wished her words didn't sound so bitter. "Are you all right?"

"Yeah."

But the way she said it--Azal heard something else. Frustration? Disappointment?

"How's the investigation coming along?"

"Well, I can't say Nathan walks the best path. He's trying to convince me his tattoos only influence free will, and that his clients could make an infinite number of choices to change their lives. His designs bring the sinful part of their nature to the surface so they can examine it," Faye said with a sideways glance. "But I think you know that already."

"Yes," Azal said. "I understand how he operates. But is he an extremist? Is he going too far?"

"I need to think about it a little more, and I'd like to meet a client who has been positively affected in the long term," Faye said.

"Will you stick with him just a few more days, maybe look for that positive example? I need to be sure about him."

"I don't know, Azal."

"Did something happen with Nathan? Has he--"

"Oh, god. Shut up already. What are you? My mother? Look, I'll spend a few more days, a week at the most on this, but that's it. I have my own life, and this little assignment of yours is already a pain in the ass."

Azal nodded. "Thank you. I'll leave you to the rest of your evening."

"Azal, what's really going on? Why do I get the feeling you've sent me to investigate Nathan for another reason?"

She moved a little ahead of him, and though he knew she hated it, he made himself invisible. Faye glanced over to the spot where he'd once been and sighed, trudging on. Azal watched, hoping he did the right thing in withholding his information. He just couldn't risk her reaction.

Though the hour grew late, one more visit would be required before he could rest. Azal doubled back to Hell's Leak. It was time Nathan knew what was at stake.

Chapter 9

The creature watched Faye walk down the dark street, and wished the time were right to approach her, to at long last reveal himself. But it wasn't. After studying her for the last few years, he couldn't take the chance, couldn't risk the exposure. She just wasn't ready yet. The little peeks he'd taken into Faye's psyche during her dreams told him that. So he kept his distance, though it pissed him off he couldn't hear what the angel--that fucking busybody Azal--said to her. His burning need to collect the angel's soul ate at him. For a few seconds, the desire overpowered him and his shields were dropped. But he tempered his urges, forcing himself to be patient.

The Others were on to him. While they couldn't know his identity, they could sense his presence. The powers he'd collected from previous angel kills kept him shielded. He knew the bitter ache of loss and could only assume the angels shared a similar feeling over their fallen comrades, which might eventually prompt them to vengeance. Of course the symbol he left so blatantly on his human victims probably piqued their curiosity too.

They still haven't told Faye about me, he mused.

Perhaps they were afraid Faye might join him if they pushed too soon. Wouldn't that be ironic? The one thing the angels were most concerned about was the very event they could cause if they didn't proceed with caution.

Influencing free will could be a real bitch.

* * * *

Nathan writhed on the floor. The pain and the hum lasted only a few seconds, but they'd been powerful enough to cause the rivulet of blood dripping from his ear.

"It will pass."

Bleary-eyed, Nathan looked into Azal's calm face.

"What are you doing here?" Nathan cleared his throat, trying to get rid of the metallic, bitter taste in his mouth. "How did you get in?"

"You're still too young to keep me out." Azal offered his hand, and Nathan pulled himself up. "I thought I'd get a tattoo."

"Hmm…I'm sure I have something that would look good on you."

"What do you think my sin would be?"

"Envy," Nathan said. "You wish your role was more like mine."

"Your methods don't suit my style." Azal walked into the kitchen and found a glass, which he filled with water.

"I can't seem to win with anyone today."

"Have a fight with Faye? Was she not impressed with your…methods?" Azal handed Nathan the water. As he watched him drink it down, he said, "I know the creature causing your headaches."

Nathan's eyes narrowed. "Who is it?"

"A mistake."

"Is that what we're calling the children of God we don't like today?"

"Don't joke about this one. He's powerful and his intentions are dark."

"What else would they be? I didn't exactly think you set Faye on my scent because Jesus Christ had come again." Azal's face darkened just a shade at Nathan's scorn. "What I don't get, Azal, is why the hell you haven't told Faye about whatever it is that's really going on? What's all this crap about me being a rogue?"

"You do things in a different fashion, don't you? You're the most unorthodox of us all," Azal pointed out.

"And yet I've heard no complaints from the Big Guy."

"You're hearing it now."

A small ripple of thunder sounded outside, and both angels walked to the window, peering out into the night sky. Lightning zigzagged through the air, leaving the scent of ozone behind.

"Such drama," Nathan muttered.

There was another rumble of thunder.

"I take it the boss is cranky."

Azal gave a small smile and asked, "Who is minding your shop tonight?"

"No one right now. My assistant is off today."

"What if someone comes in?" Azal followed him to the kitchen and pulled out a chair. He sank into it, folding his hands on the table.

"Trust me," Nathan said. "I'll hear them."

"I'm curious about your assistant, Nathan. Her name is Judith, right?"

"Yes. She's not ready to be practicing on her own just yet. Her personal feelings get in the way when she tattoos a client," Nathan said.

"And you?" Azal gave him a speculative look. "Do your personal feelings ever get in the way?"

Nathan glanced at the door, imagining Faye's body pressed to it as he kissed her.

"As angels, we aren't really supposed to have personal feelings about our jobs." Nathan shrugged. "The longer you stay on Earth, the longer you mingle with the humans, the more like them you become. Emotions evolve."

"It is inevitable."

Knowing Azal's fondness for them, Nathan lit a candle, and placed it in the center of the table. The flame bounced and danced against the wick as Nathan sat down. Why did Azal remain silent since he obviously had something to say?

"Faye is a nephilim," Azal said.

"I know. She told me tonight."

"Then you understand her parentage? How rare her kind are?"

"Her mother was a human, and her father an angel. She didn't tell me his name."

"Raphael."

"Raphael?" Nathan couldn't hide his surprise. Raphael--the angel of healing and hope. It explained why Faye's healing powers were so strong. "I know of him."

"He was destroyed seven years ago."

"I heard something about it, but I didn't believe the rumors. Raphael was a source of God's pride, a power for good." Now it was Nathan's turn to hesitate, unsure of how Azal would react to his next thoughts. "I have trouble understanding Raphael's demise over his union with the human. Surely his other deeds overshadow this one fall."

"That's not the case at all."

Nathan raised his eyebrows.

"God did not destroy him," Azal said. "His demise was caused by the creature creating your headaches, and who is now stalking Faye."

"A demon--a true rogue angel?"

"This is something in between. Not an angel, and not a human."

"Another nephilim then? Like Faye?"

"Yes, but not like Faye." Azal shook his head, adamant. "Faye would never use her powers in the manner this creature uses his."

"Why would another nephilim kill Raphael?"

"Remember Lucifer?"

Nathan rolled his eyes, disgusted. "Are you joking? How could I forget? Of all the angels who ever wandered on the earth, he's the only one that reached rock star status. He must be so pleased by the way Hollywood and the King James version of the Bible glorified him. Pompous asshole."

"This nephilim," Azal said, gazing into the candle's flame, "is Lucifer's son."

"What?" Nathan slapped his hand on the table and lowered his voice. "Does God know?"

"Lucifer never believed God would have the heart to destroy him. After all, it was his antics that kept God entertained for so long, his tales that made it into the Bible and popular culture. The idea of the two of them being enemies tickled them both for a time," Azal said. "It captured the imagination of the human population too, so much so this nephilim I'm tracking believes he is the antichrist."

"There is no such thing. That's a bullshit story Lucifer started to terrify the humans under his charge at the time," Nathan said. "Who knew those same humans would go on to write the gospel? Talk about a tale gone wild."

"I know that, but this nephilim doesn't. No one has told him about how things really are. He's untrained, uneducated in the ways of the veil, and unfortunately, powerful. Half the time, we can't even locate him, because he's learned to block us. And despite his passion for flamboyance, no one could call Lucifer a small time angel. He had amazing capabilities, which we believe he passed on to his son." Azal reached out, crushing the flame beneath his fingers and watching the smoke swirl up. "But here's the thing. When you mix Lucifer's genes with those of the nephilim's mother...well, we have an accident."

"What do you mean? Who was the mother?"

"A deranged mortal--what the humans call a serial killer."

"So this poor kid got Daddy's gifts and Momma's temperament?" Nathan shook his head. "Isn't human life intriguing?"

"He's killed many innocent people, Nathan."

"Why did he kill Faye's family?"

Azal looked into the other angel's inky eyes. Pain and sadness intermingled on his face, and Nathan noticed the room grew chilly.

"The nephilim believes Faye's father, Raphael, destroyed Lucifer. So he killed her parents and fiancée as an act of vengeance," Azal said. "But what he really wants is Faye. I think he sees it as poetic justice, a final act of revenge in choosing Faye to be his mate. He believes the two of them will make another creature altogether. Something more powerful than any of us. Not human, not angel but something more."

"His own version of the antichrist," Nathan said. "Lucifer's idle comments would become a reality."

"Yes. This creature's actions caused a rift between Faye and her association with heaven, a stroke of good fortune for him. I assume he thought once the path was clear of her family it would be easier to get to her."

"He doesn't understand Faye then. She's not a weak woman."

Azal gazed at him, curious, but he kept whatever thoughts were brewing to himself and said, "Don't I know it. But Faye is still grieving about the past, and it does make her more susceptible to suggestion. She would rush in without regard to the consequence if she thought she could avenge her parents. We need to keep her occupied and away from this nephilim for the time being."

"She deserves to know the truth, Azal," Nathan said.

"She will know the truth when we've got a better understanding of this creature and how it's gaining its powers. We need to gather more information and prepare her."

"Sounds to me as if you already have a wealth of information on this nephilim. Who is your source?"

"I'm afraid I can't tell you everything, Nathan. I hate withholding information from you, but for now I must follow the instructions God gave me. He has His reasons."

"I take it God wants me to protect Faye," Nathan said, though it irked him to realize he wasn't fully trusted.

"No. It wasn't what He wanted, but I convinced him you were the best option. This nephilim's power allows him to cloak himself physically, but it can't hide the hum of his sins. That's why I put Faye on your case. I knew if she kept in contact with you, you'd sense if the nephilim were around. With your special gifts for sin, you might be able to pick him up on your radar. That's what your recent headaches have been about. He must be powerful indeed if he can render you defenseless." Azal gave him a small smile of apology. "You can keep her safe while I locate the nephilim. Telling her the truth would only make her go after him. She's not ready for that. She's too emotional, and that's where he would prey on her."

"You care about Faye."

Azal's jaw tightened and the long scar that ran down the side of his face flexed. "I'm an honorary guardian angel for her. Raphael requested it of me, and I've grown to love Faye as much as I loved him. He was my mentor, you know. It was an honor to be appointed the duty."

"So where is Lucifer in all this? Why doesn't he take charge of his kid and set him straight about the whole antichrist thing?" Nathan asked. "I know you said the nephilim thinks he was destroyed, but we're talking about Lucifer. Nobody gets to that guy."

"We haven't heard from him directly in twenty years." Azal shrugged at Nathan's shocked look.

"Are you saying no one knows where he is?" Nathan frowned. "So all the chaos in the world, all the destruction, all the wars...that's been the humans' own doing?"

"Lucifer planted the seed long ago, and the humans' free will did the rest. I doubt Lucifer did much in the way of real work before he disappeared." Azal hesitated a moment. "Many of our brethren have vanished, Nathan. I know you are not as...in touch with our kind as I am, but we've begun to lose angels."

"I heard you say the angels were dying in my vision last night." Nathan didn't like the scrutiny emanating from the other angel. "What's going on?"

"I'm not entirely sure. It's a difficult task to destroy an angel, but we've been finding their mortal shells. They are all marked with a symbol."

"Marked?"

"Yes. Each has a design carved into them."

Nathan felt the unspoken accusation, and his own temper

flared. "Say it, Azal. I dare you."

The other angel sat quietly.

"Azal, I am an angel of the Lord. I don't kill my own kind."

Still Azal remained silent.

"You're thinking of my clients."

"You are going too far in your job."

"Says you." Nathan stood, unable to hide the flash of anger.

"The death toll you bring is high, Nathan. Perhaps it's time to set aside the job and return to heaven a while. You've been on this side of the veil a long time. I don't think you care any longer about saving them."

"Most of them are beyond redemption. That's why I hear them," Nathan said, his face dark with anger. "As I said earlier, let God bring the complaint to me."

Another low rumble of thunder sounded outside.

"He is, my friend." Azal stood. "We might be asking you to help protect Faye, but her investigation of you is not without its merits. I'll be curious to know what her assessment is. In the meantime, keep her safe."

"Isn't that your job?" Nathan watched Azal open the door.

"Yeah, but she likes you," Azal said, and left the apartment.

Chapter 10

Faye sighed in her sleep and rolled over. A little tendril of her hair slipped against her face, and the creature's hand trembled as he brushed it away, focusing on the memory he wanted to push into her dream. Taking a deep breath, he linked his subconscious with hers.

* * * *

Angry. Momma was always so angry with him. The little boy cowered under the kitchen table, sucking on the scraps of meat she occasionally tossed down. He heard her fork scrape against the plate. The sound grated, vibrating his teeth and giving him the chills. It was nothing new, though, all part of Momma's suppertime routine. He could only stare at the blue hem of her second best dress and wait for the ritual to be over.

After a few minutes, the boy heard her get up and empty her plate in the sink. Time for him to come out from under the table. A vague half smile lifted her thin lips when she looked at her son, but it didn't make it to her eyes. She ran a hand over his black hair and nodded. Reaching for the dirty knife on the kitchen counter, she pressed it against her chest as if holding something very dear. Grabbing her purse, she slipped the weapon inside. Without a word, she wrapped a long black scarf around her dirty blond hair and left.

The boy heard her car roar to life in the driveway, and knew she would not be back until very late. Often when she came home, her clothes would be stained with blood and an awful smell clung to her. He couldn't imagine what Momma had been doing.

He wandered into the living room to look at the silver picture frame with bells engraved at the top. Momma posed there, smiling in her ivory dress, her eyes a bright teal beneath her veil. Next to her stood a man. The boy liked the glow that lit the man's handsome features. Somehow he appeared more alive than Momma did in the picture. Once or twice he'd even thought the man winked at him. But of course it was just imagination.

"Momma, is that man my father?" the boy had asked once.

Momma glared at the picture and shrugged. "Could be. I ain't too sure anymore who that man was. But the person inside him…well, that person I know too well. That's the person who is your true daddy."

His true daddy? At the time, the boy hadn't known what that meant. When he'd brought the conversation up again a few months later, his momma had been drunk, her eyes red and wild with the effects of Wild Turkey. She'd sneered, "Your true daddy…I'll show you him."

Reaching over to the TV cabinet, she pulled out several VHS tapes, saying, "You want to know daddy? Then watch these. Your daddy is in all of them."

Prince of Darkness. The Exorcist. Amityville Horror. The boy read the titles and as soon as his mother left for the night, her knife secure in her straw purse, he watched the videos, not knowing what to make of them. When Momma got home, he spied on her as she dropped to her knees in the living room, weeping.

"Lucifer, come back to me."

It was the first time he'd heard her speak his father's name.

* * * *

Faye woke up. Sweat saturated her thin nightgown, chilling her skin. Or had it been the dream that left her feeling so cold? She fought to hold onto the fragments of the nightmare, but they slipped from her mind. Something about the dark-haired boy again, and a design. Right at the end, it flashed before her like a neon sign. She could still picture it--an ornate cross.

As her conscious mind grew more alert, she became aware that something wasn't right in the dim room. She felt the presence of another person. Cautiously, Faye sat up in bed, looking around, knowing there was nowhere for an intruder to hide. Everything appeared to be in its place, yet she couldn't shake the feeling someone had just left the room.

Faye snapped on the light at her bedside table and grabbed the little notebook lying there. Flipping through its pages, she reviewed her notes, noticing most of the dreams were about the dark-haired boy's childhood or his mother. Who was he? Was there any way to find out? More importantly, what did he want?

Her hand moved smoothly across the paper and after a few minutes, Faye had a decent sketch of the cross. It had scalloped edges with little circles at each of the four points. In the middle lay a small stone that Faye thought she remembered being red.

After studying the image for a few minutes, she put the notebook away and turned on the television in time to hear the news reporters of Austin Daily giving a blow-by-blow account of all the events taking place in the city overnight. She got up, made a cup of coffee and then opened the door to grab the Austin American Statesman. She tossed it onto her coffee table and it landed on the old newspaper Nathan Ink had given her. She tapped a finger against the mug and wondered what to do.

She hadn't made contact with Nathan in several days, feeling drained. Knowing that exhaustion would do her little good when it came to learning more about Hell's Leak, she backed off, giving her brain time to process things, and her energy to return. Besides, when it came to thinking about Nathan, her senses were undeniably clouded.

Nathan had kissed her. And not just some blushing schoolboy kiss, but a hardcore, deep throated, toe tingling one. She had returned the gesture, delighted when he had picked her up and carried her up the stairs. What could be hotter than a lusty angel? But it was that thought that had prevented her from going further. He was an angel. They were not supposed to consort with humans in a sexual way. She knew all too well the consequences of such a union.

Of course it was easy to simply justify her reaction to Nathan as a result of the residual energy of Curt's lust. After all, she was only human, sort of, and allowed a slip up here and there. But a little voice in her head whispered this was a slip up she wouldn't mind repeating. And she wasn't sure she could entirely blame it on Curt's lust. Surely after days of not seeing Nathan the feeling would have waned. So why did she still feel a deliciously odd tingle when she thought about him?

Pushing those feelings aside, Faye tried to focus on the death his tattoos brought. Couldn't he create less vicious designs that didn't carry horrific consequences? Was it possible for him to make something beautiful and have that influence free will in the same way?

She picked up the picture on her bedside table and looked at her lost family. How different her father had been from Nathan! He helped others whenever he could. Exceptionally talented, able to remove any kind of sickness and pain, he'd taught Faye how to do the same. Her mother, a traditional doctor, appeared to possess a special brand of magic all her own too. She could place her hands on a patient and diagnose them almost before the test results came back. Her colleagues were in awe, and there was never any shortage of interns tagging along in Estella's wake. Both her parents placed a high value on human life and the importance of caring for others.

The phone rang. Faye reached for it, surprised the thought of her family didn't hurt as much as it used to. Maybe there was some benefit in having limited contact with the other angels again.

But she wouldn't admit it to Azal anytime soon.

"Faye? Good. You're awake." Zenovia still sounded a little groggy herself. "I really need your help. I was supposed to call you about this yesterday."

"What's up?"

"Can you fill in tonight at the Black Cat? Tony left me a message, saying Trina has strep throat and can't sing. Not that she can carry a tune when she's healthy," Zenovia grumbled. "I'm going to be working all day for my mom so I wasn't sure I'd get a chance to call you later and ask."

"Sure," Faye said. "I'll fill in."

"Thanks. Oh, and Tony did confirm Barb officially quit. She didn't show up to work again last night. I'm so envious. Can you imagine suddenly having all that money fall into your lap?" Zenovia paused and Faye couldn't help but grin. She could picture Zenovia doing some serious damage at Macy's if she had Barb's money. "By the way, that was some disappearing act you pulled on Sunday night. Are you feeling better? John said he saw you leave."

"Oh. I didn't know he was there. Did you and Mr. Blue Lagoon have fun?"

"Yeah, but I think John would have had a better time if you'd stuck around. You made quite an impression on him."

"Whatever. I'm sure I was such a great conversationalist during our one chat at Katz's."

"Conversation?" Zenovia snorted. "I don't think he was interested in you for that."

"You are so bad," Faye said. "How many times do I have to tell you I can get my own men?"

"When you find one all on your own, I'll leave you alone," Zenovia said. "Besides, you should give this guy a break. He's been living downtown for six months and barely knows a soul. I think his mom passed away recently too."

"Well, I'm sorry about his mom, but I'm not the one to cure him of his shyness. I don't care how cute he is."

"Aha! See? You were kind of interested in him. That's good."

"Zenovia--"

"Shut up, Faye. Don't deny it." Faye heard the grin that must have been plastered on her friend's face. "Now I don't feel so bad."

"About what?"

"About giving him your number...and calling him to tell him you're singing tonight."

"Zenovia, I don't need another complication right now," Faye said, unable to stop the image of Nathan Ink from popping up in her mind.

"Another complication? You got a man I don't know about?"

"No. But..."

"But what?" When Faye didn't respond, Zenovia pushed on. "But nothing. I promise to butt out once you're safely married with dozens of babies. Now make sure you wear that sexy blue dress tonight. You know, the one that shows off your boobs."

"Goodbye, Zenovia."

She sat on the couch for a while longer, thinking about Nathan. Despite the things he did to his clients, Faye couldn't forget how badly she had wanted him for those few minutes, how much she wanted to feel him against her skin. He wanted it too, and it made her wonder about a whole host of other things. Did he have other lovers? Was it only the angels who created children that were destroyed? Was the sex act itself allowed? And for that matter, would the rules be different with her? She was a nephilim, part angel, after all. Maybe there were exceptions to be made.

Faye, you are ridiculous. You're supposed to be checking up on the guy. Not finding loopholes around the angel sex thing.

Easier said than done.

* * * *

The creature sat in his car. Faye had almost caught him in the apartment. He wanted her to know him, but trust couldn't be built if he were caught breaking and entering. He'd just been unable to restrain his urges, and while the wicked deed he'd indulged in earlier that morning worked toward sating his needs, the urge to share it with another had been strong. So he'd driven by Faye's place, an act he did every day. Swayed by temptation, he'd stopped the car and slipped into her bedroom. He barely even remembered doing it now, but the sweet thrill of seeing his muse up close...now that he could live on for a week.

He hadn't meant to touch her again, but his usual defenses were weakened. The last time he'd felt the warmth of her skin, just a few days ago, a strange desire started to worm its way into his heart. Self-restraint became hard to maintain.

As he watched the apartment, hoping she would come to the window, his hand reached down to massage the erection pressing against his jeans. Not much longer now. Soon he could show her his true face. And then there would no longer be a need to hide behind the mask she knew him in.

The creature glanced down at the knife. The blade gleamed in the early morning light and he tilted the handle, studying the symbol embossed into the bone at its base. The cross was his favorite symbol, a mark of the great work he was doing. Soon Faye would know all about it, and she would appreciate what he'd done for her.

He wanted her to understand him, to sympathize with what he'd gone through. All his studies indicated she helped others, and he needed her to help him.

It didn't matter what means he used to obtain that help.

* * * *

The afternoon sun beat down on The Flower Pot, but Faye stayed out of it, tending to her seedlings in the backroom and humming along with the radio. She treated each tiny plant like a small child whose welfare she alone was responsible for. The water, the earth she chose to plant them in--these things were a sacred ritual to her. In her little shop, away from angels and people, Faye felt herself a powerful being of nature at peace within her plant world.

Her hands were covered in dirt and grime when the police car pulled into the parking lot. The officer got out and walked toward the delicate flowers displayed out front. He ran his fingers across the roses before turning to look at something else.

"Can I help you?" she called out, grabbing a towel to wipe at her dirty hands.

The cop looked around and nodded when he saw her.

Still in cop mode, though he's off duty, Faye thought.

"Yeah. I need something for my wife."

"For the wife? Well, I have lots of pretty flowers to choose from. Special occasion?"

"No."

"Then your wife is lucky. Not all men stop in to buy flowers for their sweethearts just because." Faye walked out to join him. "What kind of flower does she like?"

"I was thinking these roses," he said and then shrugged. "But I don't know if she likes them."

"Are you kidding? All women like roses." But Faye looked around at the other choices. "What kind of woman is she? Fragile and delicate? Tough and steely?"

The cop smiled. An image of his wife popped into Faye's head. A tall woman with long, brown hair, she didn't need to wear makeup, a fact the cop loved about her. He thought of her as earthy and beautiful, though she never believed him when he told her so.

"What about daisies? They're earthy and just about the friendliest flower on the planet." She pointed to the brightly colored flowers.

The cop selected a pot of daisies and followed her inside to pay.

"Just getting off a shift?" Faye asked, ringing up the sale.

"Yeah. I was supposed to be home hours ago," he said. "I'm trying to make it up to the missus with these."

He handed her the money. As her fingers brushed his, another image popped into her head.

The cop along with several of his colleagues stood over the body of a young woman, no more than twenty years old. Her silky, black hair lay in a tangled mass around her face, not hiding the lifeless eyes, which stared at the night sky. She wore a black tank top, which had been lifted up, and there was no coat to hide her fragile body or the bloody hole in her side created by a knife. Above the stab wound, the charred tattoo of an upside down cross had been branded into the skin.

"Looks as if we've got another Grim Sleeper victim." The cop squatted over the body and pointed to the small cross. "How is he doing this? He can't be carrying around a branding iron."

"It's a hell of a painful calling card to leave. How many does this make?" Another cop bent over the body, his breath coming out in frosty puffs.

"Eight total if you don't include the ones from ten years ago. With those, we're looking at close to twenty victims."

"How can we not include the ones before? They all have the same mark." The second cop stood. "Maybe he left town for a while, or found something that broke his routine."

The image abruptly slipped away.

"Ma'am, you okay?" The cop stared at Faye.

"Yes. I just had...a little dizzy spell. Sorry." Faye forced a smile. "I'm fine."

"Well, all right then."

Faye watched the cop drive away and then sank to the ground, her legs no longer able to support her.

She was aware of the serial killer. God, who wasn't? Nicknamed the Grim Sleeper, because he'd taken a ten year hiatus, tales of his crimes were always on the news or in the papers, but the one detail that hadn't been made public was the mark he left on his victims--the upside down cross. The very cross she'd seen earlier in her dreams.

She understood what the symbol meant. In popular culture, it was considered a sign of the devil, though Faye knew no such creature existed. Her father always said it was just a story created by one angel to keep order in a time when it had been strongly needed. Of course only a chosen few knew that.

An awful suspicion formed in her head.

The face of the dead woman loomed in Faye's mind, bringing with it grief. That silky black hair--how many times had Faye envied it? And the silver writing on the black tank top dotted in blood, smearing the words Black Cat.

She recognized the piano bar's luckiest waitress.

Barb.

Chapter 11

Dusk fell.

Judith bent over the Book of Sinz, and Nathan watched her as he swept the shop floor. An easy read, her thoughts showed on her face. Whatever Judith examined right now had her excited. She pushed back her long, black braids and ran her finger over one of the designs.

"What are you looking at?" he asked.

"Atargatis. The mermaid goddess." Judith fanned herself. "She's a regular hottie, boss.

"I'm sure she would appreciate that."

"Is this the one you tattooed on that girl last month? You know, the one that drowned in the lake?"

"Yeah."

"Wicked."

"The girl or the tattoo?"

"Both, boss. But I really like the tattoo. You draw great work."

"They pay the rent."

Judith nodded and flipped through the other pages. She'd looked at the book many times, even tattooed a few of the designs herself. Yet she never grew tired of it, and her work improved every day. Nathan figured it wouldn't be too much longer before Judith would be ready to go it alone. She wasn't an angel, but he hadn't been one, either, when he first started out.

"Boss, I want to show you something."

Nathan stopped sweeping. Judith held out a crumpled paper. Curious, he took it and smoothed it out.

A fat frog with a backward baseball cap on had been sketched on the paper by Judith's smooth hand. Around its bulbous neck were several gold chains encrusted with diamonds and jewels. Sunglasses perched on its squat nose, but they were lowered enough to see the frog's eyes slit in sly satisfaction. She'd stenciled GREED on the baseball cap.

"Nice frog," Nathan said. "I like it."

"You don't think it's too obvious?"

"Everything about this tattoo is obvious. But that's the nature of greed." Nathan handed the paper back to her. "Put it in the book."

A glow of pleasure lit her face. She scurried back over to the book, and placed her design inside it. Picking up the yellow bucket outside the bathroom door, she headed into the small room. The scent of Pine Sol drifted through the building, bringing with it a soft peace.

It didn't last long.

The door to the Hell's Leak swung open and Faye came in.

"So…" she said, leaning against the doorframe.

"So…" he repeated, mimicking her by leaning against his counter. "I'd just about given up on you. Figured you got bored investigating me. Or did you just take some time off?"

"You can wipe that sassy little smirk off your face, Nathan Ink. I'm on to you."

Sassy. He doubted anyone in all his years had called him sassy. No one would have dared.

"Well, it's nice to see you too." He tried not to notice the blue slip of a dress she wore or the purse that swung on her bare shoulder. The cloud of unrest she carried with her had her distracted, and he took a quick peek in her head. He caught the words Damn dreams before her mind shut to him. "Don't you own a coat?"

"Are you the one sending me the dreams?"

"I haven't even seen you in a couple of days and you're already dreaming about me?" Of course that was a small fib. He'd checked up on her off and on the last few days without her knowledge. "What dreams?"

"Don't be cute," Faye said, hands on her hips. "Are you the one I keep dreaming about?"

"I'm flattered, Faye."

"Oh, give me a break and just answer the question. Are you the black-haired boy in my dreams?"

"How should I know? They're your dreams. How long have

you've been having them?"

"Months," she said. "But I can never remember them or make out the face of the boy."

"We've only known each other a few days. I don't know why you'd think I would have anything to do with your dreams."

"In my experience, anything is possible."

She stared at him, her thoughts a mystery, but he could read the suspicion in her eyes. And there was something else, something that radiated off her.

Fear.

"Have you come to lecture me on my designs again?" he asked. "Thought up any new arguments to try my patience with?"

"Don't take that superior angel tone of voice with me."

"I suppose you think I should be tattooing people with emblems of puppies and rainbows?"

"Well, since you brought it up, have you ever tried to create something beautiful on your clients? Or is actually helping them something you're incapable of? Do you like killing them?"

"I guarantee you the end result would be the same. I know you understand the concept of free will. It doesn't matter what tattoo I put on them. My gift is to make them see their sins, to give them an opportunity to change. If they don't take that opportunity, then their free will has been exercised and fate does the rest."

She glared, and he couldn't help but glare back. Few people got under his skin, but damned if he was going to let her lecture him. He was an angel, a creature of God above reproach.

Faye took a deep breath. A minute passed before she spoke again.

"I wondered if I could look at your book one more time." She nodded in the direction of Sinz, which still lay on the counter.

"Why?" Now it was his turn to be suspicious.

"I want to check on something."

He handed her the book without comment and resumed sweeping. "Are you working tonight? I noticed you're dressed up."

"Yeah. I've got to fill in for the singer at Black Cat. She has strep throat or something." Faye turned the pages, a little crease appearing between her eyebrows as she looked at the designs. "I'm a regular Girl Friday."

"Is there something specific you are looking for in the book?"

"Yes." But she didn't quite meet his gaze. "I don't think it's in here."

"Might go faster if you tell me what it is."

"It's a cross, Nathan. An ornate upside down cross." Faye shut the book with a snap. "It's been found on a lot of bodies lately associated with a serial killer."

Nathan felt the blood of his human armor quicken. Azal mentioned whoever killed the angels left a mark of some sort. He knew what Faye implied with her words, and just as it had when Azal hinted at the same thing, it irked him.

"You told me the other night the cross is your favorite symbol," Faye said.

"And so it is. Doesn't mean I tattoo it on my clients."

"I had a vision today. It came from a customer who visited the Flower Pot, a cop. He had just been investigating a murder committed by the serial killer called the Grim Sleeper. Do you know why he thought that?" Faye scrutinized Nathan's face. "Because the killer always leaves the mark of an upside down cross on his victims. It looks like a tattoo."

Nathan sat down on his rolling chair and crossed his arms.

"Is this why Azal really asked me to investigate you?"

"Seems like a dangerous move, doesn't it? What would stop me from killing you if I was this person?"

"Nothing, I guess," Faye said. "Nothing at all."

Nathan heard the low buzz of the hum as people moved on the street outside, but none of it distracted his attention from the woman who stood across from him. The little table next to the barber chair where he kept his tools vibrated and the air in the room grew heavy with the heat of his temper.

"The thing is, Nathan." She moved closer to him, unperturbed by the signs of his anger. "I'm not sure what to believe. The woman that was killed…I knew her. Barb worked at Black Cat with me. Her sins didn't fall anywhere close to the ones of your clients. And I don't know why Azal sent me to look into your activities. He could have done that himself. Oh, it might have been a challenge for him, given how you feel about other angels, but he didn't necessarily need me. But I know Azal, and he wouldn't have sent me to you if he felt I was in real danger."

Nathan nodded, and the table stopped rattling. The room cooled.

"So you tell me, Nathan. Why am I here? What's really going on?"

"You've got a stalker," Nathan said. Screw Azal and his

secrets. He hadn't asked to be the keeper of them. "He's been watching you for some time."

"A stalker?"

"Yes."

"Are you kidding me?"

"Do I appear to be a kidder?"

"A stalker? Really? That's crazy."

"Why?"

"I'm not stalker material."

"Oh? What makes up stalker material?"

"Women of great beauty. Models, actresses."

"You are beautiful, Faye," Nathan said. "And you're unique, a nephilim. I think that alone could make you definite stalker material."

"Why didn't Azal tell me?"

"He's worried how you'll take the news."

"I'm a big girl. I can defend myself against strange men. I've been hanging out with you, haven't I?"

"I know." Nathan held up his hands. "Don't shoot the messenger."

"This doesn't make sense. Azal knows I can handle myself. So why did he put me on your path?"

"Because whoever is stalking you has committed some terrible sins. This person murders humans and angels. He might be the one who killed your friend, Barb, as well as a few of my brethren that are missing," Nathan said, thinking that would explain how no one could track the nephilim. Somehow the creature used the essence of the angels he killed to hide himself from the Others. "Azal thought I might be able to sense this guy because of the strength of his sins, and protect you."

"And can you?"

"I've been having terrible headaches when this creature is near. They've occurred frequently in the past couple of days, particularly when you are around. Then again, that could be happening because you're a pain in the ass."

"What does this person want with me? Why is he killing off angels? Hell, how can he even do that?"

"You better ask Azal about it." Nathan ran a hand through his hair, hoping she would let him off the hook. He didn't want to be the one to tell her the truth about her parent's death. "Better to ask Azal all your questions."

"But you know some of the answers, right?"

"I've been asked to protect you, to keep you safe if I can. I'll do that," Nathan said. "But Azal's the one holding all the cards. He's the one you should be pestering."

Hurt flashed on her face, but she nodded her head.

"You're right. It's not your problem. I can't imagine what Azal thought bringing you in on this, anyway. You don't give a shit about your own clients dying, so why would you give a shit about me?" She moved toward the door. "Tell Azal I want to talk to him if you see him again."

This was going all wrong! She shouldn't be walking out there alone, and now that she knew someone stalked her, he doubted it would make her more cautious. Now she would try to face her stalker head-on, which was exactly what Azal told him shouldn't happen.

"Wait."

Faye paused, her hand on the door. "Yeah?"

The silence stretched between them, a tenuous rope ready to snap. Nathan debated what to say, how to stop her. He'd already said too much.

"Be careful, Faye."

She nodded and left.

A clatter of a bucket made Nathan whirl around. Judith poked her head out of the bathroom. "Uh...boss, I couldn't help but overhear some of that. I know it's not my place, and we have an agreement not to discuss your...private business...but, are you really going to just let her go like that?"

Guilt welled in Nathan. He knew he shouldn't have let Faye walk out of Hell's Leak without knowing her intentions. With a nod of dismissal to Judith, he left the shop and headed up to his apartment. Sitting down on the bed, he closed his eyes and started meditating. With his mind, he reached out to view the front of the shop and the streets around it, searching for Faye.

There. He had her. She moved up Sixth Street fast, her frustration and anger leaving a cloud of residual energy in its wake. She stopped, cocking her head to the side. Then slowly turned around where he could see her.

"Now who is the stalker? Nathan Ink, let go right now."

So strong, Nathan thought and complied with her wishes, watching her image swirl away.

He needed to talk to Azal and tell him what he'd done. Nathan shut his eyes again and willed his mind to open. It wasn't hard to sense the Others if he let himself. Usually, he just blocked them, immersing himself in humanity. He reached out, feeling for their presences, surprised when nothing came up. Wait. There. The presence was farther north but undeniably angelic. He willed himself to follow the trail, and grinned when he opened his eyes. Of course Azal would be here.

The purple neon sign for Melvin's Bingo Parlor blinked back at him.

Chapter 12

"B-24."

The bingo caller spoke into the microphone without enthusiasm as the numbered balls whirled around the metal basket. It was the only sound in Melvin's Bingo Parlor. People shut up when the game started, berating those around them that didn't do the same. The serious players studied their cards and held tight to their daubers, casting murderous glances at new players if they coughed or shifted too much in their seats. No one wanted to miss a call. Azal had seen it get ugly in Melvin's a few times for the people who didn't follow the rules.

The current game's winner would take home seven hundred dollars. But just who would the lucky winner be? Azal moved around the tables, invisible to the humans, searching for the person he felt most deserving. Like Nathan, he experienced his own special hum when he connected with a human, but tonight no one stood out.

An old woman a few aisles away sighed. The sound carried to Azal, and he moved closer to her. Little images of the woman's life flashed at him. Low income. Widow. Used a walker. Hip replacement. Home falling apart. Car stolen. He reached out and squeezed her shoulder.

"Bingo!" The old woman yelled, and all eyes turned in her direction. There was a smattering of applause from the small group around her. She called out her numbers and Azal smiled at the excitement lighting the woman's weathered face.

He sensed Nathan across the room before he turned to meet his steely gaze. Something must be up. Nathan never sought him out willingly.

"Don't tell me you're going to tattoo my new friend." Azal gestured to the old woman, gliding across the room to Nathan, unconcerned by the tables or chairs in his way, which he passed easily through. The quickness of his movement cast out a little good luck to a lady nearby holding a scratch off lottery ticket, and to her delight she discovered she'd won ten dollars.

"Only if she gets too greedy. I've got a frog tattoo that might be perfect for her," Nathan said, but his expression lacked humor. "We need to talk."

"Of course." Azal followed Nathan outside. They both looked up into the night sky. "How about we get some perspective?"

Nathan nodded. The angels lowered their heads and closed their eyes. When they opened them, they were seated on a billboard, the cityscape of Austin before them. The skyline twinkled with lights, and though cars rushed by on the highway, the city was quiet at this height.

"It's nice here," Nathan said. "Peaceful."

"You never get out of your shop, do you?"

"Not often. There's always work to be done."

"I imagine so." Azal waited for Nathan to reveal the nature of his visit, knowing it wouldn't take long. He would never have considered Nathan the most patient of angels.

"Faye knows about the stalker, Azal."

"She's seen him?"

"No. But she figured out you sent her to me as a ploy. She confronted me about it, and I told her the truth." Nathan held up a defensive hand at the look of chagrin on Azal's face. "Most of it."

"How much did you say?"

"That you wanted me to protect her, because someone stalked her."

"Did you tell her why she was being stalked or about her parents?"

"No. I left that job for you. The woman tends to get cranky with whoever gives her bad news," Nathan said. "I don't think I should have to be in the line of fire."

"Scared of her, huh?"

Nathan glanced at him. "You should have told her what was going on."

"I couldn't risk her going after the guy herself, which is exactly what she's going to do now, thanks to you."

"Look, I didn't ask for the job of protector." Nathan's anger shook the sign, causing the structure to groan under the friction.

"I know, old friend." Azal tried to contain his irritation. "Calm yourself."

After a few seconds, the sign stilled.

"There're some things you should know, Azal. Things you might want to take into consideration."

"Such as?"

"Faye told me for the past few months she's been dreaming about another person's life, a black-haired boy, but she can't remember all the details, or exactly what he looks like." Nathan ran a hand through his own distinctive hair. "There's something else too. Her friend, Barb, is dead, an upside down cross embedded into her skin. That's the same symbol you told me was found on the angels' mortal shells."

"The waitress has been killed?" Azal felt genuine grief for the woman he'd given luck to only a few days earlier. And frustration. Could the being responsible for her murder be tightening the noose by killing people Faye knew?

"She actually thought I caused this Barb's death, and that I might even be the person in her dreams."

"Would she be so far off in assuming that? Look at what you do."

"Fuck you, Azal."

"It's just an observation, old friend." Azal waited for the sign to begin vibrating again, but it remained still.

"I thought there might be a connection between Faye's stalker and the angel deaths," Nathan said, and Azal couldn't help but be amused at the other angel's attempt to ignore his harsh words. "If this nephilim has figured out how to kill us, then maybe he's using the angel essence to shield himself and to get to Faye. He could already be in her life and we just don't know it. He is attempting some type of communication with her through the dreams."

"That's what I have thought all along too," Azal said.

"And yet you accused me of it just the other day. It would have been nice of you to share information."

"I had to be sure. My source gets…confused."

"Are you going to tell me who this source is?"

"Not yet." Azal gave him a sideways look. "You're not very good at keeping secrets."

"Well, someone should get down there." Nathan looked at Azal. "Something should be done about this."

"I agree. We should tell Faye the truth. Since she knows about the stalker, we'll go ahead and give her all the facts. Then we can make a plan to protect her and get this nephilim."

"What's this we shit?" Nathan got to his feet and stood at the edge of the sign. "You're her guardian angel. Go guard her."

"I need your help. You can sense what I can't. My job is to bring good fortune."

"Then go give some to Faye. She could use it."

Azal lapsed into silence, knowing he couldn't track the guy on his own. However, the nephilim couldn't always stay hidden. His sins, the things he'd done, the crimes of his soul and mind were giveaways for an angel like Nathan to locate, and just as Azal had imagined, the nephilim gave off his own special hum only Nathan with his finely tuned ears heard. Whatever tricks he employed to block him from the Others, it didn't include hiding the hum of his past sins.

"Suit yourself then," Azal said. "If you want harm to come to Faye, stay here."

Azal closed his eyes. When he opened them, his feet were on solid ground. Though he didn't relish the task ahead, he moved in the direction of where he sensed Faye was.

It took him only a moment to realize Nathan had followed. Azal smiled, relieved his guilt tactic worked. He needed a little good fortune of his own.

* * * *

Unaware the two angels discussed her future from their lofty perch, Faye trudged up Sixth Street toward the Black Cat. Caught up in her thoughts and stewing in anger, she almost didn't hear the voice behind her.

"Faye!"

She turned and saw John struggling to catch up.

"Hey," John said, wheezing. "I've been hollering at you for a block. People must think I'm crazy."

"Sorry. I didn't hear you. I'm a little preoccupied right now."

"Yeah. I figured that out." He gasped for air. "Let me just catch my breath."

"Uh…listen, I'm working tonight. I really need to get going." Faye watched him inhale deeply, wondering if he could take a gentle hint. She just needed a few minutes to herself.

She hadn't wanted to say it out loud to Nathan, but the idea of being stalked didn't sit well. That meant someone watched her movements and knew her routines, but even more upsetting was she didn't know why or what they wanted. Nathan had passed the buck to Azal on that one. Coward. She couldn't wait to talk to her joke of a guardian angel and give him a piece of her mind.

"Are you okay?" John asked. "You look upset. Has something happened?"

"I'm fine." Faye cringed inwardly at her tone. John might be a nice guy, but she didn't need the complication right now. "I got some bad news and I'm still processing it."

"Anything I can do to help?"

"No. I'm sorry, John. I just need a few minutes to myself."

"I understand," he said, and took a step back. "Zenovia called me to say you were performing tonight, so I was headed up to the Black Cat. But I'm actually a little hungry. I think I'll stop in at the Iron Cactus and grab something to eat."

Faye barely heard what he'd said. A stray thought had grabbed her attention and she mulled it over. John's handshake had been blank the first time she'd met him. There'd been nothing there for her to see about his life. Some people were naturally better at shielding their thoughts, so John's blankness didn't necessarily mean anything odd, but still…in light of what she'd just learned, Faye's senses went on alert.

He started to walk away. Taking a deep breath, Faye stopped him. "John, wait. I'm sorry. I didn't mean to be rude. Like I said, I've just heard some bad news and I'm upset about it."

"Hey, I understand. Let me give you some time to yourself like you asked. I didn't mean to come off as the pushy, stalker guy."

Stalker? Interesting choice of words, Faye thought.

"I want to hear you sing, though." John smiled. "Is it okay if I come by the Black Cat after a while?"

"Of course it is. I'd like to see you," Faye said. "In fact, maybe I could use a little company for a few minutes, after all. I don't have time to sit down at the Iron Cactus, but how about grabbing a slice of pizza?"

"Sure, I could be persuaded to do that." John offered her his arm with mock formality. "Shall we?"

Faye smiled. She reached out and placed her hand in the crook of his arm, hoping to get some spark from his life. As before, there was nothing. She hid her disappointment, giving him a bright smile.

"Are you sure you don't want to talk about why you're upset?" John led them up the street to Hoek's. "I'm a shitty problem solver, but a great listener."

"Well…" Faye toyed with an idea. She couldn't get a read off him by touch. Maybe body language would give her some clues. "The thing is I just found out someone is stalking me."

He tensed. She felt his arm muscles tighten, and his mouth formed a rigid line. Reaching up, he covered her hand with his.

"That's bad," he said. "I can see why you'd be upset. Any idea who it might be?"

Faye couldn't help the tingle of fear that ran down her spine. His hand on top of hers made her feel he grabbed onto her in case she ran.

"None," she said.

John frowned. "Maybe it's a fan. Someone who likes the way you sing."

"Maybe."

"If that's the case, you shouldn't perform tonight."

"The thing is, I don't know much about the situation yet. I'm hoping to hook up with a friend of mine later who can tell me more," Faye said. They got into the short line outside of Hoek's where the scent of pizza mixed with the music blaring from the stereo. The sound reminded her of Nathan, but she forced herself to not think about him.

"Can't you go to the police?" John squeezed her hand and then released it. "This kind of thing can be really dangerous. You don't want to take it lightly."

"Believe me, I'm not." She ordered her pizza, but John waved her money away when she tried to pay. He handed over some cash to the guy behind the counter.

"Thanks."

"I have some experience with stalkers." John took a bite of his pizza and then gave a bitter laugh. "That sounded bad. I guess I should say my mother had some experience with it."

"What do you mean?"

"She tended to attract the wrong kind of man." Faye heard the pain in his voice. "One of them got a little overprotective with her."

"I'm sorry."

"He followed my mom around for months and then one day he snapped. He stabbed her." Though the street was getting crowded and people pushed by them, he turned to Faye. She couldn't mistake the misery she saw in him. "That's why you should definitely go the police and take precautions."

Taking a chance, Faye reached out and ran a hand down the side of his face. John closed his eyes at her touch. He really was sweet. Nathan's information had made her paranoid.

But then the air changed. The electric tingle that always told her when something was about to happen ran through her like a current, reminding her of the way she'd felt before the homeless man had stabbed Julie. Faye kept her hand on John's face, unsure if the feeling came from him or something else. She willed her senses to sharpen, and a memory came back to her.

She'd touched the homeless man that night, thrusting the arm that held his knife up and away from her. As she'd done so, the image of a cross had popped into her head. She'd forgotten all about it in the chaos that ensued, but it was the same image she'd seen on the body of Barb, the mark of the Grim Sleeper.

Faye dropped her hand and the odd tingling feeling of anticipation disappeared. John opened his eyes. He reached out, concerned.

"Are you okay?"

"Yes," she said and turned away. "But I really need to hurry now. I have to prepare for my set."

She finished the pizza, barely tasting it as they walked along, and unable to stop the thought whirling in her head: the Grim Sleeper walked next to her. She glanced around, aware there were lots of people on the street. Hopefully, he wouldn't try anything in such a public place.

John talked, but she only half listened as her brain tried to sort out a jumbled mess of information. She thought back to what the cop had said in her vision. The murders had been occurring for a while and then had stopped before resuming once again. The black-haired boy in her dreams had a knife-wielding mother. John's mom had been stabbed by a stalker. When she touched John, she'd gotten the same image of a cross that she'd seen when she touched the homeless man who stabbed Julie, the same image she'd seen burnt into Barb's skin. They all seemed to be random details and yet, she couldn't help but try and tie them together.

They reached the Black Cat, and her anxiety grew as they entered.

"There's the lovely Zenovia." John pointed to the bar where the dark-haired woman was busy filling orders. "I think I'll grab a drink. You want something?"

"No, no, I've got to go backstage and get ready," Faye said. "I'll talk to you later."

"Sure. Have a great set."

Faye crossed the stage. Some of the regulars were already there and gave a little cheer when they saw her. She waved at a few of them, trying to appear normal, and again hoped John wouldn't try anything with so many people around. Then she remembered how at Julie's death her murderer had sprung out of the darkness, unafraid of the small crowd she'd been with. Faye shivered and glanced over her shoulder at Zenovia, worried for her friend's safety.

"Oh, Faye," John called out. "Don't worry. I'll be watching after you tonight."

Somehow the thought did little to ease the confusion and fear she felt inside.

* * * *

A table of frat boys nearly drove her crazy. They'd come in just as Faye took the stage. Drunk before entering the club, the several rounds of beer they consumed through her set hadn't made them the best audience members. They kept requesting for her to sing Free Bird and when she sang a few bars of it to please them, their hoots and hollers practically brought down the roof. Normally, this would only have made her smile, but she didn't like the way John kept looking their way. Faye hoped he wasn't singling one of them out to be his next victim.

Yet even through the commotion and debauchery, Faye sensed the divine presence of the two angels, and though she wouldn't have admitted it to them, she was relieved. They could stop John if he took it in his head to pull a knife.

After her set, she'd gone straight to Zenovia at the bar. "Vodka tonic. A double please."

"Yes, ma'am." Zenovia gave her a salute. "I see John's here tonight."

"Yeah." Faye followed her gaze to the end of the bar where John chatted with a young couple. "Listen, let's hang out tonight after closing. I owe you a girl's night since I cancelled on you last Sunday. Besides, I want to talk to you about John."

"John?" Zenovia didn't stop making her drinks, but she gave Faye a look of worry. "What's wrong? You sound…upset."

"I am upset, but this isn't the time to go into it," Faye said. "Has anyone heard from Barb?"

"No. I figure she's with the players in Vegas."

So the police still hadn't released the information on Barb's death yet. Faye gave Zenovia a quick smile. "I need to talk with some old friends that are here tonight, but don't forget about later. Just the two of us."

Zenovia, too busy making drinks to question further, nodded

and Faye headed to a back table where the din of the frat boys wasn't so loud. The two angels materialized in the vacant chairs at the table at her approach.

"Well, well, well. If it isn't Twiddle Dum and Twiddle Dee."

"Hello, Faye," Azal said.

"Don't you hello me. Why didn't you tell me about this stalker person?"

"Now, Faye--"

"Uh-uh. No bullshit, Azal."

"He's dangerous. He's a nephilim."

"A nephilim?" She couldn't hide her surprise. "I'm a nephilim. What makes him different from me?" At Azal's hesitation, Faye prodded. "Just fucking spit it out. How bad can it be?"

"He killed your family."

The drink slipped from her hand, but Nathan's fast reflexes caught it. For a few seconds, all Faye could do was stare at Azal and struggle to breathe. "Is he in here tonight?"

Azal turned to Nathan who shook his head. "I don't sense him."

"Are you sure?"

"Why?" Azal watched her face. "Have you met him? Do you know where he is?"

"Yeah, I've met him. Or at least I think I have." Faye glanced toward John at the bar. He shook hands with the man he'd been speaking to and then sidled down to Zenovia. The handshake reminded her again of the first time she'd touched him. She should have known right then something was wrong with him. Nephilims were rare. She'd only met two others, and both had been tall males like John, giving off no personal information. Damn it!

"When?" Azal broke up her thoughts.

"I met him last Sunday," Faye said, and looked at Nathan. "He was also at the Crabs show that night, though I didn't see him when we were talking. I guess that's why you had that headache."

Nathan nodded and stared at the table.

"What's his name, Faye?" Azal leaned closer to her. "We really need to know as much about him as possible."

"John," she whispered. "He's at the bar right now."

Both angels snapped to attention and focused on John who sipped a Lone Star Beer, oblivious to their scrutiny.

"Are you sure?" Nathan's brow furrowed. "I'm not sensing anything but a low level hum. It's not enough to even warrant him getting near my chair. Also he's a blond. I thought you said you'd been dreaming about a black-haired boy."

"I have been. Maybe he knows how to glamour." Faye rubbed her forehead, unable to focus on anything but Azal's words.

He killed your family.

"We think the nephilim is trying to communicate with you through these dreams you told Nathan about. What can you remember about them?" Azal continued to watch John.

"I can't remember much, just pieces. He had a rough life, was on his own from an early age, has a momma obsession."

Her hands shook as she watched John laugh at something Zenovia said. If he had killed her parents, then what was she doing just sitting there? The angels obviously didn't believe her. She should take action.

"Wait." Azal placed a hand on her arm and gave her a stern look. "Wait, Faye. I can feel the pain and anger inside you. You're so good at shielding yourself that it must be very strong if I can detect it at all. Don't do anything yet. I'm not sure if this John is the right person."

"You're never too sure of anything, are you Azal?" Faye shook off his hand. "You weren't sure about my parents' death. You weren't sure of Nathan. I'm sick of nobody doing anything!"

"Can you say for certain this John is a nephilim?"

"When I touched him earlier tonight, I saw an image--the cross the serial killer the cops have been chasing left on his last victim. I saw the same symbol Saturday when I touched a homeless man who stabbed a woman I helped cross to the other side of the veil. That can't be coincidence. He must be using a glamour spell to hide his identity."

"Nephilims aren't powerful enough to do that," Azal said.

"But this isn't an ordinary nephilim." Nathan lightly tapped the table with his finger. "If we are working under the assumption he is using angelic essence to hide from us in the first place, then why couldn't he be powerful enough now to glamour?"

All three stared at John, and as if he felt their gaze, he turned his head. With a smile, he raised his beer in a toast to Faye. Azal placed his hand on her arm, feeling her surge of emotion again.

"You say you can't remember the dreams, Faye. Let's see

what I can do about that," he said. "I'm no healer, but I can certainly give you some good fortune."

Azal had never offered to use his power on her before, and Faye hadn't thought to ever request it. Her initial instinct was to refuse the gift, thinking it selfish to take it, but for the first time in her life, she needed some serious luck if she wanted to catch her family's killer. That desire overrode everything else. She sat and waited for her luck to change.

"Concentrate." Azal touched her forehead. "Don't think about vengeance. Focus on your desire to remember the dreams. I'll take care of the rest."

Heat seeped into her forehead, traveling down her face, neck and shoulders. She followed Azal's instructions, thinking only of the dreams. In her mind, she saw the outline of the black-haired boy, which triggered a tornado of images in her head. Her body jerked, but she forced herself to stay with the pictures and memories that hid in her subconscious. Pieces of her dreams flew by, but one caught her attention, because she'd never seen it before--the black-haired boy's face. She focused on it and felt a rushing sensation, propelled into the mind of another.

Faye stood in a dark kitchen. The moon cast its pale light through the window, illuminating a young man and two women in the living room just beyond the kitchen.

"You poor child." One of the women reached her long tapered fingers over, running them through the boy's dark hair as her scent filled the room. Faye recognized it as the unique smell of an angel, and she found herself hearing the thoughts and emotions of the boy. "Let me offer my sympathies."

The young man looked down at the couch where his mother lay, unnaturally still. Normally, she snored loud enough to wake the dead when she passed out. The two women stood there with somber eyes. When he knelt by his mother, he noticed how one of her arms hung down off the couch. Her knife lay just below the fingers as if she had dropped it.

"What happened?" His hazel-eyed gaze searched theirs, and there was a soft innocence in the olive toned face of the sixteen-year-old. When Faye looked at him, she couldn't help but notice how striking he was, and what a handsome man he would one day be. She moved to stand in the corner of the room where she could see the action.

The two women removed themselves from behind the couch and drew the young man toward the kitchen. How odd to be seated in there! He'd eaten under the table until finally his ever-growing form had caused too many accidental bumps, disturbing his mother's meal. After that, he stood in the corner and waited until she ate her dinner. Then he would eat the leftovers standing over the sink. To sit in the kitchen chair felt somehow sacrilegious.

"Your mother has passed on, child. Her heart gave out," the lady who had stroked his hair said. "She's gone on into the hands of the Lord."

"God will cleanse her soul now," the other lady chimed in.

"Who are you?" The young man glanced back and forth between them. "What are you doing in my house?"

"We are your guardians, dear. We're a little late in our duties, but then again, your existence comes as quite a surprise," the first lady said. "My name is Hesiel."

"I am Uriel." The other woman smiled, and he couldn't help but be dazzled by her. "We were friends of your father. Tell us your name, child."

"Sammael." A look of concern crossed both women's faces. He straightened and took a good look at them. Friends of his father. At last. Now his mission, his purpose could begin. His mother had given him precious few details about his father. Her fanatical ravings indicated Lucifer had been taken from her, killed, and all because they dared to love one another. Oh how unfair God was, how cruel the angels actually were to take Lucifer, his mother had claimed. Jealous. Yes, they were all jealous, because Lucifer had grown too powerful. He remembered her words: Someday you will take care of them all. You will make your mark.

"You do know about your father, right?" Hesiel moved to crouch in front of him.

"A little. His name was Lucifer."

"That's right. But he's not quite as bad as what you may have been brought up to think."

"Are you demons?"

As far as demons went, they were a disappointment. Sammael couldn't see any horns or scaly skin. Their eyes didn't glow and the perfume of sulfur didn't cling to them. Instead, they wore soft white dresses, which molded to their curves. Gold circlets gleamed on their wrists. One was blond, the other auburn-haired, and there was a peace about them Sammael found offsetting.

Hesiel, the blonde, gave a light laugh. "Do we look like demons, Sam?"

"My name is Sammael, and no, you don't measure up at all."

"There are no demons," Uriel said, and gave Hesiel a

meaningful look. "Right, Hesiel?"

"Right." Hesiel dutifully changed her tone. "Demons are what mortals created to explain the bad things that happen rather than accepting that it's all part of a greater plan."

"Then what was my father?"

"An angel. Like us," Hesiel said. "Lucifer is one of the brightest angels I've ever known."

"No." Sammael shook his head. "That's not right. My mother said the angels killed my father. They were jealous of his power."

"No." Hesiel said. "No. Lucifer has an ego and part of his job is to present the bad guy image. Nonetheless, he is still an angel doing God's bidding."

"What about all the people who worship him? The ones that call him Satan?"

"When people summon him, they don't realize what they're getting."

"And what is that?"

"An angel empowered by God to create chaos, which usually ruins their life. Temptation in all it's glory! Why the very word Satan means adversary. Tell me, have you ever read one story where he triumphed?"

Sammael pondered the question, but remained silent.

"That's Lucifer's job--to challenge people, to test them, to appear bad when he's...on the clock, so to speak. But he never wins, and more importantly, he doesn't want to," Uriel said with a little laugh. "He's actually quite charming."

"You talk as if he is still alive."

The two angels exchanged glances of uncertainty. Hesiel patted his leg as if soothing a confused child, which only irritated him further. "Well, we're not sure about that. He sort of disappeared from our radar. Angels can, you know. They have the option of taking a sabbatical from duties, and when that happens, it's sort of like being human for a bit. We think you were the...product of this sabbatical."

"My mother said he's dead, and she believed it with her whole heart. Momma said the angels killed him," Sammael said. How could these two be so thickheaded?

"The last we heard about Lucifer was from an angel called Raphael. They had a meeting over Lucifer's earthbound situation. We all assumed he was off to commit some mischief and return to his duties, but...well, that was some time ago. Roughly fifteen years in earth time." Hesiel shrugged and stood up. "He hasn't been heard from since then."

Sammael cocked his head to the side. He didn't believe these two crazy bitches. They obviously thought he was dumb enough to fall for their crappy angel line. And the fact they would be so disrespectful to the name of Lucifer…it angered Sammael, causing him to grind his teeth, a habit from childhood. He got up and walked back into the living room.

Behind him, Uriel called out, "Where are you going, dear?"

"Leave him be. The child is in shock," Hesiel chastised.

Sammael heard them bickering as he stared down at his mother's lifeless form. He bent over and picked up the knife, examining the blood that stained it. Those angels lied. They weren't there to help him if they told him lies.

Help me.

He squinted at the knife. He could have sworn he'd heard a voice come from it.

Help me.

"Momma?" It occurred to him this was a sign. For the first time, Momma asked him for help. He wouldn't let her down. He would begin his mission, serve his purpose and rid the world of angels.

Calmly, he walked into the kitchen, confidence flooding through him. He couldn't explain it, but he knew the knife would help him accomplish great things. Hesiel, her back to him, stared out the screened kitchen door into the night. Uriel sat at the table.

"Look." She stood. "I know this has been a huge shock, but if you'll just--"

He hadn't been sure if the knife would have any effect on her, but it tore through her skin as easily as it would any mortals. She moaned, a small glow illuminating the bone handle before she fell to the floor. He yanked it out. Hesiel turned, and without ceremony, he rushed at her, startling the other angel before she could react. He watched the knife land square in the base of her throat. Blood dripped from the wound, saturating her dress. The knife glowed, and Hesiel dropped just as the other angel had.

Sammael removed the knife, struck by the sense of power he got from the weapon. He could have sworn the blade screamed, sending out a high pitched tone, but it silenced as he examined it.

It was then he noticed the bottom of the handle, the little symbol carved there.

Make your mark, his mother's voice said in his head. Make your mark.

Sammael turned the handle of the knife, so his hand held the blade. Without knowing why, he pushed the handle against the skin of the dead angel at his feet. Smoke rose, along with the smell of charred flesh, but he was pleased with the image of an upside down cross burnt into the skin.

A sudden longing to see that same symbol burnt into the angel who destroyed his father consumed him. What had the angels called him?

Raphael.

He looked down at his hand. Blood welled from a cut by the blade. It mixed with the angel's blood, and the feeling of power grew.

He had come into his own at last.

* * * *

Nathan helped himself to Faye's drink, wary of the way her body twitched every now and then. Whatever she remembered took great effort even with the help of Azal's power. He sipped the drink, resisting the urge to put a steadying hand on her shoulder.

Instead, he turned his gaze to John. The man's blond hair shone under the dim lights of the bar like a halo gone wild. He reached out again, listening for the telltale hum of sin. Still, if his theory about what the nephilim could do with the angel essence he stole proved right, then a strong glamour was possible, even one that hid the hum of sin for a while.

Nathan's mind rifled through his long memories of being an angel, and could come up with no other occasion where a human could cloak their sin. True, if John was a nephilim, he wasn't completely human. Maybe that made it easier to block the hum, just as Faye could block him from her mind. But he doubted it. Sin was the most powerful noise he knew, and it would take a great deal to dull its tone.

"Sammael," Faye said, and her eyes fluttered open. "That's his name."

Azal looked alarmed, but Nathan found the name amusing. Psychotic or not, the nephilim's mother obviously had done her research. There could be no disputing her purpose in choosing that name. It meant poisoned angel.

"What else did you see?" Azal gripped Faye's hand as she struggled to steady her breathing.

"His father is Lucifer, and his mother thought the angels killed him. She instilled the belief in her son that there are demons in the world, and his purpose is to leave his mark. He thinks he is meant to eradicate the angels with some sort of knife that absorbs angel essences," Faye said, her voice low and shaking. "Sammael killed two angels, Hesiel and Uriel. Then he burned down the family home to hide the evidence. He's lived on the street ever since."

"What else?" Eager, Azal leaned in closer, but Nathan's ear pricked. He'd heard a slight change in the air.

"My father met with Lucifer before he disappeared or was killed…is that why this creature went after my family?" Faye's eyes welled with tears. "Does he think my father killed Lucifer?"

"Yes," Azal said. "I think so."

"I saw his face, Azal. I've never seen him before, except in my dreams. They're all coming back now. I can't believe I forgot them in the first place."

"He is made strong by the angel essence he collects when he kills our kind." Azal released her hand. "He cloaked your dreams, and cloaked himself to get to you."

"But why? What does he want from me? He already took the things I care about."

Nathan's head ached. The sound of sin steadily grew stronger. He kept his eyes on John, waiting for the glamour to lose its power.

"He wants you, Faye," Azal said, unaware of Nathan's discomfort. "He thinks two nephilims could create a new creature, something powerful enough to wipe out the angels and capture dominion over the mortals."

The hum filled the room, rising like slow moving water and heard only by Nathan's ears. Yet it remained manageable, nothing worse than what he got from any of his regular clients. So far John had not moved from the bar, and continued to chat with the pretty bartender.

Nathan took another drink of the vodka tonic. Sweating from the ice, little drops of water ran down the side of the glass. As he drank, Nathan noticed one of the drops roll off, heading toward the table with a splash. However, the drop froze in midair, suspended in time and space.

"Azal," Nathan said, and the other angel turned at the warning in his voice. "He's here."

The sounds of the club slowed down, but the hum grew. People froze in mid-movement or speech, stiff as department store mannequins. Time stopped, but not the buzz in Nathan's head. He felt the familiar pain of the nephilim pressing against his senses.

"What's going on?" Faye asked, unaffected by the time freeze.

"I'm not sure." Azal struggled to get up, his movements sluggish.

"He's here." They turned to Nathan who raised a shaky hand and pointed to the area by the bar. "Somewhere over there."

The front door to the club burst inward, flying off its hinges and smacking several frozen frat boys who fell like dominoes to the floor. A rush of wind blew through the doorway and a woman walked into the room.

"Judith," Nathan said, the pain rushing through him stronger than ever before.

His assistant looked at them, a grim smile pulling back the corners of her mouth.

"Hello, boss." She tilted her head and her long black braids fell to one side. "Surprised?"

"What do you want?" Faye stood, knocking over the chair she'd been sitting in. It fell in slow motion, caught in the same time bubble as the rest of the club.

"You, of course." Judith moved toward the trio, her pace measured and confident.

Nathan could no longer move. Whatever spell or magic Judith weaved affected Azal too. Faye looked at them, panic in her eyes.

"Oh, don't mind them," Judith said. "My little spell takes longer to work on angels. Humans are a piece of cake. I freeze time around them all the time. It has taken me longer to figure out how to do it with beings not of this world. Unfortunately, it doesn't last as long as I'd like with angels, so I'm afraid our time together is brief."

"Where did you learn to freeze time?" Faye's voice sounded far away to Nathan. Every step Judith took toward him made the hum louder. He didn't know how much longer he could stand it.

"It's part of my gifts. It's no different than you helping the woman I stabbed cross over to the next dimension. I'm surprised you've never taken the time to develop your other powers, instead of solely focusing on healing. I mean, that's nice and all, very Mother Teresa of you, but c'mon. We are the next best thing to gods. In fact, I bet the original nephilims were what the Greeks worshiped until our kind got wiped out by the Big Guy." Judith chuckled at the amazement on Faye's face. "I've been watching you a while, Faye. I know all about you. I've been in your home, your thoughts and your dreams."

"And them?" Faye nodded at Azal and Nathan. "How did you cloak yourself so Nathan couldn't detect you in his shop?"

"I'm not sure you'd approve of my…methods. But don't worry about your friends here. They're very aware of what's going on. I imagine Nathan is suffering terribly from the hum of my sins right now." Judith stood in front of them. One hand reached out and touched Faye's hair. "You are so lovely, Faye. I've waited a long time. The first time I saw you, I knew you were special, destined to be in my life."

"Cut the crap and show me your real face, Sammael," Faye said, her voice strong with anger. Judith's eyebrows twitched in surprise. "Yes. I know your name now. Azal helped me remember the dreams."

"Did he?" Judith allowed the female persona to meld into the handsome features of a young man with short, tousled, black hair and a porcelain face. Sammael. A small goatee covered his chin, but the lip ring Judith sported still hung there. The boyish quality about him reminded Faye of the countless number of Emo kids she saw downtown.

"You killed my parents, my fiancée." Faye's anger cut through the sin to Nathan's ears. He tried to hold onto the sound of her voice.

"Is that what you were told?" Sammael's eyes widened. "Then that confirms what I've believed and been taught all along. Angels are bad, corrupt beings. Their days of purity and goodness have long faded. Why just look at your friend, Nathan Ink. Most of the people he tattoos die."

Sammael pulled out a knife from his satchel. Just the sight of it was enough to make Nathan's heart pound harder. "See this? It's what allows me my power. It has angel blood on it. That's the key to it all. Every angel life I take makes me stronger and harder to be tracked. I'm eradicating the angels, getting rid of the bad seeds."

"That's not your call to make."

"Oh, you mean that's God's job?"

"Yes. Why did you kill my father?" Faye's voice filled with fury. "He was hardly a bad seed."

"No. He wasn't. And I didn't kill him." Sammael turned his attention to Azal. "Oh, I'm sure Azal told you some story to make you think I was involved, but you should really look to him for those answers. After all, he's the one supposed to be savvy to the dangers your family faced. He knew the consequences for angels and humans being together."

"What are you saying?"

"God found out about your father and mother, and their little...indiscretion. Namely, you. Azal or one of the angels probably tattled. And you know what God did? Instead of viewing what occurred between your parents as a miracle, He saw it as an abomination. More to the point, He sees you as an abomination. So He charged an angel to get rid of the one who'd fallen from grace, and who do you think that job fell to?" Sammael gave a grim smile to Azal. "That's right. Your buddy here. Your guardian angel. He got the shit job of destroying your father. God didn't have the balls to do it himself."

"I don't believe you."

"Believe it. Don't believe it." Sammael shrugged. "It's the truth."

"What about my mother or Chris? Why kill them?"

"Accidents. Wrong place, wrong time. Angel eradication can be very powerful you know, especially if the angel is old. There's always an explosion of energy. It can take out bystanders like your mother and fiancée."

Nathan twitched his fingers, the freeze beginning to wear off.

"How do you know all this?"

"I have my sources." He placed the knife on the table, and his hand snaked forward to grab her arm. "You pick up a lot of secrets when you take an angel's essence."

"You kill your sources." Faye stood her ground, though she didn't pull away from Sammael. Nathan longed to break free of the spell and put his own hands on the man. He understood all too well the direction of the nephilim's thoughts and desires. "What do you want from me?"

"Your help. My job isn't easy. But I will prevail. What the world needs is a new breed of angels. That's where you and I come in. We're nephilims, half-angel and half-human. What would happen if we got together?" Sammael smiled at her and grabbed her other arm. "You know, tried to repopulate with our kind."

"Whoa. Back off cowboy--"

"Now don't say no right away," Sammael said, his voice soft. Nathan saw the intensity of his gaze, the way his hazel eyes mesmerized. It reminded him of Lucifer, his gift for temptation, and Nathan knew it was the very angel essence Sammael used to sway Faye right now. It worked, judging from her compliant reaction. Sammael placed a hand on her waist and pulled her closer. Her mouth parted a little, letting out a soft sigh.

"Think it over, Faye," Sammael whispered before lowering his lips to hers. "We could be good together."

Nathan watched him kiss her, hoping her response would be to push him away. But the thrall he had her under was strong. Her hand reached up, wrapping around his neck and she kissed him back. Sammael's free hand ran up and down her side, flirting with her breast.

"Stop." She pulled away with an effort. "It's a trick. A thrall."

"It's temptation, one of my father's specialties. You saw me use it the other night when I infused Curt's tattoo with desire." Sammael placed a finger under her chin and forced her to look at him. "Your nephilim blood recognizes mine. It calls out to me."

Nathan noticed the room flickered. The time freeze was about to run its course. Life crept back into his body, and he stared at the knife on the table, hoping he could get to it before Sammael.

"I'll let you have some time to think. I want you to come to me willingly. When you sort through the lies and bullshit of these angels, you'll do just that," Sammael said. "And as a token of my faith in you, I'll get rid of any distractions that might keep you from the truth. I'll start with the angel who killed your family."

Sammael thrust his knife into Azal, and the handle glowed. Nathan heard faint screams, voices crying out to be saved, mixing with the sound of Faye's cries as she ran to Azal.

Apothecary.

The word cut through the hum and screaming souls, undeniably in Azal's voice. Before he could puzzle it out, Sammael turned toward him. Nathan braced for the sting of the knife's blade.

Sammael licked the blood off his fingers and winked at Nathan. "Don't worry, boss. I don't want to kill you. I respect what you do too much. You're a kindred spirit, the closest thing the angel world has to a rogue. You don't like the angels any more than I do. That's why I've been training under you, learning from you. We could still do a little business together. But make no mistake, if you get in my way with Faye, I will collect your essence. I bet I could definitely hide the sound of my sins then."

He winked at Nathan, and moved toward the door. Pausing by John who sat frozen at the bar drink in hand, he called, "Hey, Faye."

She looked over at him.

"I said I was removing all distractions. I saw you talking to this guy earlier tonight. He'll only be in our way." Sammael thrust his knife into the base of John's throat.

John slumped on the bar, blood dripping onto the floor slowly at first, but speeding up as time crawled forward. With a smile, Sammael left the Black Cat. The low murmur in the room grew louder as time caught up.

Nathan broke free of the binding spell and rushed to Faye. The pain in his head threatened to consume him, but he forced himself to focus on Azal.

The angel's eyes were glazed, his body still. Faye placed her hands on his chest, and Nathan knew she searched for something to heal. It was too late. His mortal shell was empty. She looked at Nathan, helpless.

"I'll take him," Nathan said. "Let me remove him before time completely resumes its normal pace and anyone notices."

She nodded, tears streaming down her face as she looked over at John.

"No. It's too late for him too." Nathan tried to be gentle, but he couldn't keep the urgency out his voice. "Go to my place, Faye. Don't speak to anyone. I'll take care of everything here. Just go to my apartment. You'll be safe there."

She nodded, and grief-stricken, stumbled out of the bar.

Chapter 13

Faye stared out the window and listened to the smooth voice of Diana Krall. In one hand she held a cigarette, which sparked orange at the tip as she inhaled. Silky smoke rings floated above her head like miniature halos. She had quit smoking long ago, but tonight…well, tonight had been rough. She wasn't afraid to tempt the fates by smoking a little stick of cancer.

Azal is dead.

The thought kept running through her head, but she could make no sense of it. She'd seen his body, felt the absence of his spirit. Azal is dead.

And John. She'd been so wrong about him, and because of her, his life ended way too soon. The same could be said for Barb. If it weren't for Faye, she might still be alive.

Shame mingled with her sorrow. When Sammael kissed her, she'd felt something. Desire. Temptation. There'd been no control in the action. Her own free will hadn't mattered. Faye didn't care if it had been a case of thrall or not. Sammael's words haunted her.

Does our nephilim blood call out to each other?

And then there was Azal.

The angel of good fortune killed her father. No. It wasn't possible, she couldn't believe that. Not her guardian angel. He wouldn't commit such a heinous act. He kept her from harm, not caused it. Besides, God wouldn't be so cruel.

And yet…she had doubts.

She'd grabbed a memory from Azal when he'd boosted her good fortune. She wasn't aware if he knew she'd done it, or if he'd pushed it to her on purpose. It was a recollection of the last day of her parents' lives.

Her body stiffened at the small sound behind her. She reached out with her mind and found Nathan. He stood in the doorway, his angelic smell lingering in the air.

"Did you take care of…things?" Faye asked.

"Yes. I removed both bodies and erased the memory of those in the bar."

"Is Zenovia okay?"

"Yes."

"Do you think Sammael told the truth about Azal killing my father?"

Behind her, Nathan remained silent, but she felt his mind turning over the question. She sensed doubts in him too.

"I don't know, Faye. Azal was the angel of good fortune, not the harbinger of death. I just don't know." He sat on the couch, slumping forward as one hand rubbed his forehead.

Faye rested her cigarette in the ashtray on the coffee table. Kneeling in front of him, she reached up and massaged the tender point in the center of his forehead. "I hope you don't mind that I put some music on. I love Diana Krall. I was surprised to even find a title I recognized in your CD collection. Most of the music you have seems so…angry."

"Most of the time I am angry," Nathan said, closing his eyes. Faye sensed the pain still pulsing beneath her hand, and she sent a burst of healing energy to the point.

"At what?"

"At life. At humanity. Myself."

Faye understood. In the last seven years, she'd often felt the same way.

After a few moments, he pulled her hand away, holding it in his own while he studied her face. Faye felt him gently probing at her mind.

"Stop it," she said, but her voice remained soft. "I can feel what you are doing."

"I don't care. I want to know how you are, and I don't believe you will tell me the truth," he said.

"It's not in my nature to lie."

"No. But you omit things like the best of them."

She smiled. "True."

"Faye, did you hear anything before Azal…passed?" Nathan's voice cracked on the other angel's name. "I thought I heard him pass on a thought."

"I didn't hear anything at that moment, but I did get something from him right as he helped bring back my memories," she said. "Why? What did you hear?"

"Just a word. Apothecary."

"Apothecary? That's a type of pharmacist, an herbal doctor, right?" Faye asked. "What could he have meant?"

"I'm not sure," Nathan said. "Tell me what memory he passed to you. Maybe there is a connection."

"I haven't had time to look at it." She crawled up on the couch to sit by him. "I haven't wanted to."

He took the cigarette from its resting place, sucked on it and then ground it out in the ashtray. He stroked her hair, and now it was she who closed her eyes, savoring the touch.

A soft sound flickered through the room, lingering inescapably below Diana Krall's sultry voice. Nathan's hand stilled in her hair, and she knew he heard it too. The soft golden hum enveloped her senses and brought back Azal's last memory of her family.

* * * *

The explosion rocked Azal, breaking him from his trance. He'd been staring at a woman dancing. A small crowd gathered to watch and toss coins into the sombrero on the sidewalk. Her skirt whirled around her, revealing long, tan legs as she kept time to the Spanish tune playing on her portable stereo.

Absolutely exquisite, he thought.

She flashed a breathtaking smile at the crowd, further enrapturing Azal. It was a moment he would always regret.

His ears heard the explosion before anyone else, and Azal moved from the dancing woman in the direction of the sound. Dread grew in his heart as he saw the noise came from an old warehouse. Already the smell of smoke gathered in the air, and the scent propelled him to move faster. Raphael had told him only a few minutes earlier he was headed to the building to minister to the homeless population who called the place home. Flames licked around the worn down warehouse, charring its edges. Azal entered, impervious to the orange fire raging all around.

He spotted the bodies immediately. Estella and Chris both lay dead, blood pooling around them. Horrified, Azal looked for Raphael. No sign of his essence or his mortal shell.

But someone else was in the building. Azal could just faintly pick them up as he rose above the flames. Raphael might be alive after all, weakened perhaps, and Azal whispered a small prayer of hope. He looked around, searching for the source of this presence, but saw no one. A mental scan of the building encountered a block, almost as if something threw up a black veil to keep him from identifying them. Could this be the being Raphael mentioned sensing lately and the reason he had Azal spending so much time earthbound to watch over Faye? But he didn't have time to waste on searching for an unknown creature right now. His concern was for Raphael. Already he heard the sound of sirens.

The fire fighters sprayed water on the building, battling the flames, and Azal's presence provided them with the luck needed to put out the blaze. He waited as they discovered the remains of Estella and Chris, but there was no sign of Raphael, or the mysterious other being he'd sensed. Because of the lack of a mortal shell, Azal suspected the worst, and he knew he could no longer avoid doing what had to be done.

Faye napped, exhausted from studying for finals. Her hair splayed across the pillow, and Azal watched her, unconcealed tenderness in his face. He almost got lost in the slow and steady rhythm of her breathing, but caught himself before he could become transfixed a second time.

Glancing around the small dorm room, he saw she had surrounded herself with pictures of her family and friends. Photos of Chris and Faye grinned at him from wooden frames, their happiness unconcealed. Azal liked Chris, who had been studying to be a doctor like Faye's mother. He often accompanied Estella and Raphael when they'd done community work. The love the young man felt for Faye was evident to anyone who saw the two together.

Azal covered his face and wept.

With a start, Faye awoke, sitting straight up in the bed. She gasped for breath, clutching at the T-shirt she wore as if the neckline were too tight and cutting off circulation.

"Azal, what's wrong?" She choked out the words. "Your grief is taking the air from the room."

He sought to get his emotions under control. She would need him to be strong now.

"Azal, what is it?"

"Faye." He walked toward her, his gait unsteady. "I have news."

"Are you crying?"

He sat on the edge of the bed and reached for her hand.

Without thought, he sent a small burst of energy to Faye, warming her cold fingers.

"What is it, Azal? You're scaring me."

"I was sent here today to do God's will," Azal said and then stopped. The anguish showed in her face, though she willed herself to be patient. He admired her strength, and it gave him courage.

"What do you mean?"

He looked into the green eyes he knew so well. Raphael's image peered back at him, and he didn't want to answer the question. How could he explain God wanted Raphael to give up his family?

"Azal, where are my parents?"

"I'm sorry, Faye." He bowed his head. "They are...dead."

Disbelief in her eyes.

"That can't be," she said, shaking her head. "That just can't be."

"I'm sorry."

"How? How did it happen?"

"I don't know all the details. They were going to tend those in need. At least that's what your father told me. There was some sort of explosion. By the time I got to the warehouse it was too late."

"But you were there? You spoke to my father?"

"Before it happened, yes."

"Why weren't you with him then? You could have helped him." The bitterness in her voice, the hurt, made Azal wince.

"I...needed to talk to him about an urgent matter, but Raphael asked me to wait for him," Azal said. "I followed his instructions."

"How did my father die?"

"I don't know."

"Yes, you do," Faye accused. "I can feel you're not telling me everything. I might not be a full angel, but that part of me is very strong thanks to you and my father. You know something."

"I truly don't know, Faye. I just felt it happen. I stood on the street and something severed inside me. The connection we angels have to one another is strong. One moment Raphael was there and the next..."

"Gone." She finished the thought. "Dead."

Silence stretched between them, threatening to break into a torrent of sorrow.

"Who is powerful enough to kill an angel?" she asked.

"I can only think of two beings that strong. One would be another angel." Azal spoke slowly, but an idea occurred to him, an idea that sickened his soul.

"And the other?"

He couldn't voice the thought. Too terrible a thing to be said to Faye, it would change her forever. Besides, it couldn't be true. Why the very reason he'd been trying to meet with Raphael was to warn him, to help him with the request that would be coming soon. Surely God hadn't acted on His threats.

"God?" she asked, as if she'd heard his thoughts. Perhaps she had. He couldn't seem to keep his mind guarded, soaked with grief as it was. "Did God do this? Did he take my father?"

Azal said nothing.

"Azal, tell me the truth."

He got up slowly from the bed, turning toward the window of the room.

"Don't you even think about disappearing on me, Azal." She got out of bed and stood beside him, placing a hand on his shoulder to prevent him from going. "Just tell me. Was it God? Was it because...of the relationship between him and my mother? Because of me?"

"God was aware of it," Azal said. "He sent me to speak with Raphael. He wanted your father to return to the other side of the veil."

"But when you didn't talk to my father, He acted without you."

"I don't know that for sure."

"But you think it. I heard the thoughts flow from you a moment ago."

"I don't know for sure, Faye," Azal stressed. "I was sent to talk to Raphael, and I didn't get to. I'm not sure what happened. I do know if Raphael were to refuse the request, there would have been consequences."

"Consequences? All because of me. Because I exist." Tears slipped from her eyes, but her voice turned hard. "You should have fought harder to warn him. You knew what was at stake."

"Yes. I did." Azal hung his head, overwhelmed by guilt. "I was going to help him."

"You shouldn't have listened when he told you to hang back. You should have pushed him to speak with you."

"Yes." Her words stabbed him, bringing fresh pain.

"I thought you angels were big on protecting one another."

Anger almost choked her words. "Let me guess. You were transfixed weren't you? You were off staring at some trivial little thing instead of protecting my family."

Azal couldn't refute her words as images of the dancing girl on the sidewalk came to him. He had been transfixed. He couldn't even remember how long he'd stayed there watching the woman perform.

"I've got to call Chris," Faye said, and Azal winced at the note of hysteria in it. "I need him right now."

Chris. Azal realized he hadn't told her everything.

"Wait, Faye." He saw the comprehension click in place before he said the words. "Chris was with your parents."

Her face went white and she dropped to the floor, her hands covering her mouth as if she tried to keep from screaming. But he heard it in her mind, an awful wailing that built and built until it burst forth, shaking the walls of the room. Pictures fell to the floor, smashing on impact.

"Faye, I'm so sorry." He dropped to his knees beside her.

Faye pushed him away.

"Get out," she hissed. "Get away from me, Azal."

"I can't leave you like this."

"Get out. I don't want you here!"

"Faye, please--"

"Go!"

He nodded, knowing she needed to be alone, needed time to process all that had occurred before she could heal. He stepped away, not knowing it would be the last full conversation they would have for seven years.

* * * *

The song switched and Diana's smooth voice sang The Night We Called It A Day.

"I didn't give Azal a chance. He tried to talk to me so many times after that," Faye said, and stood. "I blamed him, never thinking he might be grieving too."

"You are human, Faye. Azal is not. He spent so much time here on earth he started to feel emotion. It's a hazard of our kind, but ultimately, Azal should have been stronger for you." But even as he said the words, Nathan had to admit if he'd been in Azal's position, he didn't think he would have handled the situation any better.

"No. I should have been stronger for him," Faye said. "And I shouldn't have ever entertained Sammael's suggestion that Azal killed my family."

"Did Azal never try to talk to you again about the events of that day?"

"I wouldn't let him. I shut him out, blocked him. I know a few tricks too, you know." She moved to the windows, restless. "So who did it? God or Sammael?"

"What does your heart tell you?"

"That at the time Azal had doubts as to whether or not God had been involved. But now it seems pretty clear to me a more likely scenario is Sammael killed my father. He must have been the creature Azal sensed in the fire."

"So you're letting God off the hook?"

"Maybe Sammael just beat Him to the punch. If my father had been asked to leave us, I don't know if he would have."

"Maybe." Nathan stood next to her, his jaw a tight line. "I'm sorry I didn't recognize Judith was Sammael. She worked in my shop for six months, and I had no clue, which goes to show how powerful this nephilim is. I could only sense his sin when he either wanted me to, or when his defenses were dropped for whatever reason. The angel essences his knife takes have allowed him greater advantages than any other creature I've ever seen or heard of."

"This isn't your fault," Faye said.

"Still, as Judith, he learned things about me, learned how I worked, my habit of tuning out the Others. I'm sure that only helped him cover his tracks," Nathan said. "He called me a kindred spirit."

"He considers you to be on his level."

Nathan nodded, the air vibrating with the telltale signs of his anger.

"He's not all-powerful, Nathan," Faye said. "I think he's at his weakest when he is in his true form, when you can hear the sin. Maybe that's something we can use to our advantage. What do you think Azal meant with the whole apothecary thing?"

"I have no idea," Nathan said. "You?"

"I don't know, either."

Nathan turned her to face him. He stared into her tired eyes, probing, and then unable to stop himself, he leaned forward, touching his lips to hers. She closed her eyes and kissed him back.

He wrapped an arm around her waist, pulling her toward him,

and damn, if she didn't taste good. The fervor inside him grew, and she pressed against him, running her hands up and down his body, making him want to feel skin on skin. Nathan slid her dress down, and it pooled on the floor as his lips moved to her neck. She moaned at his touch, and the sound urged him on.

Nathan picked her up, tossing her on his bed. As he removed his clothes, he saw her eyes take in the long tattoo that wrapped around the length of his body. Before she had time to ask questions about it, he slid over her, his mouth everywhere.

He moved upward and stared into her eyes. The desire, the need for comfort in them gave him pause, but it was Faye who asked the question. "Are you sure? This could be trouble."

He found there was no question, no doubt. She closed her eyes and offered herself to him.

* * * *

On the street below Nathan Ink's apartment, Sammael gnashed his teeth, his anger coming unbound. He'd accomplished what he meant to. Killing Azal had been part of his plan, and now he felt the time was right for him to move forward. The information he'd given Faye caught her off guard and should have been just the thing to do what he wanted. He'd had her for a few minutes back there, had swayed her with desire before his time spell wore off. That's what had him in such frenzy now. That desire, the delicious sexual feeling he'd created in her was now spent on another. He could sense them up there, their guards down just enough to allow him to understand what they were doing.

Even more frustrating to Sammael was the knowledge his presence typically caused Nathan physical pain. He didn't have to be far away for that to happen. The months he'd spent working in Hell's Leak allowed him to experiment and learn about Nathan's habits. And yet here he was on the street, right outside the angel's apartment, and there seemed to be no deterrent to Nathan Ink's libido. Damn it.

What the hell was going on?

He could only hope this little act would require immediate action from the head honcho, the Almighty Himself. Problem solved! Well, maybe. What if this one little transgression resulted in Faye conceiving? That would ruin everything. Sammael had been counting on getting there first.

A chilly wind blew down the street, ruffling his black hair and cooling his emotions. Here he wondered if some rogue angel knocked up his future mate. It was laughable!

Fuck it. Nothing had happened that couldn't be fixed.

One way or another.

* * * *

Afterward, Faye ran a finger over the tattooed line on Nathan's body. Thick and black, it wrapped around his entire body starting at the base of his neck. It spiraled under his scrotum before going down one leg and ending on top of his foot.

"Nathan?"

He stared into her green eyes, feeling lost in their depths, and surprised as the urge to roll over and enter her again gnawed at him.

"Are you all right?" Faye asked. "Having regrets?"

"No," he said, pleased at the relief on her face. "I thought of a moment long ago. The first time the direction of my life changed."

"Did you die? Is that how you became an angel?"

"Yes. I was never the same after the myst came."

"The myst?"

"Yes. In the time of Queen Isabella, I was a nomadic creature of Spain, a gypsy. I traveled with my clan as a scratcher."

"Scratcher?"

"Yes." Nathan ran his fingers through her hair. He'd never talked about his transformation with anyone. "I grew up with no memory of my parents. There was always just my tribe, and everyone looked after one another. Early on I showed a talent for drawing and fortune telling."

"Fortune telling? Really?" The idea seemed to amuse her, and she propped herself up to see him better. "Did you have a crystal ball too? Or did you just read palms?"

"Neither." Nathan chuckled. "My methods were a little more unconventional. See, I wasn't like the old gypsy women of my tribe who could look at someone and instantly know everything about the person. My gift was related more to the auditory senses."

"The hum." Faye nodded in understanding. "Even as a regular mortal you heard it."

"Yes. But not in the same way I do now. What I hear as an angel causes me pain, discomfort, but back then the sound was golden and pure. It's hard to describe something you don't hear anymore."

"Why don't you hear that tone? Why is it always the other?"

"Part of the deal I made when I became an angel."

"I figured pillow talk would be interesting with you, Nathan. You have to tell me how you became an angel. Please. I'm dying to know."

Nathan thought back to his transformation. Though centuries ago, the memory was still fresh. He closed his eyes, picturing the cliffs of the Mediterranean where his tribe settled for those last fateful months. The smell of the salty sea lingered in his mind, and for a second, he could almost hear the crash of waves against the rock wall of the cliff.

"I made scratches for people," he began. "When I heard the golden hum, I would look for the source, knowing someone needed my help. After touching them, my senses would tell me what their needs were. Instead of mixing up some elixir or potion to help them like others in the tribe would do, I would scratch a picture onto their skin with a knife. Before the blood dried, charcoal would be rubbed into the image, so it would stay even when the wound healed. My primitive tattoo would influence the outcome of whatever the person desired."

"So even back then you had clients," Faye said.

"You would have approved of my designs in those days, Faye. They weren't intended to do anything but heal or help. It's ironic my good intentions actually turned me into what I am today." Nathan frowned. "One day I took a nap on the cliffs overlooking the sea. When I woke, a man stood over me holding a knife. I didn't recognize him. He told me his wife, Marta, had come to me many months ago, begging for help because she couldn't bear children."

Nathan paused, remembering the desperation and agony in the man's eyes as he described how Marta had come home, her heart light, because of the three intertwining circles carved into her arm--a sign of fertility. Marta had grown heavy with child in the following months, but during childbirth there had been a complication, and the poor woman died. Angered, her husband sought out the young gypsy scratcher, the person he felt should be punished. If Nathan could see the future, why hadn't he seen Marta would die? Why would he allow her to have a child?

No amount of talk would convince the husband Nathan could only see so far into the future. He had no control over fate. Or did he? For the first time, the young gypsy wondered at the influence his designs might have over others. After all, if he hadn't scratched the intertwining circles into Marta's soft skin, she might not have had any hope of getting pregnant. She might still be alive.

"You helped her, but something went wrong," Faye said, understanding in her eyes. "Sometimes, even the best intentions aren't enough."

"True. The woman died in childbirth, and the husband felt I could have prevented it by never tattooing her in the first place. Maybe he was right. At any rate, he was angry enough to murder me. There on the cliffs, he caught me off guard and killed me," Nathan said. "As I lay there, feeling life slip away, the golden hum sounded out. I remember thinking how nice it was to die to such a peaceful sound. And then I saw it. The myst."

It had unfurled its gray arms toward him, a cloud bank of fog pushing in from over the sea, and carrying an odd acrid scent, reminding him of burnt feathers. Death had come, drowning out the beauty of the hum.

"I heard a voice in the myst," Nathan said. "It told me God wasn't through with me just yet. I could go on to heaven, or I could change into something else, do something more for humanity. Help others take the path away from sin."

"So you became an angel," Faye said. "You took the deal."

"I did."

"Any regrets?"

"Only one." He shifted in the bed, a little ashamed to admit to any regret at all. "I never heard the golden hum again."

"Tell me about your tattoo." Faye ran a finger down the line starting at his neck, following its path around his chest.

The tattoo vibrated at her touch, giving Nathan an uncomfortable sensation and he sat up, pushing her hand away.

"What are you doing?" he asked.

"Nothing," she said, and her eyes widened at the sudden anger in his voice. "I was just touching it."

"What were you thinking about? Were you trying to heal it?"

"No, no." She pulled her body farther away. "I was just touching it. I felt it vibrate, though."

"Don't do that again," Nathan said. "I don't want you to remove it. When I woke up from the myst, this was the mark left behind. All angels have a mark, something that cleaves them to the Lord. This is mine. It binds me to my mission. Don't try to heal it."

"I couldn't," she soothed. "I can't even remove the ones you put on your clients."

"Yes, but you can dull them a little. Don't dull mine."

"Nathan, your tattoo comes from divine powers. I don't think I could dull it if I tried. And I didn't try. Whatever has you so freaked out is not because of any special skill of mine."

He lay back on the bed, contemplating her words, never having felt anything like that before. Her touch on the thick black line stirred his soul, twisting it into dizzying knots. The little vibration startled him, and for a moment, he'd heard...no...that was impossible...

"Shh...it's okay." Faye leaned over him. "I won't touch it again."

"It's just I thought I heard..." He trailed off, struggling to make sense of the strange emotions running through him.

"The hum you get from your clients?"

"No. That's what is so strange. As I told you, once I got the gift, I never heard the hum the same way again. Before the myst, it had been a gentle sound that pleased me, and allowed me to know who needed aid. But along with my transformation, the hum changed too, becoming harsh and painful. I spent a great deal of time behind the veil, learning my purpose. When I encountered humans again, I found myself incapable of serving them as I once had. I could only assist those with the worst tone I've ever experienced, the sound I now associate with my clients."

Nathan stopped speaking. How he missed the sweet hum of his youth. He knew the tone represented the goodness in life. For just a few seconds when Faye had run her fingers along his tattoo and earlier, when they'd shared Azal's memories...

She dropped down beside him again. He felt the pounding of her heart as he pulled her to him.

"I'm sorry," he whispered. "I didn't meant to suggest you..."

"It's okay."

Nathan held her tighter. He couldn't imagine what it meant or how it had happened. In five hundred years, he hadn't heard it, and yet when she'd placed her fingers on the dark, thick line of the tattoo...

He'd heard the golden hum again.

Chapter 14

Angels snored. The steady roar coming from Nathan's mouth made Faye smile. Wrapping a blanket around her, she slipped out of bed and walked to the windows. The early morning sun crept up over the horizon, and the light touched the downtown area, illuminating it street by street.

She'd woken up, pleased with what had occurred between her and Nathan, but the realities of their situation tempered the pleasure. Here she was, enjoying herself when others she'd cared about had been destroyed by Sammael. The sly voice of her conscience whispered her attentions should be on finding and putting a stop to him. Destroying his knife should be at the top of her to-do list.

Not to mention what occurred was a violation of holy laws. But damn it, Nathan always seemed so mortal, so human-- definitely different than any other divine being she'd ever encountered. She couldn't deny her attraction to him.

Get a grip, she told herself. Focus on what needs to be done.

But just what was that?

Azal had given them a clue in the word "apothecary". He wouldn't have used such a specific word without it having a meaning. But none of the local herbalist and healers she knew were associated with the word.

Glancing around Nathan's loft, she saw no sign of a phone or a computer. That meant a Google search was right out. She had a dim recollection of leaving her iPhone in her apartment to charge.

Hell's Leak. She bet it had a phone and a phonebook. Perfect. She would just go down to the shop and find out what she needed. It took her no time to slip back into her dress, replace the blanket on the bed and grab her purse. Rifling through Nathan's closet, she located a green army jacket with the thrift store tag still on it.

"I had no idea angels shopped at Goodwill," she said softly.

Nathan ripped another huge snore, and Faye smothered a giggle as she tried to decide whether or not to wake him. Going out of the loft would be a risky move. The night before Nathan explained his apartment was charmed with an "angel alarm" capable of stopping intruders. But Sammael would know how to get into Hell's Leak, having worked there for six months.

Waking up Nathan would be the smart thing to do, yet she couldn't bring herself to do it. Azal's death, fresh in her mind, reminded her that the sleeping angel she found herself suddenly attached to could be killed. She didn't want another death on her conscience. Maybe she could just slip into Hell's Leak, get the information and then come right back.

Holding her breath, Faye slid the front door open and stepped out. The stairwell looked clear.

The front door of Hell's Leak opened easily, and she figured there was really no need for Nathan to lock it. Not everyone saw the place, and he sensed the ones that could. The interior was dark, but light from the front windows showed her she was alone. As a precaution, she turned the inside lock of the door.

The phonebook lay underneath the telephone on the counter. She leafed through it, discovering one match. A listing toward the bottom of the page read simply "The Apothecary". No number was listed, but it did show the street address, which wasn't too far from Hell's Leak. Still, it would be a hell of a hike. Much easier to drive there.

Pushing away thoughts of how much Nathan would disapprove of her going out alone, Faye unlocked the door and moved quickly down the street. Since she hadn't gone home the night before, her orange MG was still parked beneath the overpass a few blocks away. Soon she sped down the side streets of downtown Austin.

The Apothecary sat tucked in between a vintage boutique and a used bookstore on South Congress Avenue. Two tall windows flanked the green front door. A white candle had been painted on one window and it was surrounded by gold angel wings. Curious she parked and got out.

A bell tinkled, announcing her presence, and she expected to see a clerk hurry out, but the place was quiet. The scent of lavender hung heavy in the air, passed around by the whirling ceiling fans overhead. Everywhere there were shelves full of plants and herbs, neatly arranged and labeled. Many of them were things she grew at The Flower Pot, but a few were unfamiliar even to her practiced eye. One area held candles of varying sizes and colors. All of them were meant to help the user summon angels. Old books were on another set of bookshelves, though she couldn't decipher all the titles. There were charms dangling from the sidewalls and empty potion bottles in an old glass cabinet. Whoever owned the shop knew about angel lore and understood the importance of color. The hue of the bottle helped contain the strength of whatever potion lived inside it.

Movement at the back of the store distracted her, stopping further inspection. A man stood behind the counter. He scratched his head, staring at a blue bottle in his hand.

"That should do it," he said, and looked over at Faye. A smile of recognition lit up his elderly face, and his blue eyes warmed. "Well, hello. It's nice to see you again, young lady."

Faye gripped the counter, shock pouring through her like icy water. She knew those eyes.

"Are you all right?" He came around and reached for her arm. A yellow spark sizzled between them. Startled, he stepped back.

"Daddy?" The old man's face turned confused. "Daddy, is it really you?"

The man tilted his head, puzzled. She moved to him, grasping his hands. He pulled away when the yellow spark jumped again at her touch.

"Why didn't Azal tell me?"

"Azal? Is he here?" Raphael looked around the room.

"No, Daddy, he's not," Faye said. "He's--"

"What's that you say? Daddy?" He squinted at her. "You must have me mistaken for someone else."

"What's happened to you?"

"You reminded me a little bit of..." He shook his head, frowning. "Never mind. I made a mistake."

"No. Listen to me. Your name is Raphael. You were married to my mother." Faye leaned on the counter. "I am your daughter. My name is Phaedra McCoy. I was named after you, but everyone calls me Faye."

"I'm sure you're a nice girl, but you're confused. My wife, Estella, and my child, Chris, died," Raphael said. "They were killed in a fire seven years ago."

She took a good look at the man behind the counter. What had happened to her father? The energy and vitality always surrounding him were gone. She stretched her mind and found his brain muddled, bruised.

"I'm sorry to hear about your loss," Faye said, unable to keep the tears from springing into her eyes. "I've lost family too."

The old man's face softened. "There, there, sweetheart. I didn't mean to bark at you."

Faye blinked back her tears, determined. Okay. He didn't know her, but her father was alive. Right now that was more than enough.

"So...you're an apothecary," she said, brushing her tears away with the back of her hand.

"I dabble in herbs and healing." He smiled. "What about you? You must be interested in natural medicines if you're here."

"Yes," she said. "I grow some of the same plants in my shop, The Flower Pot."

"You own The Flower Pot? I've been meaning to stop in there." He scratched his head again and shook the bottle. "Now what was I doing with this?"

Faye moved away, afraid she might start crying again.

"Faye?" She turned toward him, her heart thumping with hope. "Is that you?"

The puzzled demeanor was gone. The old man behind the counter stood, straight and tall, recognition in his eyes, and for a moment, she saw the father of her youth.

"Daddy?"

But then, as quickly as it had come, the comprehension flickered out, and once again he was a confused old man.

The bell above the front door tinkled again.

"Hey, Ralph." A young man stomped in, his work boots loud against the wood floor. He peeled off his coat and knit cap.

Faye noticed he was missing a hand.

"Can I help you?" The man looked over her shoulder at Raphael. "Everything okay here, Ralph?"

Raphael stared at the bottle, but nodded.

"Sorry. We're not actually supposed to be open yet." The man crossed his arms. "Sometimes Ralph comes in early, though. Were you looking for something in particular?"

"No, I was just curious about this place."

"Bob?" Raphael looked at the newcomer as if seeing him for the first time. "When did you get here?"

"Just walked in, Ralph." Bob turned to him. "I don't think you've had your daily dose of memory yet, have you?"

Bob walked behind the counter, disappearing into another room. He came back with a small red vial. "Here's your medicine, man."

Raphael gulped the contents down.

"Excuse me, what's that he's taking?" Faye stepped toward the counter.

"His medicine," Bob said, but he eyed her with suspicion. "This is just something I'm supposed to give him every day. A friend of his pays me to make sure he gets his dose. It's nothing illegal, lady."

"What's the friend's name?"

"Why do you want to know?" Bob moved in front of Raphael and studied her again. "Who are you, anyway? You an undercover cop or something? Listen, I don't do the hard stuff anymore. Not even weed. So back off and--"

"I'm Faye. I was directed to this place by a man called Azal."

"You're a friend of Azal's?"

"I've known him a long time."

Bob relaxed a little. "Well, if you see him again, tell him to come here. I'm almost out of Ralph's dose."

"How long has he been taking it?

"Shoot…I don't know. I only started working here a few months ago. That's when Azal hired me." Bob leaned on the counter, and Faye watched her father pick up the blue bottle again as if transfixed by its color.

"How did you meet Azal?"

Bob shifted, uncomfortable with the question.

"I'm sorry," Faye said. "I know you don't know me, but this is really important information. I think…I think I've met Ralph before."

"Do you know who he is?"

"Do you?"

"Hey, all I know is he's some sweet old guy Azal says took a hard blow to the head. Ralph can't remember anything about his life except for bits and pieces. Apparently Azal found him in some homeless shelter a couple of years ago and has been working with him to get better. It sounded as if Ralph functioned pretty well for a while, but I guess about a year ago he deteriorated. I'm not sure why. Azal started looking for someone to keep an eye on him on a daily basis," Bob said. "That's how I came into the picture."

So Azal had known for some time about her father. Faye tried to ignore the heated flush of anger creeping up her neck.

"You okay?" Bob frowned at her. "You look pissed."

"I'm fine." She struggled not to grit her teeth. "How did you get the job as caretaker?"

"I got a tattoo."

"What?"

Bob lifted the nub where his hand used to be. "I got rid of it."

Faye fought a surge of revulsion at the scarred flesh. "You actually took off your hand? Why?"

"I can't talk about it, or the voice will start again. I don't hear him much anymore, but every now and then he flares up."

"The voice? Whose voice?"

Bob glanced around and then with a sheepish grin, said, "The goat's voice."

"You hear a goat's voice in your head?" Faye recalled seeing a section of animal tattoos in Nathan's book of Sinz. "What does he sound like?"

"George Carlin."

Faye fought a laugh.

"Really?"

"Yes. He has a raspy voice and tells dirty jokes while puffing on a cigar."

"Your goat puffs a cigar?"

"Well, he used to. I cut my hand off so I wouldn't have to look at him, but I still hear him sometimes." Bob's eyes filled with tears. "I fuckin' hate George Carlin. He can shove his seven forbidden words straight up his ass."

Faye fought the urge to laugh again. The poor man found nothing comical about his misery. She watched as he massaged the nub.

"Bob, did you get your tattoo at Hell's Leak?"

"Yeah. I looked for the place again when I met Azal." He looked Faye over, surprised. "Since you've heard of it, you must have been a client too. Where's your tattoo?"

"I'm not a client. It's kind of a long story, Bob," Faye said. "Why would you go back there? You couldn't have been too pleased with the tattoo artist's work if you cut your hand off."

Bob lifted his nub, perhaps seeing the hand as it used to be. Rubbing it gently, he said, "No. I didn't like the tattoo, but I got what I deserved. I was a lazy prick, a sloth. Never did nothing for nobody. Cared only about me because it was easy. I fucked over so many people, people I called friends. The tattoo opened my eyes. I cut it off before I'd learned my lesson, but even then it wasn't gone. I could still hear its voice. The only way the damn thing will shut up is when I give to others. So I give all the time. I volunteer to help those in need. I do my part to clean up our town. I support everyone's equal rights, and I try to not think about me. Whenever I forget, that's when I hear the voice. It keeps me on the path. When Azal found me, I was going back to Hell's Leak to thank the guy who gave me the tattoo."

Faye couldn't help the tiny flood of happiness Bob's story gave her. Hadn't Nathan told her it was all about free will? If the client chose to see the light, to change their ways, then the tattoo lost its power. Bob was doing everything he could to rectify his sins, to make it right. She'd been looking for someone who had been positively impacted by Nathan's work and here he was. Again she wondered about the wheel of fate, and just how much it influenced her life. What were the odds that one of Nathan's former clients would end up tending to her ill father? Hadn't Azal instructed her to look for the one positively influenced by Nathan? Had he meant to lead her down this path all along?

Raphael came back into the room. Clarity lit his eyes once again as he held out the blue bottle. "This is for you."

She took it, making sure her fingers did not brush his. "Thank you, Ralph. What is it for?"

"I don't know. I just know you need it." The old man smiled. "Let me give you one more thing."

Raphael walked to the bookshelf. As he rifled through the books there, Bob said, "He must like you. He doesn't give out the elixirs he makes to just anyone."

Faye watched her father, surprised when he pulled a small thin book off the shelf and handed it to her. Printed in gold letters on the front cover were the words The Book of Raziel.

"I once gave a copy of this to Noah," Raphael said. "And then I lent it to Solomon."

Faye smiled, uncertain what to say. She'd never heard of the book, but she gripped it tightly before slipping it and the blue bottle into her purse. On an impulse, she wrapped her arms around her father and sent as much of her healing energy into him as she could.

She felt him tremble in her hold, and sparks of light flew off their bodies. Still she held on, concentrating on her purpose. Odd images danced in her head, residual energy from Raphael's time on earth. The air grew thin and mixed with the lavender scent of the shop, causing her head to throb with a dizzy fever as her body grew weak. With a mighty thrust, Raphael pushed her away.

She fell to the floor, but he remained standing, sparks of light encircling him. His skin glowed and pulsed, while his blue eyes brightened to an unnatural shade. The lights in the shop flickered, and books fell off the shelf, vibrating with energy.

"Daddy!" Faye worried his mortal shell wouldn't be able to handle the stress he was under. "Calm down."

Everything stopped. The vibrations and the sparks all disappeared, leaving a panting Raphael standing in the center of the room. He stared down at Faye.

"What the hell was that?" Bob peeked from where he'd taken cover behind the counter.

"I think you should go," Raphael said to Faye. "You need to prepare."

"For what?" She pulled herself off the floor, clutching her purse.

"For fate."

* * * *

Sammael saw Faye come out of The Apothecary, and watched her cross the street toward him. He couldn't quite decipher the mix of emotions on her face. As she unlocked the car, he allowed his heightened defenses to drop away.

Her head jerked up, and she took a tentative sniff of the air. When he stepped from behind the tree where he'd been hiding, her eyes narrowed in derision, not fear. This pleased him. He would much rather have an equal for a mate. Of course a little control over his partner would be nice too.

She would learn. He would see to it.

"Hello, Faye." Sammael watched her slip the purse inside the car. She didn't get in, though. Instead, she moved until she stood only a few yards away.

"I thought I smelled shit," she said, crossing her arms. "You either have a lot of guts, or you're really stupid to show yourself to me. I prefer to think you're stupid. What do you want?"

"To talk," Sammael said. He hooked his thumbs into his belt, hoping he appeared nonthreatening, though her words stung. "There's so much I want to say to you. Last night your companions wouldn't have allowed it. They've gone to great lengths to keep us apart. And who could blame them? After all, if we got together we could be a force to be reckoned with."

"You killed Azal." The coldness in her eyes grew stronger. "Not to mention my family. You took my heart away from me in one move."

"Hearts are fragile things, indeed, Faye. I wouldn't break yours for anything. What I wish is that I could remove the lies your so-called 'guardian' told you," he said. "Azal wiped out your family. I did you a service by killing him. A sweet girl like you would never have the strength to do it."

"No. I saw his memory of the day my father died," Faye said, and stared at the shop across the street. "He didn't kill my family. Azal was there to talk to my father about something."

"Sure he was." Sammael didn't like the adamant tone of her voice. It had been a long shot that she would buy the story he'd told her about Azal, anyway. He'd hoped it would further the rift between her and God, allowing her to easily choose between the angels and himself. "Angels are crafty, deceitful beings. Azal showed you the memory he wanted you to believe. Trust me, Faye. I've learned enough in my studies to understand their powers give them a phenomenal leg up with humans. Altering a memory is nothing for a creature like him."

"You're crazy, and I don't know why you think I would actually help you exterminate angels." Faye uncrossed her arms and stood straighter. "We both have a parent with angel blood. It's like destroying our heritage."

"Heritage? We are the red-headed stepchildren, Faye. Always creeping around, hoping not to be discovered. You know why God created the Great Flood, right? To rid the world of our kind. Is that a merciful being? We weren't worthy of God's love. But the real kicker is the angels allowed Him to do it!" Sammael felt the anger twisting in his words, making it difficult to breathe. He had to make her understand. "I didn't choose my heritage, Faye, but I can choose my future. I see a new race of beings, beings of infinite wonder and power who never have to live under the threat of being wiped out."

"You don't know everything, Sammael." The wind lifted her hair as she studied him. "Nor do I. When I think about the love my father showed to me, it makes me think those angels who lost their children must have suffered too. They were powerless to stop God. If you must be angry, at least direct it in the right place. Not toward the angels."

"My father wasn't around to show me love," Sammael said. Oh, how he wanted to hurt her, to scratch at her pretty face. Because of her fucking father, Lucifer was dead. But he fought the words and the urges that shook him. "My mother showed me my path. She knew how evil the angels truly are."

"Your mother," Faye said, looking him straight in the eye,

"wasn't well."

He couldn't argue with her there, but it pissed him off just the same.

"I need you, Faye," Sammael said. "I want you to help me create my new race of beings. Avenge the others of our kind by wiping out the creatures who did nothing to stop the nephilim from being exterminated."

"You're so dramatic, Sammael. You don't know we would actually create anything new. Doesn't matter, anyway. I won't help you." He'd been prepared for resistance. Long studies of her revealed time and again just how stubborn she could be. Still, he had some inkling of her feelings toward God and hoped she might be a little more open-minded.

"I guess I'll have to try a new tactic then. I'll start killing the people closest to you until you change your mind," he said, enjoying the sudden anxiousness in her eyes. "I'll begin with Nathan. I know you've developed a fondness for him."

"If you hurt Nathan you'll only be guaranteeing I won't help you."

"Oh, I'll get what I want. There's such thing as force, you know. My powers are much stronger than yours. I'm afraid there would be no contest in fighting me," Sammael said. "But why would you choose that option when all you have to do is help me. In that scenario your friend lives, and you know I can kill him, Faye. An angel of sin is nothing against my blade."

Her eyes strayed across the street to The Apothecary shop.

"What's it going to be, Faye?"

"No. The answer is still no." She moved to the driver side of her car and slipped in. The MG roared to life and pulled away from the sidewalk.

Damn. The little bitch was going to play hard to get.

* * * *

Nathan sat up in the bed. He'd heard a voice in his dreams, someone familiar, and it told him to wake up. He struggled against weariness to hear the voice, to understand its request. There. Just a whisper in the room.

Help her. She needs you.

Nathan got out of bed, stretching his mind for the source. Where the hell was Faye? He stretched farther and sensed her a few blocks away, but she was with…

The pain brought him to the floor. His head ached, the hum

so loud blood dripped from both ears. He tried to retract his mind, but to his dismay, the sound boomed with power, catching him in a sonic net. Blood streamed from his nose, and another rivulet of it ran from his eye.

Nathan staggered to the kitchen, knocking over chairs and books as he covered his ears. He ripped the kitchen cabinet door off, hardly aware he'd done so as he searched for the elixirs that helped his pain. Damn it! He was out of them, and Azal was no longer around to keep up his supply.

Faye? Where was she? Desperate, he made it to the door of the loft and flung it open. He would go to her, even if it killed him. Someone had to protect her.

* * * *

She'd wanted to strike out at Sammael, but fear he would discover her father across the street, alive after all this time, forced her to drive away. Faye hoped he would follow her, and it looked as if the plan worked. Cars were beginning to move in slow motion, caught in the same type of time freeze he'd weaved the previous evening. People froze in mid-step on the sidewalk, and her car shuddered as the effects of the spell caught it. She pushed the accelerator down, but nothing happened.

"Screw this."

Faye hopped out of the car, clutching her purse. She darted down the street. How long did she have before she too froze? Weaving in and out of the sluggish oncoming traffic, her only goal was to get to Hell's Leak.

But her pace slowed until she could move no more.

"Don't run from me, Faye. There are rituals to be performed."

Sammael's breath tickled the back of her neck as he placed a hand on her shoulder.

"This is not the way I wanted things to go."

Faye tried to speak, but her mouth refused to cooperate.

"Don't worry. I'll be quick and gentle. I had hoped to begin the blood ritual in a more private place, but you make it necessary for me to mark you a little now in order to maintain control." He pulled off Nathan's jacket, exposing her to the cold morning air. Goose bumps popped up on her skin as Sammael ran a finger down her back. "This may sting."

The blade of his knife chilled the base of her neck as he started to make a long incision down her spine. The prickle of pain it brought caused a soft whimper to escape her.

"Sammael."

She heard Nathan's voice before he materialized, unaffected by the same paralysis holding her prisoner. Blood streaked his face, but the fury in his eyes warmed Faye's spirits. She hoped it would cause fear in the nephilim carving away at her skin.

"What are you doing here?" Sammael's voice filled with anger. "I told you to stay out of the way."

"I'm here for Faye."

"She's mine now."

Sammael moved in front of her, the bloodstained knife glittering in his hand. As the sun bounced off it, Faye heard voices. A great mass of whispers echoed in her head, and the knife gleamed with a pure, clean light.

Nathan's eyes took on a feverish white glow, and electricity crackled in his hands. He moved toward them, predatory, his head tilted at an angle as he observed his prey. But it was Sammael who made the first move.

He lunged. Pavement greeted Sammael's face as he fell against it when the angel vanished. Nathan reappeared in front of Faye, his back to her as he blasted his foe with a powerful white current of electricity. Pinned against the wall of a nearby building, Sammael struggled to break free.

"What's the matter, Sam? Not used to actually fighting with those you intend to kill?" Nathan growled before dropping his hands.

Faye blinked, feeling the effects of the time spell loosen. Sick with fear, she focused on moving her body. The sight of Sammael peeling himself free from the wall spurred her on. Summoning a burst of energy from deep within, she took a halting step forward.

"I told you not to mess with me on this," Sammael said, brushing the dirt off his clothes. "Now I'm gonna have to show you who the real boss is."

"Get back," Faye hissed, and without thinking, she raised her hand, tossing out a yellow ball of energy that hit him in the face.

Nathan reached up and gripped her hand.

"Hold on," he said.

A torrent of wind whipped up around them, swirling them away from the street and into an eerie darkness. Nathan's familiar scent comforted her, though she heard Sammael's angry roar in the black, pursuing them. With a whoosh, the noises stopped and her body hit hard ground.

They were back in Nathan's loft. Sunlight glinted in from tall windows so bright it hurt her eyes. She raised an arm to shield them, breaking Nathan's hold. His body collapsed onto the hardwood floor of the room, his face ashen underneath the red sheen of blood.

"Nathan? Can you hear me?"

"Close the door."

She hurried over to the partially opened door at his weak command, taking in the chaotic state of the apartment. The door slid shut, and though Faye knew it to be charmed, she doubted it would keep Sammael out for long. As if to reinforce her fears, there was a loud bang on the other side, followed by a steady pounding.

"Ardos!" Nathan flung out his hand as he shouted the word. A scream of anger ricocheted outside the door, but the pounding stopped.

"Are we safe here?" Faye hurried back over to Nathan, examining his face.

"For now. My charms should hold, and I just sent out a little spell to push Sammael away for a few minutes. He has trouble balancing all his powers when he's angry. He's never learned how. I imagine he'll be back, though." He moaned as she touched a sensitive spot on his face.

"How did you know I was in trouble?" She hurried over to the kitchen sink and wet a rag.

"Hard to explain." Nathan's normally stoic face twisted in pain, though her touch remained gentle. "I woke up knowing something was wrong. I reached out with my mind to search for you, but found Sammael instead. His sins were uncloaked, almost as if he'd dropped his defensive shield, and the pain in my head was overwhelming."

"I don't know how you did it," she said, stroking his hair.

"Had to save the girl."

Faye gave him a shaky smile. "Thank you. How are you feeling now?"

"Better. I wish I had some elixir left."

"What elixir?"

"I have little bottles of elixir I take sometimes if the pain of the hum gets too bad. Azal gets them for me." He propped himself up and looked at her face. "What's wrong?"

"Do you know where those elixirs came from?" He shook his head. She said, "I think they came from a place called The Apothecary. That's where I was this morning. My...my father was there."

"Raphael?"

"Yes. He's alive," she said, fighting back tears. "Something has happened to him. He didn't know me, but it was him."

She retrieved her purse and pulled out the two items Raphael had given her. Handing him the blue bottle, she said, "I think this must be for you."

Nathan opened it and sniffed before taking a deep draught. Energy infused his skin, and his eyes grew alert, losing the sheen of pain. He sat up and took a deep breath.

"That was better than the stuff Azal brings me," he said. "Stronger."

"My father already had it made when I walked in. It was as if he knew I was coming."

"Maybe he did. Let me see the book."

She handed it to him.

"Do you know what this is?" he asked.

"No, but he said something about giving it to Noah and Solomon," Faye said. She reached behind her neck and gingerly touched the mark Sammael had carved into her neck. "What is the Book of Raziel?"

"Turn around. How bad did he cut you?"

"Nathan, tell me--" Faye began, but he cut her off, inspecting the thin lines on her back.

"It's a superficial wound. I have some salve that will help with scarring," Nathan said. "It reminds me of the scratchers work I used to see before the advent of the tattoo gun. It's primitive, but definitely heading for symbolic."

"It was going to be an upside-down cross, right?" Faye turned to face him. "The sign of the devil."

"In modern culture, yes, that's what the symbol represents, but it has no real meaning."

"Just another story spun by angels to keep the mortals in line."

"Correct, but not everyone knows it, and I think God prefers it that way," Nathan said. "Take your friend, Sammael--"

"He's no friend of mine."

"Easy." Nathan rummaged in his kitchen cabinets. "Sammael is a nephilim like you, but unfortunately, he didn't have the education, the family support you did. He didn't have the benefit of his father explaining it all to him. Instead, he had a mother who was touched in the head. She would be considered a serial killer, unable to control her urges and desires, the first phase of the Grim Sleeper persona."

"I remember the dreams now, and that would be an apt description of the woman." Faye shuddered at the memories. "But you're wrong about something, Nathan. The symbol does have meaning to Sammael, just as the symbols you tattoo have meaning to you. That's what makes them powerful."

Nathan brought the salve back.

"Lay down on the bed so I can put this on your neck."

She complied, and he worked the lotion into her wound. Faye winced but did not cry out.

"Sammael almost had you today, Faye. You shouldn't have gone out alone."

"Sometimes I can be a little impulsive."

"Really? I hadn't noticed."

Faye laughed, but sobered up quickly when she remembered the conversation with Sammael. "He threatened you. He said he would kill you if I didn't help him."

"Then we'll make sure that doesn't happen."

"Do you think he will be able to get past your special security system?"

"I don't think we're in danger right now. I charmed the place pretty well. Only a few angels are allowed entry, and luckily I never had Judith up here. We might be in trouble, otherwise." Nathan glanced at the Book of Raziel. "That's one way the book over there comes in handy."

"It's a book of magic?"

"Not that particular copy. The one Raphael gave to you can be bought in many religious stores," Nathan said. "The real book holds the secrets of angels and their powers."

"Why would my father give it to me?"

"You're sure the man in The Apothecary was Raphael?"

"Yes." She told him all about the conversation with Raphael and Bob, ending with Sammael's attack. "Why do you think Azal didn't tell me my father was alive?"

"I think Azal wanted to keep him safe."

"From who?"

"From Sammael maybe, or God," Nathan said.

"I understand the God part--Azal wanted to save his friend from God's wrath for disobeying." Faye picked up the book. "I also understand because I'm a nephilim, Sammael wants to get cozy with me. But there is something I'm unclear about. The angels in Sammael's vision, Hesiel and Uriel, indicated my father was the last person to talk to Lucifer, which is what prompted Sammael to get revenge. He thinks my father killed his."

"That's the rumor in heaven too."

"Okay. But why? Why would he do that?"

"Why was Azal sent to speak to Raphael seven years ago?" Nathan saw the understanding dawn on her face. "Is it so far-fetched to think God asked Raphael to do the same thing?"

"That theory doesn't make any sense," Faye said, "and don't tell me I'm just in denial because he's my father. Raphael was guilty of the same thing as Lucifer. He'd married and procreated. It's a little hypocritical don't you think? If God knew, wouldn't he have destroyed my family then?"

Nathan shrugged. "Perhaps that was part of Raphael's punishment for disobeying. He had to see the consequences on another."

"No. If my father did destroy Lucifer, it was over something else."

"We might never know for sure, Faye. The point here is Sammael thinks Raphael killed his dad," Nathan said. "He doesn't know Raphael is still alive, does he?"

"I don't know." She looked stricken. "He did see me come out of The Apothecary, but everything happened so quick after that. I ran from him in order to get him away from that place. What I keep thinking about is how he threatened you."

"I think it might be time to go behind the veil and get reinforcements."

"No!" She grabbed his arm. "You can't do that. What if God punishes you for last night? You might never come back and then what would I do."

"Faye, I punish sin. I can't hide from mine."

"Just wait. Let's see if we can't come up with a plan on our own to stop Sammael."

He studied her, his eyes dark.

"I want to do something about Sammael. I'm a nephilim, and he even hinted I have untapped powers. Maybe it's time to use them." But Nathan turned away from her. Desperate, she grabbed at his arm. "He took everything I valued away from me. I should be in on how he's punished."

"That's up to God."

"It's been up to Him for a while now, but He has done nothing. Doesn't everything happen for a reason? Isn't that the whole fate mythos? Maybe that's why I'm finally finding out about all this," Faye said. "Maybe this is fate's way of saying it's time to do something."

"Could be. Or maybe fate is trying to warn you."

"What would happen if two nephilims had children together? Could those children wipe out the angels?"

"I don't know."

"Hasn't it ever happened before? Surely in all the time since the world began something like this must have taken place."

"Nephilims aren't found on every street corner, you now."

"Maybe two nephilim can create a being that is extraordinary."

"Maybe."

"What should we do about Sammael? How can we destroy him? I think the key is the knife. If I can get that, maybe use it on him--"

"You can't kill him Faye. That would be an unforgivable action on your part, a stain on your soul, even if he is deserving. You are a healer. Besides, all the angel essence he has collected makes him too powerful. I only held him off today because I caught him off guard. He won't make it so easy next time," Nathan said. "But we can slow him down."

"How?"

"He's a sinner. I need him in my chair. His human side is still susceptible to my designs."

"I see." She mulled the idea over. "Let free will have its shot at destroying him, huh? Just like any of your other clients."

"And just like many of them, death is a possible end result."

"So you would just be doing your job."

"Exactly. And while he's dealing with the havoc my designs cause, you can destroy that knife."

"I don't know how we are going to get him in the chair. He knows what you do, since he worked side by side with you for six months as Judith. I doubt he'll come willingly."

"You're right," Nathan said. "I'm going to need your help."

"Tell me what to do."

Nathan placed his hands on her shoulders. Gently he bent down, kissed her lips. With a smile, he pulled away, but did not release her. "Faye, I need you to get into the chair first."

Her eyes widened. "I don't think so."

"I want to protect you."

"Then use good ole Raziel's book over there and cast a magical circle. Burn a sacred candle or something," she said, taking a step back. "Work your magic, but I don't want one of your tattoos."

"Faye, it wouldn't be from Sinz. I have something I scratched on paper long ago. It's the last design I created before I became an angel. When I made it, I knew it was going to be special. I just didn't know five hundred years ago I created it for you." Nathan waved his hand and an ornate silver box slid out from under the bed. Curious, Faye picked it up. She studied the lid, unable to identify any of the symbols or designs carved into it.

Nathan took the box and removed the top. He pulled out an old book with a giant sapphire in the front cover. The stone sparkled, shooting rainbows through the air. For a moment, Faye thought she saw writing in the gem. She looked to Nathan for an explanation, but he avoided her eyes and set the book aside along with a ring and some aged coins. He rummaged in the box until at last he held up a faded piece of parchment.

Faye tried to keep the wariness out of her expression. His proposal startled her, and all instincts told her to say no. What Nathan tattooed onto people changed their lives, and not usually for the better. She didn't know if she quite trusted him when it came to his art.

Nathan handed her the paper. She studied it before handing it back to him, unable to hide a pleased smile.

"I'll take it," she said.

Chapter 15

Raphael sniffed the night air. It held a multitude of scents, and he sorted through them, finding the one that had caught his attention several times throughout the day. An awful smell, like rotting meat and sulfur mixed together. It made him nauseous, but he recognized it from somewhere. He just couldn't quite put his finger on it. Whose soul was so badly tarnished that it gave off such a stench?

Certainly not the young woman he'd met earlier. Faye. Her scent, a constant puff of fresh flowers, never threatened him. He'd liked talking to her, though parts of the conversation confused him. Something about her, something just on the tip of his memory--it wouldn't quite come out. Instinct made him create the elixir in the blue bottle. He just knew she would need it. The Book of Raziel had also been the product of instinct. Something about the title was important too.

Frustrated, Raphael went back into The Apothecary. He stared at the shelves and plants, reflecting on how he'd ended up here. Sometimes he couldn't remember, but tonight the memories drew close.

Azal had saved him. He'd been raving like a madman in the shelter, plagued by bad dreams about fires and death. He didn't know how Azal found him, but suddenly his mind cleared, and he looked into the face of a friend. The other man's expression-- a mixture of shock, relief and happiness--caused Raphael to take the hand offered to him. "What are you doing here?" Raphael asked.

"Making my rounds, old friend. Looking to offer someone a little luck." The man smiled at Raphael. "What happened to you?"

"Do I know you?"

The smile froze on the man's lips. "I am Azal. Your name is Raphael."

"Azal." A peculiar name, but he knew he'd heard it before. "Where have we met?"

After that the memories became fuzzy. Azal took care of him with food and clothing, providing him with some sort of elixir. Later he showed Raphael how to make it himself. From time to time, they would have exhausting memory sessions. Azal would place his warm hands on Raphael's head and probe the muddled mess of his mind. Sometimes the other man would act as if the information he found there made him happy, but most of the time Raphael felt whatever Azal saw wasn't good. He wished he could be more helpful to his friend, but try as he might he couldn't recall his life before living in the homeless shelter.

Until today. The woman, Faye, held him in her arms, warming him, and he felt as if something inside him healed. All day long, his thoughts were crisp and clear, and constantly of her. She'd called him Daddy, and though he could picture his wife and a son in his head, he couldn't recall much about them. He knew they were dead, but when Faye addressed him as her father, he'd been sure for a brief second she was right to do so.

He'd watched her walk across the street to an orange roadster. Raphael could picture himself in the car, driving along some deserted road at top speed, the wind ruffling through his hair, Estella laughing in the seat beside him. Estella. An image of her popped into his head, and his heart ached with longing. What was happening to him?

Before he could wonder too much, another person approached Faye. The smell of rot and decay drifted to Raphael, rendering him helpless for a few minutes. When he'd recovered, both Faye and the man she'd been talking to were gone.

"Hello, Raphael."

He turned, shaking loose the puzzling memories of the day and found an old woman standing behind him. There was a smile on her face as if she were pleased to see him. Raphael couldn't help but smile back, and love flowed through him, pushing away his many anxieties.

"Lord," Raphael said, and bowed his head. "How good to see you."

"It's good to see you, my child." The old woman's hand reached out and lifted his chin. "You have no idea how worried I've been."

"Worried?"

"Azal told me about your situation here. That you were split from your angel essence and remember nothing of the last seven years. I'm afraid the time has come for that to end." She slipped her arm through his and guided Raphael toward the back counter. "You see, I wanted your mind to rest, to come back on its own, but something has changed. I can't sense Azal."

"Angel?" Raphael recognized the Lord right away. The brilliant light, the warm smell and the comfort--all undeniably holy and familiar, but the talk of angels confused him. It sounded as if she said he was some sort of angel.

"Yes, Raphael. You are an angel. One of the most powerful. I'm not sure how you escaped this nephilim's grasp, but I need your help. Faye needs your help too." The old woman reached beneath the counter, pulling out three of the colored glass bottles he kept there. "It's time I showed you how to make a healing potion to bring back all of your memories. It won't restore your angel essence, though. You'll have to work on that yourself."

"What are the other two bottles for?"

"To ease the mind. We have friends in need of it."

Raphael had no idea what she meant, but it felt right. As he'd done countless times in a past he couldn't remember, he put his faith in her and got to work.

* * * *

Faye leaned against the bar. Outside she heard the sounds of early evening joviality getting underway as downtown Austin prepared for its usual Friday night assault from the masses. Tonight the doors of the Black Cat would remain closed. The news stations reported a fight had broken out there the previous evening, resulting in injuries for some witnesses. Faye preferred this version of events to the true one and almost wished Nathan could adjust her memory as he'd done for Zenovia and the others.

She looked around the dark club, her eyes skimming over the spots where she'd last seen Azal and John.

Don't think about it, she told herself, pulling out a small vial of liquid from her jeans pocket. Stick to the plan.

As she poured the liquid into a large circle on the floor, she reflected on all she and Nathan had accomplished that day. He'd pushed her to delve into her subconscious mind, to access and control powers she'd never known existed within her. The yellow energy ball she'd produced to defend them from

Sammael had only been the start of what she could do. She'd spent a great deal of her time practicing her newfound skills while Nathan worked on creating what he called an angel snare.

Her shoulder pulsed. The tattoo she'd allowed Nathan to put on her body had a mind of its own, and at odd times throughout the day she found it seemed a living thing, moving up and down against her shirt. She supposed the movement made sense given what the tattoo was.

Faye found the process of getting tattooed uncomfortable. It wasn't just the pain the action itself brought, but the sense of her mind being invaded. Nathan probed at her thoughts and memories, the secrets she held close to her heart, looking for energy to infuse the special tattoo. Which emotion he looked for, Faye couldn't tell, but she found herself drifting in and out of memories. Thoughts of Chris flowed back and forth, mixing with feelings of love for her family. She heard the buzz of the tattoo gun, but just below it, the soft murmur of Nathan's voice tickled at her ear, warming her. With the tattoo's completion came a sense of wellbeing and peace she hadn't felt in years.

Exhilaration flushed Nathan's face as he surveyed the work. She could tell the design pleased him, and the perpetual grim mood he carried with him had eased just a little. He caught her gaze and grinned.

"How is it?" she asked.

"It's good," he said. "It's been a while since I created something so simple and beautiful."

"Maybe you should start tattooing puppies and rainbows. Perhaps your work could go in a different direction."

"Perhaps." They stared at one another for a moment before Nathan asked, "Do you want to see it?"

"Sure."

Faye stood and took the hand mirror he offered, holding it so the small tattoo on her upper left shoulder could be reflected into the wall mirror of the shop. She flinched at the sight of the nasty cut going down her back, but it was forgotten as she examined the Sacred Heart tattoo.

A heart shaped vial had been branded on the skin. Only half full of bubbling red liquid, a banner stretched across the design with the word Faith rippling on it. At the top of the vial sat a gnarled cork, and around the cork were decayed vines connecting with a lopsided crown. There were seeds scattered around the bottle and rising around the tarnished crown were flames.

"What the hell is that?" She wrinkled her nose. "It doesn't

look like the one you showed me. It looks like something from your book of Sinz."

Nathan laughed. The rich noise of it, pure and honest, echoed around Hell's Leak.

"You sound so disappointed," he said. "I wondered if you'd be any different than my regular clients."

"I'm not perfect, but--"

"Oh, don't go getting all upset. You misunderstand. The Sacred Heart looks different to everyone. What you saw might not be the same to someone else, which is why it's the most powerful tattoo in my arsenal. You glimpsed the actual beauty of the design when I first showed it to you, but I got a good look in your head, Faye. You often doubt the things right in front of you. Right now, you see what you want to see--a symbol that has often let you down. Notice the liquid in the heart is only half full. It represents right where your faith is at." Nathan chuckled again, but his voice was kinder than she'd ever heard it. "Give it time to work on your soul, though. Perhaps you can fill the heart again. The flames offer you protection. I'm counting on them to keep you safe when the time comes."

She stared at the tattoo again, not liking the decayed vines or the rotted seeds hanging around the heart. Seeds of doubt--Faye knew that's what they were and seeing her inner most feelings unmasked for all to see left her feeling disgusted, vulnerable.

"C'mon, Faye. We can have a philosophy lesson later." Nathan patted her other shoulder. "Right now we need to get to work on our snare."

She let him cover the tattoo with a soft white bandage before slipping her shirt on over the camisole top she wore. "Snare?"

"We are going to catch an angel."

"There's a way to do that?"

"Of course. I suspect even Sammael uses one from time to time. It's the only way he could collect some of his angel essence without being harmed."

"How would he have learned about it?" But she shook her head. "Never mind. He told us last night each angel absorption reveals different secrets. I'm sure he picked it up from one of his victims."

"Probably."

"Do you know how to make an angel snare?"

"Nope."

"Well, we can't exactly call Sammael and ask him for help."

"Good point."

"Nathan, are you feeling okay?" Faye watched him move around the room. The lift in his shoulders, the lightness of his walk--it puzzled her. "You're...cheerful."

"Yeah." He sounded surprised. "I am."

"We're facing possible death here."

"Would you prefer me to be somber again?"

"No. I'm just used to your usual 'I am Lord of the tattoo. Mess with me and I'll kick your soul's ass' attitude. I didn't know you knew what cheerful looked like."

"I'm out of practice. We can debate my attitude later. If we are going to make this snare, we need the Book of Raziel."

"I brought it down here."

He shook his head. "No, the real book."

He kissed her, and for a moment everything, her worries, her fears, it all went away. When she opened her eyes, the sterile walls of Hell's Leak had faded away, replaced by the confines of Nathan's apartment.

"You are in a good mood," Faye said, watching him go to the silver box, which still lay open on the coffee table. "Cranky Nathan would have made me take the stairs."

He held out the book she'd seen earlier with the blue sapphire in its cover.

"This is the true Book of Raziel."

It vibrated in her hands.

"How old is this?" she asked.

"It was gift from the angel Raziel to Adam. You do the math."

"Why haven't I heard of it?"

"Good question, especially since your father was keeper of it for eons," Nathan said. They sat on his couch where she ran a finger over the sapphire. "Raphael sheltered you from a lot, Faye."

"I guess," she said. "He wanted to nurture the humanity in me."

"Today we nurture the angel in you."

With that, they'd gotten down to work, slowly coming up with the plan that led her back to where they were now, the Black Cat. Nathan emerged from the hallway.

"All clear still," he said.

"Are you sure you'll be able to hear him coming?"

"Pretty sure."

"That's not very comforting."

"I've caught the tune of his sin," Nathan said. "I don't think he's as focused on hiding it as he used to be. Why should he be? He's too full of pride to think we might be able to conquer him. Now that his secret is out, he can use that energy for other things."

"It's the other things that have me worried. I don't want anything to happen to you." Faye sat down at a table, gently rubbing at the tattoo on her shoulder. It visibly thumped against her shirt.

"Hurts, doesn't it?"

"What?"

"Your heart."

"Just a little twinge. Nothing major."

"Sometimes hearts need to hurt. It's how they get stronger."

"Why do I feel as if we're not discussing the tattoo anymore?"

"We're discussing your heart. Right now it's visible for all to see."

"How is this going to help us against Sammael?"

"Because you have one and he doesn't. Have faith, Faye. It will protect you."

"We'll see."

"Shh…" Nathan moved toward her. "He's coming."

Fear jumped in her belly.

"Are we ready?" she asked.

"Just remember, don't light the snare until you've got the knife. And be careful. Even in the snare he still has one strong power left. Temptation."

"Will this work?"

"The snare will hold him for a little while. Work fast."

He moved to go.

"Wait…Nathan…I…." she started the words, the heart's thump loud and clear in the room as it beat faster.

Nathan smiled and gestured to the tattoo. "I know the words in your heart."

He took his place in the other room, leaving Faye alone to face Sammael.

* * * *

Sammael sensed the woman. He'd watched the activities at Hell's Leak, frustrated he couldn't tell exactly what went on.

Despite having weakened Nathan, the angel appeared to have the strength to keep him out of the shop, after all. Where he'd gotten the boost of power, Sammael didn't know, but it worried him. Being in control, calling the shots--he wasn't comfortable when those things weren't within his grasp.

He'd retraced her steps a little while ago, curious to know where she'd been going this morning. What could have been important enough for her to risk leaving the safety of Hell's Leak? For a long time he'd stood outside the little apothecary shop, taking in the night air and trying to figure out what brought her there. He'd seen the symbols in the window, and though he couldn't say for certain, he thought they were meant to keep evil out. He struggled with the desire to go in and the stronger need to walk away--to run from the peculiar feelings the symbols evoked in him. Finally, he managed to shame himself into going inside with thoughts of what his mother would think of having such a coward for a son.

It had been worth the trouble.

The old man recognized him and fought hard, but in the end, Sammael emerged triumphant.

Before he'd had time to savor the victory, she'd popped up on his radar, her scent and energy flowing down the street to him. He'd followed the telltale signs of her to the Black Cat. For several minutes, he stood on the street, stretching his senses to gather information. Pain. Fear. They flitted out to him, tasting of Faye's essence. Good. She was breaking down. And now he had another ace up his sleeve. Cautious of a trick, he patted the knife tucked into the back of his pants and entered.

Faye sat in the middle of the floor, knees pulled up, arms wrapped around them for support. She rocked a little, humming a song under her breath. Her head lifted at his approach, and he was struck by her eyes. Dark shadows had replaced the sparkle he usually saw in them.

"Sammael?" she whispered. "That you?"

Her gaze darted everywhere and her body twitched, restless. He could practically hear the pounding of her heart. It pleased him.

"What's going on?" Sammael narrowed his eyes. "Where's Nathan?"

Glancing over her shoulder, she lowered her voice, the fear in it unmistakable. "You were right, Sammael. I didn't want to believe you, but you were right."

He looked over her shoulder. There was a noise like someone beating softly on a drum. Where did it come from?

"Do you hear that?" she asked, looking at him. "Tell me that's not just in my head."

He lifted an eyebrow, questioning. The beat grew faster, louder.

"It's my tattoo." Tears filled her eyes. "He got me."

A tattoo? On Faye?

"Why would he do that?"

"Because you were right." Her voice turned cold. "God only wants our kind dead."

Sammael surveyed the place again. Where was Nathan? He pulled out the knife, gratified at the anxiety the sight of it caused her. She scooted back from him, practically crawling on the floor to get away.

"Please. Don't hurt me. I'm sorry for what I've done. I...I didn't want to believe you. I wanted to believe in a God who loved all his creations." She lowered her head, sobbing, but the movement under her shirt garnered his attention. Something on her shoulder blade caused the thin material to pulse up and down. "But Nathan laughed at me when I told him what I thought. And then he told me the truth. That you and I are both going to be killed, punished, just as you said, for being born. The past few days have been nothing more than a round up. They brought me to Nathan in the hopes of drawing you out. That way they could kill two birds with one stone."

She wiped her face, and rubbed her hands on her upper arms.

"I tried to run, but he...was too powerful. My gift is for healing, not fighting." Her next words were soft and Sammael strained to hear them. "He marked me, stained my soul."

"How did you escape?"

"I didn't. He let me go. Now that I have one of his tattoos, he can always find me. You know how it works." Her eyes widened and she stood, staggering a little. "He knew you would find me. You've got to get out of here while there's still time."

Sammael wanted to believe her, wanted to think his time of loneliness was at an end. It would be good to share his burdens with another, someone sympathetic. To have Faye actually on his team! But his mind whispered this must be a trick. Faye had a plan. But what?

And there was the tattoo.

He contemplated it, watching the rise and fall of the thing on her shoulder. Nathan's symbols were meant to be deadly. Having worked side by side with the man, Sammael knew Nathan never branded anyone without the expected outcome of death.

It was one of the many things he admired about his former boss.

"I can handle Nathan Ink. It's you I'm worried about," he said. "Nathan's designs only bring death."

She shivered at his words. The beating movement on her shoulder picked up its pace. "There's no way to get rid of it?"

"None that I know of." He studied the shoulder. "Tell me, what did the angel of sin tattoo you with? I don't think there's a symbol for being gullible."

"Haven't you guessed?" She reached up and touched her shoulder. "A heart."

Sammael smiled. Nathan hadn't lost his sense of irony. Hard not to admire the master! He couldn't think of a better symbol for someone like Faye, whose heart had been broken. It didn't take a genius to understand why she'd given up on love a long time ago.

"Sammael." He loved the small submission he saw in her as she took a shaky step toward him. Nathan had really done him a favor. "I can feel it growing. I want you to get rid of it for me. Cut it out."

He couldn't hide his surprise at her request. Could it even be done? The rapid thumping of her shirt drew his attention again, and he moved toward her, knife extended. She backed against one of the round tables, her eyes on the weapon, the fear unconcealed.

"Look at me." After a moment's hesitation, she did. "Take off your shirt."

Her hands trembled as she struggled to lift the material, and he realized the action pained her puffed up shoulder.

"Could you help me?" she asked.

Putting the knife on the table, he reached down to her waist and pulled the shirt off, unable to keep from staring at her bare skin and the way the black camisole underneath showed the swell of her cleavage. He dropped the shirt on the floor, and Faye gave him a small grateful smile. Her trembling hands reached out and she placed them on his biceps.

"Thank you for making this easy," she said, closing her eyes.

Behind him, a flame sparked, quickly forming a half circle around them. She brought her knee up into his groin and he doubled over in pain and surprise. A swift kick brought him to the floor. Before he had time to react, she stepped toward the table and the knife, the circle of flame closing in around him.

The bitch! She stood on the other side of the circle

triumphant, the crocodile sadness gone. Sammael studied the flames, feeling the barrier they presented. An angel snare. He'd trapped enough angels in one to recognize it. He raised his hands and summoned his powers.

Nothing happened.

"Sucks, doesn't it?" she taunted, holding the knife in one hand while she tapped the flat side of the blade against her palm. "It's not much fun to be helpless."

"An angel snare." He nodded. "Very good. Now you're thinking like one of them. And the tattoo?"

"Oh, it's real enough, if that's what you mean."

"Why would Nathan mark you?"

"I asked him to."

"You're ready to die then?"

"She's not going anywhere," Nathan said, stepping into the room.

The confines of the snare made it hard to keep his head clear, but the fury he felt at seeing Nathan, at being tricked, went a long way toward creating clarity. The knife. He needed it back. She would only hurt it, maybe even destroy it. Momma cherished that knife. It was his only gift from her.

"Faye, let me out of the snare." Sammael tried to keep his voice normal. "You're going to regret this."

"You get a lot of power from this thing, don't you?" Faye studied the weapon. "It's evil. It's hurt people I care about."

"Give it back to me."

"No. I can't."

The rage sucked every other emotion out of him.

"Give it back to me, you lying little bitch," he snarled. "Or when I get out of here, I'm going to cut your real heart out and feed it to you."

As he spoke, the flames flickered. He felt a tingle of energy coursing through his body and realized the snare couldn't contain the strength of his powers forever. He needed to buy time.

"Faye," Nathan said. "Get started. The sooner the knife is destroyed, the sooner we can move to phase two."

"Right." She grabbed the purse stashed behind the bar.

What to do? Sammael paced the circle, grinding his back teeth together hard enough to hurt his head. He didn't mind the pain. It brought clarity. He watched her pull a dark blue cloth out of her bag, setting it on the floor along with candles. The sight of these preparations made him want to howl in agony, but that would be admitting defeat. Momma wouldn't have liked that.

As she moved behind the bar again, he remembered the little gift he picked up at The Apothecary. Thank God he'd been graced with a little of Azal's luck.

"Give me back the knife," Sammael said. "Give it to me or I'll kill him."

"You can't touch me," Nathan said. He'd been standing in the shadows, making preparations of his own, though Sammael hadn't been watching him. For the first time he noted what Nathan had laid out on the table.

The tattoo gun.

Their gazes met. Sammael shuddered, understanding the angel's intentions.

"I didn't mean you," Sammael said. "I meant her new friend. The little old man who works at a place called The Apothecary. You know, her father."

Faye stiffened.

"Give me the knife or you'll never know where poor Raphael is."

"Nathan--" Faye looked toward the angel, uncertain.

He felt the angel snare give a little more. Able to press it now with his mind, he could touch the strengths and weakness of the barrier. Soon he would be able to get the knife back on his own. He just needed to keep them talking, distracted.

"It's a trick," Nathan said.

"Are you sure?" Sammael asked Faye. "It's an awful chance to take."

"Nathan, if he has my father..."

"Faye, don't listen to him, he's buying time."

"And every minute I'm stuck here is a minute poor old daddy suffers. He's alone in the dark, Faye. I cut him a little as punishment for slipping through my fingers seven years ago. I just hope I didn't hit any major arteries," Sammael said, pleased at the shade of white her face turned as the bandage covering her tattoo lifted and fell rapidly. "He called out for you, and I told him you were too busy shacking up with an angel to care about him. You should have seen his face! I guess no father wants to hear about their kid having sex."

The knife lay on the blue cloth. He reached out with his mind. It gave a slight shake. Good. Not much longer.

"Do you have any idea what a screamer he is? For a healer, he sure can't take pain." Sammael licked his lips. "And his blood...so clean compared to some I've spilt."

"You're lying." Faye moved closer to the wall of flame, studying him.

"Am I?" Sammael gave a little push with his mind and felt it brush against her subconscious. Time to reel her in. "He begged me to stop, promised he would do whatever I asked if I would only stop the pain."

Nathan moved to stand in front of Faye, hiding her from Sammael's sight, though the sound of her pounding heart filled the room. The angel crossed his arms and shook his head.

"You're not getting her," Nathan said to Sammael, the thinning wall of flame separating them by inches. "Your thrall won't work."

"I don't need it to." Sammael reached out his hand, and the knife sprang from the blue cloth, through the air and into his hand.

The flames parted. With an upward thrust, Sammael planted the knife deep into Nathan's gut.

Chapter 16

She screamed as Nathan collapsed against her.

"Not death," he whispered.

Then his soul was gone.

The cold crept into her veins as she stared down at the man in her arms. His tousled black hair obscured his face, but not his eyes. They stared lifeless and dark into the room. Faye slid down to the ground, resting his body on the floor.

She raised her head, unable to hide her fury. The grim smile Sammael gave her only increased her rage, and without thinking about it, she hurled her body into his. Surprised, Sammael fell back, dropping the knife. It clattered to the floor, skimming the wood until it rested a few feet from Faye. Too incensed to care about the weapon, Faye used all her energy to thrust two flaming yellow energy balls at him. Deftly, he blocked them, sending the energy hurling back at her. One of the balls missed, but the other hit her midsection, tossing her into the bar. Dazed, she lay there trying to regain her senses.

Sammael forced her to a standing position. He stood before her, placing the tip of the blade against her throat, blood already leaking from a small slit the weapon made.

No.

The word startled both of them.

No…

It came from the knife.

"They're still in there." The truth dawned on her. "The people you killed…their souls are trapped."

"Shut up," Sammael said, but she'd seen the flicker of guilt in his eyes.

"Where's my father?"

"In his shop where I left him," Sammael said. "Of course I didn't leave him the way I found him. I'm pretty sure this time he's dead." The heart tattoo thumped louder, and his face twisted into a malicious grin. "Come on now. I bet we can still be friends."

"Friends?" She gave a hard, brittle laugh. "I don't imagine you've had many friends."

"Friends are luxuries. Most people don't understand me," Sammael said. "Take Julie, the girl I stabbed last weekend. You were so kind to help her out."

"You were using a glamour to make yourself look like a street person."

"Yes. I actually wasn't sure I'd be able to do it. I'd already exhausted a lot of energy acting as Judith and helping Nathan with Curt's tattoo. I'll miss that shit. I'm far more powerful, but I can admit I'll never be as good as Nathan at creating symbols." Sammael sighed. "It can't be helped. Julie had it coming, anyway."

"What do you mean? I helped her cross over peacefully to the other side and I saw nothing that warranted her death."

"Then you didn't look deep enough into that spoiled little bitch's heart!" Sammael said, frustrated. "That girl never wanted for anything a day in her life, and she sure as hell didn't appreciate what she had. People like that should be removed body and soul from this life. They pollute it with narcissism. The day I spotted her, laughing with her friends at some trendy fucking coffee shop, I knew she was the next target on my list. Offing her in public while her rich friends just stood around and watched was fucking amazing."

"You're disgusting."

"Oh, but it's okay if Nathan kills people. Right? It's not disgusting then, because he's a fucking angel." The words poured out. "It's exactly the same thing. Julie could easily have been one of Nathan's clients, but she just didn't make it to the chair. I took care of her and much quicker than one of Nathan's stupid tattoos."

"Nathan's tattoos teach a lesson and offer a choice," Faye said. "Your knife offers only death. That's the difference between the two of you. I'll take Nathan's methods over yours any day."

Sammael shook with anger and his thoughts unleashed into the air, a whip of venom and anger.

Bitch. I'm gonna enjoy dominating you.

She knew he would breed with her. That's exactly how he would think of it too. There would be no warmth or compassion in the act, just a filling of a need, a plan he'd been waiting to put in motion. When her usefulness was over, he'd take the knife, kill her and enjoy every moment of it.

Her heart tattoo pounded again, betraying her anxiety.

"God, that sound is so annoying," he said. "I think I will take your earlier suggestion and cut it out of you just to see what happens. Turn around."

He helped her follow his orders, pushing her so she leaned across the bar. The white bandage on her shoulder pulsed, and she braced herself. Nathan had told her the Sacred Heart tattoo would take on different meanings for different people, but ultimately it would protect her. She held her breath when Sammael pulled back the white bandage.

"Oh…" he said, wonder in his voice.

A mirror ran along the bar's wall, and she lifted her head to see Sammael. He stared at the tattoo. Faye saw the rise and fall of the heart in the mirror. Even in her fear, she couldn't help but be fascinated by the texture it had taken on. It almost looked like the real thing.

Sammael's face twisted in horror. Whatever he saw in the heart didn't agree with him. A burst of flame shot up from the tattoo, shooting straight into his eyes. He howled in pain and the edges of his eyelids turned black, charred from the powerful light.

He covered his eyes and blood seeped between his fingers, dripping to the floor.

Faye.

A voice whispered to her, and she turned to look at the knife.

Not death.

She picked it up. The blade gleamed, singing with power as she held it. Thoughts filled her head, images of the lives taken by the instrument. She allowed the feelings of anger and bitterness to swallow her healing urges.

"Sammael," she said. He lowered his hands, blinking at her through the blood clouding his eyes. "Look what I've got."

"Give that to me."

"All right."

The pounding of her heart cannoned through the club. Gripping the bone handle, she half ran, half flew, throwing her body into his. She raised the knife and blindly brought it down.

Blood squirted from his chest and the howl of pain he let out rivaled the guttural sound she heard herself making. The knife glowed and a surge of energy shot through her arm. Voices screamed inside her head, and power gave her a drunk, lightheaded feeling that blocked the rage.

Faye gripped the handle, swaying in the rapture of the essence caught in the knife's blade, oblivious to Sammael's movements. He was nothing to her, nothing she couldn't trample or crush under foot. In fact, there wasn't a thing in the world able to stop her now. She could go anywhere, do anything. She could--

"Faye. Let go of the knife."

Her father's voice jolted her back into the present. She could still feel the residual energy of the knife and the temptation to ignore Raphael, to do exactly as she pleased, was strong.

"Faye, you don't want to be like the sad, pathetic creature you see before you," Raphael squatted next to her, placing his hand on top of hers. "Let this go."

She wanted to, really she did, but a little voice in her head whispered to her about the power she could contain in her soul. There would never be a sad day again, or a time when she would feel lonely or unloved. The knife sang tempting promises causing her hand to shake with indecision.

"It's all lies, darling," Raphael whispered. "That thing wants to pull you away from me, away from the people who love you."

"And who is that?" Faye looked into her father's familiar eyes. "Mom and Chris are gone. Azal is dead. And Nathan--"

She didn't finish the sentence. Raphael sighed and reached out to touch her hair.

"I know, honey. I know you've been hurting."

"This is their killer. This thing is what butchered them!" She raised the knife, prepared to end Sammael's life. "Let me do this for everyone he's hurt."

"There are better ways to punish him," Raphael said. "Death would be an easy out, not nearly as satisfying as you think."

"But this is my fault." The words ripped from her. "If I'd never been born God wouldn't have punished you. He wouldn't have killed Mom and Chris."

Sammael moaned on the floor, his hands covering his eyes. Raphael placed a hand on the young man's leg and said, "Steady."

Sammael stopped moving and grew quiet.

"You were the greatest gift in my life," Raphael said. "I

would gladly be punished again and again if it kept you alive and well."

The guilt Faye lodged deep in her heart moved a little. Without a word, she held out the knife to Raphael. He retrieved the blue cloth from the floor and draped the material over the blade before taking it from his daughter.

The heart on her shoulder quieted, deflating against her skin. She got up, resisting the urge to kick Sammael who lay silent and still on the cold floor of Black Cat.

"We should go before he rouses," Raphael said. "He is still powerful, and we need to destroy this knife. Then we can take care of him."

"Nathan wanted to tattoo him in order to control his human side. Our plan was for me to destroy the knife first. It's the key to his power."

"It's the key to a lot more than that," Raphael said. "Perhaps destroying it will allow Sammael a second chance to do some good with his natural gifts."

"I don't care about his natural gifts."

"We should go out the way I came in. Through the backdoor."

"What about…Nathan?" She couldn't bear to look at his inert form.

"I'm without my angel essence, or I'd take care of it. I'll come back when the knife is destroyed," Raphael said. Putting an arm around her shoulder, he led her from the room.

Chapter 17

Nathan's domain was as they'd left it earlier that evening--tidy and vaguely smelling of sandalwood from the clean-up they'd done. Faye ushered her father through the loft, making sure the door locked behind them. They'd spoken little on their way back to Hell's Leak. She hardly knew what to say to Raphael, anyway, but he didn't appear to mind. He took in Nathan's apartment, curiosity on his face when he saw the bookshelves.

"Are you sure you're okay now? Sammael said he'd hurt you. He made it sound as if--" Unable to finish the thought, Faye went to get him a glass of water and discovered her hands still shook. Raphael took the water, but instead of drinking it, he placed it on the counter. Taking her hands in his, he looked into her eyes, breathing deeply.

The shakes stopped and the awful anxiousness she felt eased. It still lingered within her, but she could manage it now.

"Better?" Raphael asked. "It's not much, I know, but it's the best I can do until I get my full angel essence back. And that nephilim did nothing to me I couldn't handle. I'm pretty good at knowing when to play possum."

For a few seconds, Faye managed to forget everything going on as she enjoyed the sight of her father's kind face, but reality interceded. "I want to know all about what's happened to you, but we've got to take care of Sammael first. I've got to destroy the knife."

"I understand." Raphael released her hands. "I remember seeing it when I met him at the warehouse all those years ago."

"Then it was him that tried to kill you? Not...not something else."

"Of course it was. The little bastard caught me off guard," Raphael said, and lifted her chin. "God had nothing to do with it."

"I see."

Raphael pursed his lips and peered into her face, searching for something. "You've had a hard time of it. Azal didn't know the truth about what happened that day. He tried all these years to get it from me, but the memory was locked too deep inside. How he must have suffered too."

"I thought he let God take you." Weary, Faye sat on the couch. "I thought Mom and Chris died because of my existence."

"No. Sammael is the one who broke apart our family. He wanted revenge because he thought I killed his father."

"Did you kill Lucifer?"

"Oh, goodness no. I wouldn't have dreamed of attempting such a thing. Besides, Lucifer was a friend. Poor creature. He gets such a bad rap."

"Where is he?"

"I don't know for sure," he said. "But if I had to guess, I'd say he's in that knife you're holding."

Faye stared at the weapon. She'd sensed there were actual beings trapped within it, and had caught glimpses of them when she'd held it in her hand, but it hadn't occurred to her Lucifer might have been one of the knife's victims. "Does that mean Sammael killed his father?"

"I doubt it." Raphael took it from her. "He would have been way too young. More likely it was the mother."

"I don't understand," Faye said. "Sammael's mother always believed an angel did it, or at least that's what she told him."

"I'm just making a guess here based on what I know. You're well aware of Lucifer's reputation, right? People call him the devil, Satan, master of all things evil." Raphael's face grew wistful. "What fun titles to have."

"Oh, Daddy."

"Well, it's true. Anyway, the problem with Lucifer's job is he carries a lot of negative residual energy around with him. This energy tends to infect the humans he's around too long. It's similar to how Azal's good fortune works," Raphael said. "Lucifer settled down with a bright, intelligent, normal woman, but two years later, she'd turned dark and psychotic--all due to the energy."

"That's why you went to see him," Faye said.

"Yes. He asked me to heal her, but I could only do so much. After a time, as much as I hated to tell Lucifer this, I felt it best if he removed himself from her. I hoped his absence would ease the negative side effects she experienced." Raphael took the knife to the kitchen. "I thought that's what he did, and I heard nothing more from him for many years. However, after a time, it became clear no one heard from him."

"What do you think happened?"

"I think Lucifer's wife trapped his soul inside here and couldn't admit it to herself."

"How? She wasn't an angel or a nephilim."

"How she did it is easy enough. The real question is who made this weapon," Raphael said. "I've got a few theories about that too."

"We need to destroy it," Faye said. "Nathan and I worked out a spell that will obliterate it, but now I...well...I wonder if our plan is the right thing to do. All those souls--what will happen to them?"

"It's a powerful weapon." Raphael raised an eyebrow and stared at the knife speculatively. "You need to be careful with any attempts at destroying it. I think my angel essence is in here. I'd really like to get that back."

"If your essence is in there, is it possible that...that Nathan and Azal could be in there too? Is that what Nathan meant when he said not death?"

"Perhaps."

"What about Mom and Chris?"

Raphael said nothing to that, but she could tell he turned the question over in his mind. He laid the knife on the table and headed to Nathan's bookshelves. Faye had leafed through a few of them earlier in the day and noted they were in various languages, none of which she understood. Her father prowled around the shelves, and she glanced at the clock. How much time did they have left before Sammael recovered enough to hunt her down?

"Daddy, what are you looking for?"

"A book. A very special book by an angel called Raziel."

"You mean the book you gave me this afternoon?" Faye picked it up from the coffee table.

"No. That's a copy. I need the real book. I gave it to an angel named Nathaniel hundreds of years ago. Of course you know him as Nathan Ink," Raphael said, pulling out a book and then re-shelving it. "I don't know where he might keep it."

"I can help with that."

Faye walked over to Nathan's bed and pulled out the silver box. She felt her father's curiosity at how she knew where it was, but offered no explanation. Hopefully, there would be time to explain the situation between her and Nathan later.

Her hands shook again as she lifted the lid and sorted through its contents. How she would have loved to linger over the items, to examine them more thoroughly, but there was no time. She removed the small leather bound book Nathan used earlier to create the angel snare, letting her fingers run over the smooth sapphire stone. It tingled beneath her palms, and she held it out to her father.

He took it and flipped through the old pages carefully. There were words written in strange symbols and pictures of things Nathan had drawn, their meaning as unclear as the words. Raphael, however, seemed to have no trouble with the language despite the lack of his angel essence.

"Here we go, Faye," he said and held it where she could see the page better. "I think you should take a look at this."

Drawn in black ink, the picture on the page reminded Faye of a comic book drawing. A robed and hooded figure knelt before a tall child in a plain tunic. The smile on his youthful face belied just the smallest hint of mischievousness, and in one hand he held a sharp looking dagger. Faye could make out carvings in the curve of the blade. Unlike the knife in her possession, the handle of this one was metal and appeared a little more ornate with jewels encrusted in the handle. As Faye examined the picture, the tall boy's head turned and met her gaze.

"Come," he whispered.

Faye blinked. A roaring sound rushed through the room, and before she knew it, Faye was in the picture.

The kneeling man spoke, and though Faye knew he spoke a language unfamiliar to her, her brain processed the words in English.

"Please." The man begged the boy, unashamed. "Please. I will pay any price."

"That's what all the men who visit my kind say." The boy narrowed his eyes. "But then they try to cheat us."

"Not me," the man said. "My intentions are true. I have no desire to bring your kind harm."

"But you'll turn on us at the first sign of trouble. There is no loyalty to a nephilim."

"I can't speak for those others." The man tugged at the

bottom of the boy's robe. "I only know what is in my heart, and I must have that weapon."

"What do you need it for?" The boy kicked at the grimy fingers clutching the robe and stepped back. "Tell me the truth."

The man hesitated and then looked into the boy's eyes, his emotions raw and true. "Vengeance."

"And who is it that you seek to destroy?"

"The man who murdered my beloved daughter. He took her innocence and left her for dead on the desert floor outside the village." The man's voice could barely contain his anger. "He must die."

The boy shook his head in disgust. "There are many men in the city of Chaldea who have dark natures. You could easily dispatch them without my help."

"Yes, but I've heard of your kind, of the...special things you can do. I don't want this murderer to die a quick death. I want to punish him first, and for him to understand the pain he caused me."

"I see," the boy said.

"Then you'll help me?"

"Yes. But be warned." He bent close to the man's face. "You won't kill the man with this blade."

"He doesn't deserve to live."

"This will be a different kind of death. He'll live in darkness, trapped without light, only the thought of his sins to keep him company. There will be no chance at redemption for him." The boy straightened to his full height, towering over the desperate man. "Can you live with that?"

"Yes. Anything.... please, help me."

"Hold out your hand."

The man complied, allowing the boy to take the knife. He winced as the sharp blade of the dagger cut across his palm.

"Your blood," the boy whispered and then ran the blade against his own hand. "My blood."

He began to chant, holding the knife in both hands. The blood mixed on the blade, blackening it. After a few seconds, the metal glowed, and a white light shot up from it. The boy's eyes pulsed with the same light, and the man stepped back, frightened as the child moved toward him, offering the weapon. After a small hesitation, the man took it. Immediately, the white light disappeared, and a strange calm filled the older man's features. He reached inside the long robe he wore to pull out a leather bag. The jingle of coins could be heard as he tossed the bag to the boy.

"Thank you, child," the man said.

The boy watched the man walk away into the city streets before turning to stare out at the desert. "Why are you here, nephilim?"

Faye gave a start. She'd thought he'd been unable to see her.

"I've come for knowledge," she said.

"You are one of my kind. Are you not knowledgeable enough?"

"I need to know how to break a knife similar to the one you just gave that man."

"Again, are you not knowledgeable about your powers? You should be able to do it without assistance. We might not be as strong as our angel parent, but we are not weak."

"I...don't think I'm as powerful as you."

The boy turned to her with a smile. "And yet you were powerful enough to jump into the past and visit me in Chaldea. You need to look deeper within yourself. Have faith."

"I'm just a healer."

The boy shifted, impatient with her answer.

"If you believe that, then you're right. You are not as powerful as the rest of our kind." He moved away, headed to the desert where in the distance purple storm clouds gathered. The wind picked up, pushing the scent of rain toward them.

"Where is Chaldea?" Faye followed after the boy.

"In what you would have called ancient Mesopotamia. Where life began," the boy said. Fat drops of rain fell. "God is going to punish us soon."

A crack of thunder sounded in the distance.

"Look in your heart, nephilim. Gather your angel strength and begin your own chant of desire. Visualize how the process is done and it will be," the boy said and pointed to the desert. "Look."

Faye followed the direction of his finger. The purple clouds had somehow touched down in the sand. It took her only a moment to realize what she saw were not clouds at all, but a great wall of water rushing toward them with terrifying speed. She couldn't fathom where the wave had come from but there it was, annihilating everything in its path.

"The Flood comes," the boy said. "Our time is at an end."

Faye closed her eyes and concentrated. She felt a change taking place, but the sound of rushing water was still loud. Faye could have sworn she felt the spray of it and heard the screams of doomed people. But the sounds faded, and she cautiously opened one eye, relieved to find herself back in Nathan's apartment.

"Did you find an answer?" Raphael picked up the book from the floor and held it close to him.

"Maybe. I'm not sure," she said, frustrated. "We should get down to Hell's Leak. Nathan will have the tools we need to break this knife there."

Raphael nodded, but said nothing as he handed Faye the book. There was no time to wonder over all she'd experienced in it. She felt Sammael coming, felt his anger soaking the air. Faye clutched the Book of Raziel and the knife. As she headed down the stairs, she hoped an idea on how to destroy the blade would come to her.

* * * *

That bitch had fucking blinded him!

Sammael could hardly see a damn thing through the haze covering his eyes. He couldn't hold back a whimper at the pain that rocketed through his head too. And the knife. She'd taken the knife and that bastard, Raphael, helped her.

Rage screamed from every pore as he found his way out of the Black Cat. He stumbled down the street, ignoring the whispers and comments his gruesome appearance evoked.

Sammael knew where the bitch had gone. Hell's Leak. He made his way over there. This time he wouldn't be so gentle with her.

* * * *

Faye brought the sledgehammer down with a mighty whack. Nothing happened. The knife remained intact, looking as pristine as ever. She tried again, but met with the same results.

"Daddy?" She turned to Raphael.

He shrugged.

"Faye, what did the nephilim in Raziel's book tell you?"

"That I have the power to change this knife."

"Then you do. I saw you do things a little while ago I know I never taught you. You have reserves of strength you've only begun to tap into."

"I don't think so. All that fighting stuff came out because I was angry," Faye said, staring down at the knife. "The boy was wrong."

"Faye, the person at fault here is me." Confused, she turned to look at him. "I taught you what I thought was most important. Healing. I didn't push you to nurture any other powers you might have, because I didn't want you to draw attention to yourself. I'm all too aware of what happened to the nephilim so long ago. I couldn't bear losing a child that way. You have been far more in touch with your human side because of me. That's one advantage Sammael had over you. He might not have got a proper upbringing, but he does know a great deal about what his powers can do."

"So I can do this?"

"It requires a great deal of faith in yourself," Raphael said. "Something you seem to have lost these last seven years."

His words stung. Tears welled in her eyes and one slipped free, falling the short distance to land on the knife. She had lost her faith. For the last seven years, she'd only been half alive, full of anger and doubt. She'd barred from her life all those capable of providing love and understanding, preferring to keep them at arm's length. What she felt now was shame and a need to make up for her lack of faith in God, heaven and herself.

The tattoo on her back thumped, pulsing against her shirt.

The nephilim in Raziel's book mixed his blood on the dagger to create power. She'd seen Sammael use his own blood to infuse the knife. On the street this morning, he'd been marking her, needing to perform a blood ritual on her to make it complete.

Faye picked up the knife. Being careful not to grip it too tight, she studied the bone handle. The carvings in it were intricate, and she recognized them as being similar to the ones on the lid of Nathan's box. She ran the blade across her hand, wincing at the pain and the sight of the crimson liquid that welled. Making a fist, she squeezed the blood onto the knife's handle, watching the porous bone soak it up.

The pounding of the tattoo heart filled the room, but now she found herself steadied by its sound. Calm washed over her and a warm heat fizzed on her shoulder beneath the bandage. She could do this.

Faye held her hand over the knife and visualized the handle and blade separating. A low vibration filled the room. White light pulsed from the knife, and Faye concentrated on it, willing the metal to weaken. The light shot up, and her green eyes glowed. The souls trapped in the blade screamed, mixing with the Sacred Heart's beat and with a deft hand, Faye picked up the sledgehammer, bringing it down once more on the weapon.

The blade separated from the handle, and the two pieces rocked back and forth, two magnets trying to find their way back to each other. The white light dissolved, and the voices grew silent.

Nothing happened.

"Shit." She turned to the front door, alerted by a sharp smell of rot and decay. "Sammael is here."

* * * *

Darkness everywhere. He could see nothing else at first. Then the cold hit him, sinking into the bone, making him feel there would never be warmth again. He couldn't imagine what it would be like to be trapped here indefinitely.

The moment the blade severed, Nathan knew. The cold stopped. All the souls listened. Something changed in the darkness. A heartbeat could be heard. Light grew in the space they were trapped in, and all the inhabitants could see each other. There were at least fifty souls trapped together, some angelic of varying levels, some mortal.

Nathan watched as one by one the souls departed, swept away in the warmth of the light. Peace washed through the space, warming the others. Three remained behind, including himself, but there was no need to speak. They all knew what to do.

The third soul surprised him. That one nodded at him before turning away from the ones departing to heaven. They focused on the red light steadily growing in the distance, and the sound of the heartbeat that would lead them back to earth and Hell's Leak.

* * * *

Sammael pushed open the door. His bright red eyes gave him the demonic look he'd always thought the angels who worked for his father would possess. Through the blurred vision, he could just make out two people standing behind the counter of Hell's Leak. One of them was Faye.

"Now what the fuck did you go and blind me for?" Sammael snarled, squinting. His hand pressed against the aching wound in his chest. "You didn't have to stab me, either. Now I can't play nice with you anymore."

"You killed my family, my guardian angel and Nathan," Faye said, her tone even and cool. "Our friendship is kind of in the crapper."

"Where is my fucking knife?"

"Here." The masculine voice came from the person standing next to Faye. Raphael. "This is what you are looking for."

Sammael wiped at his eyes. Through his blurred vision he made out an object resting on the counter. The knife. Relieved, he moved forward, but his joy was short lived.

"What have you done?" He grabbed the two separated pieces, squinting to see them better.

"Broke it," Faye said.

Sammael hated the smug serenity he heard in her voice.

"You bitch." He lunged across the counter, his hands reaching for her neck. She didn't move, remaining calm in the face of his extreme anger and to his surprise, he felt his body being flung through the air. He hit the wall with a hard thud. A crazed little laugh slipped from his lips. "Somebody got their powers back."

"No thanks to you," Raphael said, and squatted down next to Sammael, giving him a pat on the shoulder. "You look like shit, son."

"Don't you fucking call me that! You're not my father. Powers or not, I'm going to kill you this time, old man. You should be dead already."

"You couldn't quite manage it seven years ago. Nor could you pull it off earlier this evening. Why would right now be any different?" Raphael reached out his hand, yanking Sammael's face up. "Oh, you put on a great show, and we had a good battle. You almost succeeded. Remember?"

Sammael shrank back from his touch, but it didn't matter. Raphael's firm grasp pulled him back to seven years ago, back to when he thought he'd avenged his father. He'd watched the McCoy family from the rafters as they tended to the homeless who infested the warehouse, praying over their worthless souls. Watching Raphael caused the anger, always so ready, so easy to access, to flare inside him.

It had been strong enough for Raphael to stop and move farther into the darkened interior of the building.

"Who are you?" The angel's voice boomed with authority. "I've sensed you many times over the last few months. I'd like to help you understand things a bit better. You have no need to be afraid of me."

"It doesn't matter who I am, but what I'm going to do." Sammael watched the angel peer around the room.

"Show yourself."

"You can't scare me, angel," Sammael hissed. "I've killed your kind before. I hardly consider you a threat. But I would get the young man and the pretty woman out of here, or else I might be tempted to take some time and play with them."

"And you don't scare me." Estella spoke, coming up behind Raphael. Chris joined her and both took a defensive stance, ready for anything. "My husband asked you a question."

"Husband? Oh, you've been naughty indeed, angel. Very naughty."

"How do you know what I am?" Raphael remained calm and seeing that made Sammael reckless. He wanted to break that calm, to see it shatter into a million jagged pieces.

"Because I am of your kind," he said, and jumped down from the rafter, landing easily. "You knew my father, Lucifer."

"We are all children of God."

"Not all of us." He laughed. "Some of us are children of the damned."

A flash of light lit the warehouse, and something flew through the air. Chris's long lanky form fell to the ground, and blood dripped from his neck. The bone handle of a knife protruded from it. Estella got to her knees beside him, covering the wound with her hand.

The knife flew back toward Sammael and he plucked it from the air with a wicked grin.

"Raphael," Estella called, panic coloring her voice. "I need you."

"Listen to that, angel," Sammael mocked. "She needs you."

Raphael moved toward his wife. Another flash lit the room, and Estella dropped next to Chris, her eyes already lifeless as blood leaked from the back of her head where the knife now rested. Raphael stopped short, his face stretching in anguish, pain building in his eyes. His unearthly scream shook the walls of the building.

"Temper, temper." Sammael willed the knife to work its way free from its victim and back to his hand. "It hurts to lose the ones you love. I saw how my mother suffered over the death of my father. I never even knew him because of you!"

"Lucifer left because he tried to save your mother." Raphael cradled his wife in his arms. The building shook and energy crackled in the air. Flames licked the walls of the room.

Sammael approached Raphael, knowing he must act quickly. Holding the knife outstretched in front of him, he hoped he would get the chance to look into Raphael's eyes when he stabbed the angel through the heart.

"Raphael," Sammael said. "Look at me."

The angel turned, and Sammael saw the confusion and sorrow that racked Raphael's body.

"I just want you to know," Sammael said, "that I don't plan to kill your daughter, Faye. She is going to be my mate. We'll start a new breed of nephilim who will get rid of abominations like you."

With a grunt, he shoved the knife at the angel. Raphael shot out his hand, which pulsed with a white ball of energy. The ball bounced off Sammael, knocking him back, but not before he'd seen the telltale white light of Raphael's angel essence leap into the knife.

The angel collapsed on the floor, and Sammael picked himself up, wiping blood off his face. Triumph lifted him up and out of the building. If he'd waited just a moment longer, he would have seen Raphael, confused and afraid, stagger from the flaming warehouse.

"Your knife scratched me." Raphael's wise voice brought Sammael out of the vision and back to Hell's Leak. "It took most of my angelic essence, but not the life of my mortal shell."

"Damn you." Spittle flew from Sammael's mouth as he gazed with hatred up at the angel.

"I think it is you who is damned."

This new voice came from behind all of them. A man came forward, his movements sleek and graceful. The pale porcelain of his skin was set off perfectly by the shiny brown hair that curled becomingly around his face, and his hazel eyes sparked with energy. At the sight of Sammael, the man's full lips curled into a smile.

"Who are you?" Sammael struggled to sit up, pushing away the hand Raphael offered him.

"I am Lucifer."

The room stilled. All his life he'd heard stories about Lucifer. But none of those stories came close to capturing the vitality exuding from the angel before him. Easy to see how so many fell to temptation. His power crept around the room, drawing them all in. "Father." Sammael rose, shocked. "Is this a trick? You were destroyed. Mother told me so."

"I was trapped in the knife."

"But…I don't understand. How could you be…"

"Your mother trapped me in there." Lucifer said. "She killed me."

"No…she told me…"

"She lied. She was angry, very angry, and as I'm sure you know, she wasn't quite right in the head, Sammael. I blame myself for that. When I first met her, Lana was pure and innocent. Such rare qualities for me to be around! But…an angel of my stature carries around residual energy from past deeds. I'm afraid I infected her with that energy." Lucifer shook his head, his beautiful face marred by genuine sorrow. "She went off the deep end. I went to Raphael to cure her, but she would have none of it. We argued about it later that evening. You were only a toddler then and upstairs asleep. In a rage, Lana stabbed me with the knife. Imagine my surprise to find I was suddenly sucked out of my mortal form and deposited into the wasteland."

"Momma lied to me?" Sammael whispered, his voice doubtful.

"So it would seem. But now the knife is broken, its magic gone. It's over, son. You know the truth now." Lucifer grew stern and his hazel eyes lit up with a yellow glow. "You must stop your plans."

"No." Sammael lowered his head. "No. You're the one lying. You're not really Lucifer."

"Oh, I assure you I am."

"This is a trick. You're teamed up with the others."

"I work for no one but God."

"Liar. I will eradicate you like the others. I won't stop until all the angels are dead and punished for the things they do. They might as well be demons with the chaos they cause."

"Don't you see? Chaos is part of the world. Man cannot have a utopia. Chaos, misery--they are what glue life together. Happiness couldn't fully exist without the other two. There must be balance," Lucifer stretched out his hands. "Come to me, son. Let me help you."

"No."

"Don't make this harder than it has to be."

"Stay away from me."

Out of the corner of her eye, Faye saw something move. She turned her head and saw Nathan staring calmly at her. He put a finger to his lips, and she nodded, unable to keep the relief off her face.

He looked at the counter, and she followed his gaze. Understanding what he wanted, she quietly removed the Book of Sinz from its resting place. He would need it to tattoo Sammael, but to her surprise, Nathan shook his head.

"Sammael, you must ask forgiveness for your sins, for the people whose lives you took. I can't know what your fate will be, but forgiveness is the first step," Lucifer cajoled, holding out his hand.

"Don't try to tempt me." Sammael backed away. "It won't work. I'm stronger than you. I am the antichrist."

Lucifer gave a mirthless chuckle.

"You're weak. Look at your eyes. It's a wonder you're still alive."

"It's from that pathetic little tattoo…"

"Pathetic?" Nathan spoke up.

Fear skittered across Sammael's face as he recognized the sound of Nathan's voice, and Faye saw his eyes were much worse now. They pooled with blood, dripping over the eyelids and staining his face with red tears.

"I'd say what you saw was hardly pathetic." Nathan's cold words reverberated around the room. "Perhaps you need a second look."

Sammael shrank against the door of Hell's Leak, unsettled by that idea. He groped behind him for the handle, but the lock turned on its own accord with a resounding click.

"Faye, come here please." Nathan guided her to the wretched creature pressed against the door. He murmured in protest when Nathan pulled back the fabric of Faye's shirt. Sammael closed his eyes, unwilling to look again. "The Sacred Heart is the most powerful tattoo I've ever created. One look and you know your place in the world. To some, it's beautiful beyond description, an affirmation of the wonders of life and God's love. For others, it's the hell of their worst nightmares, and of those people, the lucky ones die. There are some that remain alive, maimed by its power and forced to remember what they've seen. You weren't one of the lucky ones."

"Please…" Sammael thrashed, pinned to the door by the angels' power. "It has no control over me."

"Really? Then how come you are afraid?" Faye asked. "I've looked at it too, you know."

"Wh…what…did you see?"

She glanced over her shoulder, not surprised to see the symbol changed. Now the vial was full of red liquid, and the seeds blossomed into flowers, wrapping around the sparkling crown and lit by radiant flames.

"Humanity and love. That's the true face of God." At his grimace, she said, "I'm guessing that's not what you saw."

"He saw hell, the madness in his own heart." Nathan touched Sammael's arm. "Come sit down."

"No." Sammael jerked his arm away.

"Now, son, don't be like that. It's for your own good." Lucifer moved to his child, peeling him from the wall by slipping an arm around his shoulders. The younger man struggled, but whatever he'd seen from his earlier experience with the tattoo had weakened him, and the angel essences he'd relied on were gone. Powerless, he found himself guided to Nathan's chair.

Nathan muttered a few words under his breath and straps appeared, lashing Sammael into the seat. He shook with rage, but Faye sensed fear emanating from him too.

"Don't let them do this to me," Sammael appealed to Lucifer. "Why would you let them do this to your son?"

"And yet only moments ago you denied our genetic bond," Lucifer pointed out.

"No father would allow his child to be tortured like this," Sammael screamed, his face contorted with madness.

"Oh, I know a father who put his son through much worse than a mere tattoo." Lucifer leaned in close to Sammael and ruffled his hair. "I allow this to happen for the same reason. Be grateful there are no wooden crosses nearby. It could always be worse."

"Fuck you."

"Hah! Is that the best you've got? You were such a braggart all those years. I heard your voice going on and on about how you would be bigger than me. As if such a thing were possible. And your plan. Eradicating angels? Ridiculous. It's not even a very original idea." Lucifer's voice dripped with scorn. "Now if your plan had been to kill God…that would have been much more creative, not to mention ambitious."

"You talk too much, Lucifer. Always did. I don't know why God always liked you the best." Raphael turned to Nathan. "Where is Azal?"

"We decided to have him hang back. We don't want the angel of good fortune accidentally turning the tide for Sammael." Nathan nodded to Faye. "Do you have Raziel's book?"

She'd forgotten about the book she'd brought down from

Nathan's room. Now she handed it to him, wondering what would happen. The three angels clustered around Sammael, their eyes on the book. The sapphire stone glowed.

A heavy silence fell over Hell's Leak, and celestial energy moved in the air. The angels joined hands, chanting, and while Faye recognized none of the words, she thought they might be in old Hebrew. Soft at first, the chant grew louder until it shook the windows of the shop. A hum filled the small area, the most beautiful sound Faye had ever heard with each tone lovelier than the last. Her heart filled with joy, and she couldn't quite catch her breath.

But then another sound overtook it. Harsh and ugly, it beat down the beautiful hum. Faye covered her ears, and dropped to the floor.

"Nathan, it's time." Raphael's commanding voice rose above the screeching noise.

Faye realized the noise must be what Nathan heard every time he'd encountered Sammael. How would he get through this ritual if the sin was that strong?

Her father. She noticed his hand rested on Nathan's shoulder and a great glowing light issued from it straight into Nathan. Raphael, the healer, would keep the pain at bay.

Nathan bent over Sammael, the tattoo drill in his hand. The nephilim's eyes were opened wide. The iris mixed with the normal hazel color there before turning into white, cloudy cataracts, absorbing the blood in them. His mouth opened in wonder, and a thin line of saliva ran out. Nathan pressed the tattoo gun into the skin as the other's continued to chant. A long howl of pain came from Sammael, and he thrashed, helpless against the restraints.

Faye huddled on the floor, stretched apart by the ritual, her mind unable to absorb everything. Her eyes focused on the glowing light surrounding her father, and unable to concentrate any longer, she passed out.

Chapter 18

Sammael couldn't quite remember all the details of the night. Faye. Something about Faye. He'd been close, almost had her in his grasp. And the knife…where was it? He couldn't for the life of him remember where it had got to. There had been pain. In his eyes. A flash of light. He shook his head, frustrated. The thoughts just wouldn't get clear.

Hell's Leak. That was the clearest thing in his recent memory. He recalled standing outside the shop staring at the red neon words. Hell's Leak. A tattoo shop. He'd stumbled away from it afraid, though he didn't know why. The deep black of night gathered around him, and he'd walked, leaving the awful little shop behind. His right arm throbbed.

That's when the singing began. Low at first, the sound reverberated in his head until he gnashed his teeth in misery. An old hymn, it irritated his already confused sensibilities. The odd thing was it appeared to be coming from somewhere on his right arm.

He stopped in the middle of the street and rolled up the sleeve of his shirt where a white bandage rested across his bicep. Curious, he pulled back the gauze and then gave a shout of anger. "Son of a bitch!"

The image of an angel had been branded into his arm. It had great curving wings folded neatly behind its back as it knelt in prayer. The face struck Sammael as being very lifelike with its pale complexion and just a hint of pink in the cheeks. Clothed in white flowing robes, the lips moved as it sang the hymn. The angel looked up and met Sammael's gaze, saying, "You be good now."

It all came back. Nathan Ink. He'd probably tattooed him

thinking this would stop him from his destiny. And the other angels...they'd all been in on it. Son of a bitch! Well, no way would he allow some tattoo to influence him. He was beyond that and much too powerful. He could still carry out his plans. He could still get Faye. He'd get a new knife but--

"Ouch," Sammael said at the sharp pain in his right arm. "What the fuck?"

A glance at the area showed the angel shaking his head. "I told you to be good. Start thinking nice thoughts."

"Screw you. You can't affect my free will. I am a nephilim."

From within its robes, the angel brought out a sword. With a smile at Sammael, the angel stabbed the skin. Sammael cried out with pain.

"You asshole!" Sammael said and was rewarded with another sharp pain as the angel stabbed again.

"Watch your language," it warned. "You don't have powers anymore, boy."

"Not true."

"Oh, yes it is. Raziel's book was just the thing to bind your black little soul."

Sammael mashed his lips together and walked. His mind raced still trying to recall the events of the last few hours. He'd had Faye. She'd escaped with the knife. He'd known she would go back to Hell's Leak, even though he killed Nathan. But where was she now? And what the hell had happened to the knife? How had he gotten the angel on his shoulder?

"All good questions," the angel said, though Sammael hadn't spoken out loud.

Sammael ignored it and tried to block out the sound of the hymn it hummed. He headed back to his apartment, a little one room hovel on the East side of Sixth Street. Still early in the morning, he hoped none of his neighbors would be up yet. He didn't need curious do-gooders meddling in his business. Fix his arm. That was at the top of his to-do list and then he would take care of Faye.

"Don't do anything stupid," the angel said. "You've already made your fair share of idiotic mistakes."

"Shut up," Sammael growled.

"I'm not going anywhere," the angel said. "We are going to be together for a long time. That's the beauty of a tattoo. They're permanent."

"Maybe." He stumbled up the stairs to his apartment building, jabbing at the dim buttons of the empty elevator. The angel's humming grew louder. He caught a glimpse of himself in the elevator's mirror, surprised by the dried blood covering his clothes.

When the door slid open, Sammael trudged down the hall to his little sanctuary of darkness where normally he could go to rest his mind. Too agitated to relax, he stood in the middle of his kitchen.

Tucked in the corner behind the trashcan sat an axe. He'd needed it once, during his experimental phase of bringing death. But dismembering a human being had been time consuming and messy. After that one attempt, he'd been content with using only the knife.

Cut it out. He remembered Faye's earlier request to him, wishing he'd been able to do that. He'd cut out her real heart when he caught up to her.

"Just what do you think you are doing?" the angel asked as Sammael hauled out the axe.

"I'm about to get rid of you."

"I don't think so, Sammael. You're about to be in a lot pain. I don't think you're quite right in the head."

"Shut up."

Sammael balanced the axe in his left hand. He'd always been ambidextrous--a good thing considering what he planned to do to himself. Briefly, he wondered how much blood there would be and then laughed. Fuck it. He was covered in blood already. What was a little more? Wait. He'd better get the phone ready so he could call 911. And towels. Towels would help with the bleeding. Vicodin. He thought he had some in the bathroom.

"Do you really think cutting off your arm is the right thing to do? You are not invincible, and your powers don't work anymore," the angel said as Sammael gathered what he needed. "Even if they did, you are no healer."

"I won't live with an angel," Sammael muttered. "I hate your kind."

"Then you must hate yourself since half of you genetically is of my kind."

"I'm superior to an angel. I have the best of both worlds. Human characteristics and divine power. I'm going to be a force to reckon with when my plans are complete."

"Poor Sammael. Your plans are over. This is punishment for your pride. Death was too good."

"Hah! That's bullshit. They can't kill me. It would be a sin. They're trapped by their own laws." Sammael gathered the towels and gripped the vicodin bottle in his hand. "Did they really think I wouldn't go to any extreme to be rid of you?"

"I guess they didn't think you would be dumb enough to chop off your own arm," the angel said. "By the way, are you sure that's going to work? You worked with Nathan Ink. You know his tattoos are special. I'm in your soul now. Will you be able to chop that away too?"

Sammael stood at the kitchen table, his thoughts going a mile a minute. He had to get the damn thing off him. Already the first tinges of defeat crept in his brain, and it sickened him. He couldn't let go of his ideas, of his plans, of all he worked for. He popped two vicodin and steadied his body. Kneeling down by the table, he rested his arm on the top. With his other hand he grasped the axe.

"Think about this," the angel advised.

"Shut up."

With a swift whack, he sliced into the flesh. The pain was cold and blinding, but Sammael gamely lifted the ax again and again until he severed his arm from the socket. It lay limply on the table and he felt the first tremors of shock run through him. A terrible and nauseating pain followed. He dropped the axe and grabbed at the towels, howling as they pushed against the open wound.

Through the pain and screaming, he heard a sad voice say, "Sammael, Sammael, Sammael. You should have listened to me."

He calmed himself enough to look at his arm on the table. It was bare and clean of the tattoo.

"Down here."

His foot. The sound came from his foot. Grunting against the pain, Sammael kicked off his right shoe and worked off his sock. The angel stared at him, its wings fluttering with excitement. "Hello."

Frustrated and on the verge of blacking out, Sammael picked up the axe. Due to the blurring of his vision, it took several whacks before he succeeded in removing the foot from his body. He watched as the tattoo faded from the dismembered limb and wondered where it would resurface this time.

Darkness infiltrated the corners of his vision. And just as he as blacked out, he saw them--two angels. They stood across the room, one grim, and the other with just the smallest bit of sympathy in his eyes.

They faded from view and darkness claimed Sammael.

* * * *

"Nice kid you've got there," Azal said.

"He's got a lot of his mother in him," Lucifer said. "Or at least the way she became."

"You really think you caused the change in her?"

"Yes. My gift of darkness and corruption of the soul influences humans, even the ones I love," Lucifer said. "Sammael's mother, Lana, was the most beautiful thing I'd ever seen, the embodiment of purity. So I put aside my job and loved her. The human world never even missed me. But I noticed changes in Lana. That's when I took her to Raphael."

"I'm sorry it didn't work," Azal said. "Do you think you are what made the knife so strong? Chaldean daggers are unheard of in this day and age."

"No. Sammael did that."

"What do you mean?"

"They came home one day with the knife. Sammael was very young, maybe three at the most. Lana said they'd been in an antique store browsing. He'd gotten away from her, and she found him holding the knife. She took it from him, scolding Sammael, but she told me the knife...tingled in her hand. It called to her." Lucifer ran a hand through his brown hair. "I should have known something was wrong."

"Sammael must have given it power. The old stories claim that's one of the talents of nephilim children. I suppose we'll never know for sure." Azal stared at the wounded man on the floor. Blood covered the kitchen. "Well, Lucifer? Is now a good time?"

Lucifer studied Sammael. "Yes. Now would be a good time to have a little change in luck."

"I guess you do have a few paternal feelings."

"He's my son."

Azal heard the sincerity in the statement. It was easy, even for one who'd been around as long as Azal, to forget Lucifer was still an angel.

"Someone just called 911," Azal said and closed his eyes to concentrate. "They'll be here in five minutes. If they work fast, he'll live."

"He'll live?" Lucifer shuddered. "You call that good fortune?"

"Life is a miracle," Azal said. "What would you have me do?

Make it so they don't get here in time?"

"Perhaps that would be better luck for him."

Azal frowned. If Sammael lived, there was no guarantee of what he might do. The binding spell would hold, but what kind of life would Sammael have? Azal knew it was not for him to decide. "All I can do is my job. The rest is up to free will."

"I know," Lucifer said, "but still…"

They were silent, listening to the sounds of the ambulance in the distance. Then as if by mutual consent, they both disappeared in a flash of light.

Chapter 19

Faye awoke to a quiet world, conscious of no longer lying on the shop floor. She opened her eyes, relieved to find herself in her own apartment, the shades drawn. Gingerly, she pushed herself up to a seated position and stretched her arms. The tattoo ached a little at the movement and she reached over, pressing the fabric of the shirt covering it.

"Hello, Faye," Raphael said.

Seated a few yards away, his steepled fingers propped up his chin. Old and tired, Raphael stared at her, his face blank. She wondered how long he'd been there watching her.

"What happened?" Faye asked, sliding her feet to the floor.

"It's done. Nathan completed the task."

"Where are the others?"

"Behind the veil. Nathan is...recovering."

"What's wrong with him?"

"What he did tonight took great effort. The tattoo he etched into Sammael is like nothing he's done before. It took all of us angels to infuse it with our power. I only hope our combined efforts were enough. I had my hand on Nathan the whole time so he wouldn't be drained entirely. He is resting at his place. "

"And Sammael?"

Raphael frowned. "He's alive."

Faye's feelings mirrored his, and she couldn't keep the sarcasm from her voice. "Good for him, but after what he did to you, Mom and Chris, it's hard for me to jump for joy over it."

"Careful, Faye. I know you're frustrated, but it's all part--"

"Of God's plan. Don't you get tired of hearing that, though?"

"I am tired, Faye," he admitted, lowering his head. "When I saw Estella murdered all those years ago, I felt such anger, such despair. Forgetting it was almost like a balm on the pain. And as for God's plan? Yes, I do get tired of it. But it's my job to carry those plans out and live with them. Things happen for a reason. At least your mother is safe behind the veil now. As is Chris."

"Will Chris be okay?"

"He's at peace," her father said. "And you know he'll always be in your heart."

She touched the tattoo again, thinking of Chris, surprised when she noticed the lingering pain at the mention of his name was gone.

"Will you be punished further because of your relationship with Mom?"

"I don't know, Faye. But whatever happens, it was worth it to live like a mortal if only for a little while."

"Daddy, I don't know how to…bring this up," Faye said, slowly. "But Nathan…Nathan and I…we…"

"I know," Raphael said. "And now you're worried about what might happen to him?"

"Yes."

"Do you care about Nathan?"

"Yes." The answer surprised her and slipped out with little thought. She despised how he carried out his job, but there were feelings there for him. He wasn't Chris. But then no one ever would be.

"He's an angel, Faye. That path isn't possible."

Nathan wasn't for her. But still…she harbored a little hope that maybe…well, it didn't matter now. She only hoped Nathan wouldn't be punished for their one night. She would go to him, say goodbye and be done with it. The thought hurt a little, and she leaned in tighter to her father, breathing in his strength.

"You need more rest, Faye. I made a cup of tea for you. Drink some. It's guaranteed to ease the troubled mind," Raphael said, pressing a warm mug into her hands that had been on her bedside table. "All of this will feel different soon."

Like a child taking her medicine, she sipped from the mug, wondering at the small hint of sadness she saw in her father's eyes.

* * * *

Nathan sat alone in the long shadows of Hell's Leak. He

hadn't bothered to turn the lights on. No customers were coming that night, and after the session the day before with Faye and Sammael, he didn't know if he had the strength to pick up the tattoo gun. The Sacred Heart required considerable energy, but Sammael's angel wiped Nathan out. He had no urge to scratch anything onto anyone, which was strange. Never in his life as an angel or as a mortal could he recall feeling that way.

The Book of Sinz rested on the counter. For some reason, looking at it brought him a strange feeling of revulsion. The last two tattoos he'd created had moved his thoughts about doing his job in a different direction. Neither design had been from Sinz, which came as a bit of a revelation to him. Perhaps his work could go new places after all. Faye had been right.

He got up and threw the Sinz in the trash can. Closing his eyes, he held out a hand. Smoke puffed up from the can before the book burst into flames. Satisfied, Nathan watched the pages of his designs curl in the fire, turning to ash.

A tap at the glass door of the shop drew his attention. Outside, an old woman with white curly hair peered into the window, cupping both hands around her eyes to see better. She spotted Nathan and tapped again.

He moved to the door, curious. The old woman wore a black dress and comfortable leather shoes. Around her neck rested an onyx cross attached to a beaded necklace. As Nathan unlocked the door, the cross glowed.

"Come in, Lord." Nathan opened the door. She entered with a smile and the faint smell of baby powder drifted in after her. "Won't you sit down?"

With surprising spryness, the old woman hopped into the chair and opened her black beaded bag, pulling out a silver flask.

"Are you having a barbeque? I smell smoke." She offered the flask. "Have a drink with me, Nathan."

"As you wish, Lord." Nathan took the drink and sipped deeply. "And might I compliment you on your choice of mortal looks."

"Ah, yes, I like this form the best. It's so easy to wander amongst them in this guise. People expect an old man in flowing robes, or a flaming bush these days. I prefer simplicity and surprise all at once." The woman chuckled before growing serious. "So I hear you had some trouble the last few days."

"Yes. But it's resolved," Nathan took another swig from the flask, enjoying the sweetness of the elixir inside.

"Nasty bit of business with that Sammael. Lucifer ought to have been more careful with his seed, not that any of my angels should be planting roots anywhere," the old woman said, giving Nathan a reprimanding look. "But then, that's Lucifer. He's incorrigible, that one."

"Will Sammael live?"

"I don't know."

Nathan lapsed into silence, waiting for the Lord's purpose to be revealed. He had expected the visit, just not so soon. His mind went briefly to Faye and wondered if punishment for their indiscretion would be doled out.

"She'll be fine, you know," the old woman said, though Nathan had not spoken out loud. "She's scrappy. Despite my feelings toward the nephilim, I like her."

"I do too."

"Yes. I think you must like her a lot to chance my wrath. It's not like you to fall prey to temptation. In the five hundred years since we struck our bargain, you've never faltered."

"I'm sorry to have let you down now."

"I forgive you."

Nathan looked at the old woman, hope in his heart. She smiled at him sadly, answering his unspoken question. "No. Nathan, you must be punished. What would the others think if you weren't? Raphael lost his Estella and his memory for seven years. That's punishment enough. Lucifer has to deal with the stigma of his reputation, time served in the wasteland and a psychotic son. That's another sentence served. But you...well, you get the short end of the stick, I'm afraid. I know you were instrumental in stopping Sammael, and I thank you for it. But if I make the exception for you, then I have to for everybody. Then what would we have? A bunch of angels out to get laid every chance they get. They would breed all sorts of interesting children, the very same children, by the way, I attempted to wipe out with the Great Flood."

"So that rumor is true? The flood was your way of getting rid of the nephilim?"

"Damn right it was. Those kids were out of control, and if they had started breeding with each other, well...shit. Who knows what I would have had on my hands. Don't get me wrong. They exhibited some extraordinary gifts, but their propensity for violence was truly frightening. Something had to be done." The old woman rubbed her forehead. "It was a powerful lesson to the angels. No one wants to see his or her children harmed. That's why so few of these nephilim exist these days. Just look at Sammael. He reminds me so much of that first batch of freaks."

"And Faye? Does she remind you of them?" Nathan couldn't hide the anger in his voice, and the old woman looked at him, interest sparkling in her eyes.

"No. She doesn't. Faye is what I would have wanted a new race to be. Next to the humans, she is perfection," the old woman said and then added sharply, "And watch your tone, Nathan Ink."

"I'm sorry, Lord." Contrite, he drank again from the flask. "Will you harm Faye?"

"What? No." The old woman hopped out of the chair and marched to him. "I have a plan for that girl, though--something to keep her safe. Sammael isn't the only nephilim out there, you know. Others might get ideas if they were aware of her. Especially now."

"What will you do? Can you take her gifts from her?"

"I could, but I don't want to." The old woman gazed at him, and he had no clue what she might be thinking. "No. She still has other things to do. Another complication is growing for her as we speak. However, I intend to make the gifts dormant and erase her memory of who she really is."

"Why?"

"This way she won't remember you or anything that could draw attention to herself and attract undesirables."

"But--"

"But nothing. I'm afraid, Nathan, it's already been done. I had her father brew her something special to help erase her memory." she said. "But I visited her in a dream. We had a lovely chat about you. Did you know she loves you? She despises how you do the job I've assigned you, but yet she loves you, anyway. That Sacred Heart tattoo is extraordinary."

"And you, Lord? Do you despise the way I do my job?"

She considered the question. "You know, Nathan, what you do is not what I expected. But after careful consideration, it's my belief some people need a little harder dose of reality than others do. You provided that."

Nathan nodded, unable to stop the sadness welling inside him.

"Take another sip, Nathan," the old woman said. "You look like a man in need of a drink."

He complied, drinking the sweet liquid and thinking about Faye. She wouldn't remember him. The thought caused an ache in his heart. She wouldn't remember the time they had spent together or that she loved him. She wouldn't know how much he loved her. It staggered him to think such a thing possible.

Wait. Something was wrong. The world had grown quiet. Used to the hum being in the undercurrent of everyday life, Nathan looked at the old woman, confused. What had she just said?

You provided that.

She confirmed his thoughts with another sad shrug. "It's working I see."

"What's happening?"

"The drink. Raphael is good at his job. It's making you human again."

The pain in his heart grew.

"That ache within you is called loss. You haven't really experienced it in a long time, and as an angel, your emotions were stifled, though you spent so much time earthbound you felt a great deal more than most of your kind. Right now you are having what the humans call heartache. I hear it passes in time," the old woman said, taking the flask from Nathan and tucking it back into her purse, all business. "You are still a scratcher. Your senses will be heightened, and you might see things others can't. But you are no longer an angel. The hum of sin will be gone."

"This is my punishment?"

"No. Becoming human again is a gift to you for a job well done. Your punishment is that you will remember all that has occurred. Everything. Including Faye. You'll remember her, and what could have been." The old woman moved to the door. "Maybe it won't be so bad. As a human you could actually be with her."

Nathan fell to his knees, overwhelmed by emotions he hadn't experienced in a long time. He watched the old woman push open the door, and to his further amazement, he heard the golden hum. The sound was sweet and soothing, just the right balm for his exposed feelings. For the first time in five hundred years, he wept.

Bookmark:20

20

Nathan sat in the back of the bar and listened to Faye sing. Unaware of his presence, that knowledge made it easier for him to just watch and enjoy. He liked the way she closed her eyes when she sang the song, lament in every lyric. She wove a spell of enchantment, and Nathan allowed himself to be caught in her net.

Three months had passed. He'd been mortal for ninety days, and it wasn't completely unpleasant. The ebb and flow of human life fascinated and inspired him artistically. A new series of designs covered the walls and floors of his loft, though his favorite he kept next to the bed. The picture of the smiling woman with green eyes and a teasing smile often got him through the night.

He dared not approach Faye, preferring to watch her sing. Nathan always seated himself in the back of the remodeled Black Cat and tried to be unobtrusive. Once he'd caught a glimpse of the Sacred Heart on her shoulder. He wondered if anyone else saw the magnificent glow it gave off now.

God wanted her memory erased so as not to attract attention, and he could agree with that, which was why he hadn't pursued her. But he couldn't fight the desire to see her, even if from a distance. Oh, he would keep tabs on her. Especially now. His eyes fell to her stomach. The signs of the life inside it were starting to show. He would always keep track of her. Of that he was certain.

Faye finished her set, and Nathan got up to go, walking across the floor in front of the piano.

"Excuse me." Her voice stopped him cold.

Nathan turned and looked into her green eyes. The quick spark of recognition in them jolted his heart, but it faded as she tilted her head to the side. Her eyebrow lifted. "You're becoming a regular, aren't you?"

"I suppose."

"So why haven't you given me a song request? I've been waiting, you know. My friend Zenovia and I have been speculating for months over what your taste in music really is. You don't seem like the Black Cat type."

"I'm eclectic in my music preferences."

"Well, give me a request and I'll make sure to sing it for you next time you come in."

"All right."

"What's your name?"

He hesitated. "Nathan."

"I'm Faye." She extended her hand. It felt so small in his, and he flinched at the little jolt of electricity her touch gave him. "You've been coming in several nights a week for the last three months. I make a point to visit with the regulars."

"I like your voice."

"Thanks." She withdrew her hand from his and rested it gently on her stomach.

"When are you due?"

A little sadness blossomed in her eyes. "October."

"Your husband must be excited."

"I'm not married." She looked down. "My husband passed away a few months ago."

He'd wondered what story had been placed in her brain.

"I'm sorry."

"Well? What's your song request?"

Nathan thought a moment and then said, "Something by Diana Krall."

"You have good taste," she said. "All right then. Next time you come in, I'll sing one of her songs for you."

Nathan nodded and left, knowing there would be no next time. He couldn't take the risk of starting up a friendship, couldn't bear it if he somehow drew attention to her or the child.

But as he walked along Sixth Street, hope surged into his chest, and since it had been a long time since he'd really had any, he embraced the feeling. It carried him away from the bar and into the future.

Nephilim grew from a short story that Mary Ann Loesch wrote about Nathan Ink. Intrigued by the idea of an angel working as a tattoo artist, she decided to take it a little further by writing a series of stories about Mr. Ink's clients and what transpired with them after they received their "special" tattoos. Eventually she found that there was enough material there to create a novel and Nephilim, along with the Hell's Leak series, was born.

Though she writes a little of everything, Ms. Loesch finds that urban fantasy with a dash of romance is her favorite genre. Interested in learning more? Visit her website at www.maryannloesch.com.